Agnes
TREADiNG
WATER

CHARLOTTE FRENCH

banjo publishing

A catalogue record for this book is available from the National Library of Australia

ISBN: 978 0 6458 2941 9

Cover Artwork by Hannah French / Cover Design by Charlotte French

www.charlottefrench.com.au / hello@charlottefrench.com.au

First Published 2023

Content notes: Contains mature themes

For You the Reader

Who invites my words into your world

1
today

The diamonds in her ring catch the light from the work lamp as Agnes yanks and twists the surgical tongs. They're peripheral glints that nudge with each jerk of her hand—only hours to go.

Her small attic is dim. Her house is quiet. Her mind is not. She came up here while still dark, hoping to centre herself. However, she's sitting upright with her bare feet tapping the smooth floorboards, working with anything but her usual methodical calm. Tufts fly and mohair settle like a weightless blanket over her lap and the bear she's inflicting the treatment on, while her mind wanders. Through her body—gut, organs, nerves—there's a twitchy edginess as if she's gulped down three cups of Niina's Colombian.

She stops abruptly with the tongs held mid-air like a weapon. He just sneaked in—Guy. Guy, before he proved a first-class arse. It's his warm breath on her face, his stubble, his scent. If she'd close her eyes, she'd be back there, onboard Felicity with him.

With a sigh, she sinks into her wingback chair, stretching out her legs and placing her toes on the floor-level sill of the window. There's condensation on the glass, and outside the morning is colourless, more March than May. The sun casts a hazy yellow past the dark silhouette of the old oak up on the canal. The leaf-out of the trees seems delayed this year.

So what if she always imagined a June wedding? You can't trust Swedish summers, anyway. There's nothing wrong with a ceremony in her sunroom. It'll be charming. If anything, it's an advantage. They can't squeeze more than a dozen people in which means she won't have to look like the friendless reclusive she is.

Agnes drops the tongs back on her side table and eyes the ring. It's slim, the inset diamonds tiny, tiny. Up close, it looks as if a cookie cutter has pressed into the gold and lifted out the star shapes to reveal diamonds hidden underneath. Thomas chose the opposite of loud with her in mind, wanting to get it right. And he's insisted on an impromptu, unassuming home wedding to make it easy for her. It's so sweet. Yet, when her mind wandered just then …

What does that tell ya?—Niina's voice in her head as always.

'Residues,' whispers Agnes. 'That's all it is.' Not that Guy deserves to be her residual memory.

You're rushing this.

'No, I'm not.' Agnes pulls the ring off her right finger and slides it onto the correct one. It feels as awkward as holding scissors with her left hand would.

Australia. That's what's bothering her.

Last night Niina confirmed, 'Look, Agnes, people play mind-fuck games. You got caught in the middle.'

So Agnes had played as well, then? 'Should I tell Thomas?' she asked.

Niina slapped her lightly on the forehead. 'Oh, Ness, we know you're daft as a brush with no bristles, but surely, you know the *What happens in Vegas*?' Then she'd pulled a typical Niina face—one brow up, one down, a crooked smile. 'Actually, forget the Vegas thing. Tell him. Or I can.'

Agnes lifts the bear from under the pile of fur to inspect the damage, which sets off the mechanical growl. 'Let's hope she didn't hear that.' Agnes is not mentally ready for in-the-flesh-Niina just yet. She blows forcefully and brushes the last bit of mohair off, then holds in a swear word. Collectors love tattered vintage style, not plucked clean bodies.

Agnes places him back on her lap, careful not to produce another growl. 'It's wedding jitters,' she says. The bear contemplates this with his deep amber glass eyes. 'A bit of anxiety is normal,' she consoles herself, fumbling for scissors in her toolbox. She finds her old pair and touches the dull blades before guiding one tip into the bear's belly. The point is too blunt. Only stretches the weave.

Niina doesn't get it, not really. Like Agnes, she has no family. But she has lots of friends, and no problem meeting men. Agnes doesn't want to meet any more men. One will do with a family she'll become part of. A family she's already met might have been preferable, but it'll be fine. His cousins, and what have you, won't be coming today. Mind you, it would have been nice if Pernilla was.

Not there for her dad's wedding. What does that tell ya?

'Oh, shut up already.' It's probably better if she doesn't have to face his daughter. It'll be enough to have his mum, stepdad, and friends scrutinising her. 'I've not met his mum.' That's it. Britt-Marie is it. Agnes had the opportunity five days ago but opted for the bus home instead. It was a mistake for sure, yet she had no choice.

She forces the scissors through the material to its base and pushes, using too much power. In one swift action, she rips along the mid-seam, from the crotch to less than an inch below his neck. This time she lets the cussing out. The wood wool stuffing protrudes, a compressed lump wanting to escape. An opening this length is not aesthetic. There's a fine line between meticulously crafted imperfections and an obvious misfortune.

'Third thing I clocked about you,' Niina told her once. 'Beaten by your eyes and killer smile, but only just.' And she'd laughed. Then she'd pointed out that external scars are nothing compared to internal ones.

True. However, there will be new people and all of them looking at her. Too much sun brings it out, and she's come home with the customary pale line across her tanned forehead. It looks like a worm, trapped under her skin.

4

Too many new strangers checking her out—that's what's bothering her. But Niina will do wonders with the makeup.

She will.

Niina! Of course. Will she behave today? 'That's it,' she whispers to the bear. 'Niina is my anxiety.'

Agnes sighs and draws her thumbs along the raw edges of her cut. How could she be so careless with the scissors? She who's never dressed a bear before or sold seconds for years will have to knit a little jumper to disguise the damage and drop the price.

She applies anti-fray along the cut and lets it dry while opening the bag with coconut fibre. Using the tongs again, she crams the fine frizz into the opening, easing it in under the raw edges, covering the wood wool. When she's finished stuffing, Agnes sits back, assessing the result. The poor bear does not look a little wear-and-tear-loved. He looks knifed by a madman. Next is the ladder stitching. Rough and arbitrary. She doubts that'll fix the disfigurement.

'Beauty is in the eyes of the beholder.' she whispers. 'Someone will fall in love with you.'

'Talking to stuffed things again?' says a hoarse voice from the doorway at the other end of the room. 'Sewing on your wedding day. Who does that?'

'Just doing some touch-ups. I need to stitch—'

'Your Maid of honour is about to put a nicotine nail in the coffin,' Niina interrupts. 'And she wants company. So your

5

arctophile blabbering will have to wait. I will, however, offer more than a growl in response. After coffee, that is.'

2

twenty-eight days ago

Where was Thomas? The serpentine line-up was shrinking, one or two shoves at a time, as other travellers patiently herded towards check-in. She'd been waiting at the end of the queue for well over an hour, keeping her suitcases out of the way, letting people past. The queue was shortening, and she was no longer part of it.

While the terminal cacophony of voices, announcements, and anything on wheels or feet echoed around her, Agnes kept looking around searching for him. She took a break from biting her nails, unfolded her ticket for the umpteenth time. Terminal five. Australian Airways. And she had the correct flight number. Of course, she was in the right place. So why wasn't he here? Was he stuck in the Stockholm traffic with a flat battery? Why didn't he answer his phone? They would miss their flight. Agnes lifted her shoulders, held for a moment, and let them drop. It did nothing to release the tension, and a nail was between her lips again.

'She'll be right.'

Startled, she turned around.

'Didn't mean to give you a fright.'

The English-speaking man smiled, his top teeth white against tanned and weathered skin, his beard and shoulder-length curls, sun-kissed. His face gave the impression of a man who'd spent a month crawling through the desert, and you'd half-expect torn clothes, and sand gathered around bare feet. In reality, his jumper over a shirt, jeans, leather boat shoes, a light parka on one arm, and a massive duffel bag over his shoulder made him look as if he'd stepped out of an advertisement for one of those outdoor adventure mags.

Agnes brushed her fringe, suddenly self-conscious about her choice of travelling outfit—worn out sneakers, favourite home tights, an oversized jumper. She had opted for comfort right at the last minute, knowing full well Thomas wouldn't approve. Ten minutes before the taxi arrived, she'd decided that a leap into the unknown was better achieved if she felt comfortable. Now she wished she'd made some effort.

'You had a worried look on your face is all,' he said, and then slower, 'I didn't mean to scare you.'

Had he been observing her?

'Apologies. My Swedish is no good.'

This is where you say something, Agnes.

'You don't speak English?'

'I am waiting for someone.' She'd practised around the bears for weeks, pleasantries she might need. Now she didn't like how she sounded. Pretentious. Stupid. Very school English.

'Visiting Australia?'

She nodded.

'Been Down Under before?'

Agnes shook her head. She'd been nowhere, except to Stockholm twice. Disorientated, she'd asked Thomas about north and south every five minutes. Drove him mad. Touching her fringe lightly, Agnes wondered how she could let him know to move on without being rude.

'Where to?' said the man.

'Sydney.' *He knows that, you dummy.*

The man from outdoors laughed. 'I hope you get to see more than the city. We got the best beaches in the world.'

Agnes looked around for Thomas. 'It's a business trip,' she said. It sounded worldly like she knew what she was doing. 'Exhibition and a holiday.' She added, 'With my fiancé.'

'He might miss his expo.'

'Actually, I'm the one ... I have an expo.'

'My bad.' The man placed a hand on his chest. 'Blame it on my backward, prejudiced upbringing as an Aussie bloke.'

Talk about a broad accent. Language had been one of her better subjects in school. She sold bears all over the world, had no problem with written communication, but this, actually speaking with a foreigner, was different. Yachts from all over the world took the trip past South Hamlet during summer, and the town filled with tourists. But you didn't talk to the visitors. At least she didn't.

'Poor excuse, really. I've got a heap of industrious sisters,' he said. 'So, what kind of exhibition?'

Agnes couldn't help but touch her fringe again. If Niina was here, she'd elbow her. 'Oh, it's just a niche,' she said, pressing Thomas's number again, willing him to pick up.

'Have you had the help desk put it over the speakers?'

'I don't think he's arrived at the airport yet. If he has, he should be here.' She held up the phone. 'Not answering, and I'm worried something's happened.

'Right.' The Australian dropped the duffel bag at his feet. 'Anyone else you can call?'

Agnes shook her head again, like a dimwit. She'd never had numbers for his family or for any friends of his. There had never been a need.

'We'll figure this out.' He held out a hand. 'Guy Ventura.' His name sounded made up, but his hand was warm and firm. Was he too friendly? Guy held on, giving her a quizzical look. 'And you are?'

'Agnes.' When he didn't let go, she added, 'Andersson.' Should be safe. Such a common name. But she too could have made something up. The phone went off in her other hand so unexpectedly, she dropped it. Guy was quick. He let go, caught the phone mid-air, and handed it back to her, all in one effortless sweep.

'Hey.' Thomas's voice sounded thick and woolly.

'Where are you?'

'You won't believe this, but I'm home. Fever, headache, aching body. I got it all.'

Thomas—who freewheeled through life, feet off the pedals, hands off the handlebars, forever breeze in his hair—was still in bed? 'I've been calling you.'

'Been out like a light, Agnes.' He coughed. 'Guess you checked in by now?'

'Not without you.'

'This came on in the middle of the night, didn't want to worry you. Slept through the alarm this morning. I'm so sorry babe. Just woke up.'

'So ... What are you saying?'

'I won't be going anywhere today. You better check in.'

Agnes couldn't imagine boarding a plane, flying for the first time in her life, and arriving in Sydney on her own, trying to figure out where to go, how to get there. 'Might go home,' she said.

'You've got an expo. This is your chance.'

'I don't want to go alone. I can sell them online. And I don't mind. Honest.'

'*I* will mind.' Another cough. 'You have to go.'

This had been his idea. He'd seen the advertisement in one of her bear mags, asked why she'd never exhibited. There'd never seemed to be a good time. If not for her mum's stroke, at some stage, she may have gone somewhere. Maybe a London show, if Niina could have been trusted for support. Her best friend's travels were short and—according to Niina, herself—cheap debauch Mallorca trips. Agnes would have liked to invite and pay for her. The problem was, Niina would have all the best intentions but wasn't trustworthy in the men-department.

When Thomas had suggested the Teddy Bear Exhibition in Sydney, she'd thought him mad. You couldn't get much further than Australia. Besides, it was so last minute. But Thomas had phoned the organisers who said they'd be delighted to have a Scandinavian artist, and his enthusiasm and theirs had made it sound exciting. That's what she needed, he said, something exciting. They would go on their first holiday, and abroad. After the expo weekend, they'd rent a car and spend two weeks sightseeing. Driving on the other side of the road didn't faze Thomas. Nothing did. This trip was to be *their* trip. The thought of doing this on her own? No.

'I know it's hard to understand, Thomas, but I ... I can't do this. Her voice sounded tremulous. That's how she felt internally—shivering as if she'd just been pulled out of bitterly cold water.

'Don't be silly. You'll be fine. For crying out loud, it's a civilised country.'

Agnes bit a nail while listening to Thomas cough again. He didn't get it. How could he? He was normal. She was not. People travel all the time. It was nothing. Absolutely nothing. Why was she like this? Her teeth bit down hard. A sliver of nail came off. The pain gave a sharp second's relief.

Guy had not picked up his duffel bag and walked off. He was waiting as if the two of them were in this pickle together. He was watching her. Self-conscious she dropped her hand.

'Look, Ness,' said Thomas. 'I feel bad enough as it is. I know you're worried, but you've got the address for the hotel. All you need to do is find a taxi.'

Agnes brushed her fringe across again. It wasn't meant to be this way. 'What on earth will I do in Sydney for three weeks?' Renting a car was out of the question. The two times she'd travelled to Stockholm, she'd ended up in the wrong suburb.

Thomas laughed and coughed at the same time. 'You do the weekend as planned, silly, and I'll be there as soon as I can. I'll sleep it off in a day or two, you'll see. I'll be there by Tuesday, latest Wednesday.'

'I don't know.'

'Isn't he coming?' said Guy.

'Sick.'

'I'm on the same flight. I mean, if you want company.'

'Thanks, but I'm going to cancel.'

'No!' Thomas's voice was so loud even Guy reacted, giving her a funny look. 'You need to do this,' said Thomas. 'You know that.'

'Please, don't tell me what to do.' She needed to think. Agnes stared at the phone, trying to decide while Thomas talked about how she had to do this for herself. Did she? Would going home be so bad? Would it prove her a useless human being? Guy looked at her, at the phone, then back to her. He offered a faint smile and raised his eyebrows. In the background was Thomas's motivational speech. He was on a roll now.

Guy abruptly grabbed the phone, hung up on Thomas, and held it in his open hand as if it were contagious. 'Don't worry. You'll get it back. I just think you look like you need a moment to think.'

Agnes gawked at him, said nothing, didn't know if she was pissed off or thankful. She should snatch it off him, grab her suitcases, and walk out of there. Niina would. If that was her wish. But Niina would have jumped for joy if she travelled with Thomas, and he got sick—an absurd comparison.

The phone rang. Guy didn't hesitate. He pressed the red button. 'You said you have a business expo.'

'Oh, it's not that important.' Wasn't it? Wasn't her first-ever exhibition important? She'd prepared for months and even designed a unique kangaroo, especially. 'I make collectable teddy bears.' Agnes tapped her brand new vintage-style suitcase. Thomas had shaken his head when he saw it only minutes after she'd paid for it. 'I should have stayed to make sure you didn't spend a small fortune on something like luggage,' he'd said. But she would use it at home as well, find a spot downstairs and let the bears hang there. And she'd claim it as an expense.

'There are bears inside of this beauty? I say they travel in style.' Guy crouched by her suitcase and moved a hand over the leather. 'You've got good taste. Superb craftsmanship. I hope the handlers won't scuff it.'

'That's okay. My bears have a scuffed look about them.'

'Now I *am* curious. A travelling teddy bear artist. That's pretty cool.'

'Well, actually ... I've not really travelled much. Anywhere. On my own. Or at all.' Why on earth, did she tell him that?

He smiled up at her. 'Australia is my neck of the woods. We're more or less a friendly lot. You'll be fine.' The phone rang again. Again, Guy pressed the red button. 'We don't bite, not us two-legged critters.' He reminded her of Crocodile Dundee, not in looks, age, or outfit but something about his joviality, and the way he spoke. 'See! I've put you at ease now, haven't I?'

Agnes squinted at him. 'What about the ones without legs or the ones with too many?'

He stood and grinned. 'Brown snakes are not to be trusted. But the spiders stare at you wearily with their eight eyes, hoping you'll let them live. And the cockroaches? I reckon you'll get good with the shoe in no time.' With an amicable smile, he pressed the red button again. 'It's your choice, not his, and certainly not mine, but for what it's worth, when thrown in the deep end—swim.' He handed her the phone. 'But you are running out of time.'

Over at the check-in, the counter was empty. The air hostess looked up and waved.

You had a chance to travel. And you came home with the tail between your legs. Shame on you, Agnes. Fucking shame on you. I should fucking disown you.

Niina would never disown her, but Agnes would hear about it for months, if not for the rest of her natural life. Agnes nodded to edge herself on. 'Let's go then.'

Guy swung the duffel bag back over his shoulder, stepped past her and grabbed the handle to her suitcase. She let him lead the way to check-in while sending Thomas the one desired word—going.

At the counter, she handed over ticket and passport, hoping neither the air hostess nor Guy noticed the tremble in her hands. As her suitcase set off on the conveyor belt, she suppressed panic, wishing she'd not capitulated, wishing she'd slept in herself, which is what she'd dreamed the previous night—instead of her usual nightmare.

While Guy checked in, she texted Thomas, let him know she'd email on arrival at the hotel. He texted her a heart and a sleeping emoji. Agnes suppressed her frustration. It wasn't his fault that she was forced out of her comfort zone.

'I hope you don't mind, but I took your fiancé's seat,' said Guy. 'The plane is pretty full.'

She should have seen that coming. Thirty hours, right beside a stranger. If he touched her inappropriately, if something went weird, she'd call it out, ask to sit somewhere else. *Talk about paranoia. He's being helpful.*

'Agnes, relax,' said Guy. 'Flying's a bit like sailing. I reckon you'll love it.'

She didn't. Apart from the obvious—getting from A to B—her virgin flight was not a success. She knew where she went wrong. He'd wanted a beer while waiting. And did she mind? And would she perhaps like a drink? She and alcohol would never be a good combination, yet she'd agreed to a small bottle of wine. He'd suggested it would help if she was nervous about flying, and he'd been nothing but helpful, and they were surrounded by people in broad daylight. When the departure was delayed, she'd ordered another one because he had. By then, drinking wine seemed like the best idea.

The rest was a haze—the lineups, the cool air as they stepped into the plane, the roar of the jet turbines, and the force of the giant beast pushing her into the seat. When Guy's hand patted hers, Agnes had grabbed it like a fish snapping its prey. The retching that followed, the stumbling to the toilet on shaky legs, the apologising to Guy and the businessman in the aisle seat—that was all foggy. Waking up in London drooling on Guy's shoulder wasn't.

They were in the next airbus at an altitude of 35,000 feet with an empty seat between them. Agnes was sober with a headache, and dressed in airport-boutique *tracky-dacks*, as Guy called them. She looked sick in yellow, but that's all they'd had with 7/8 legs, and they'd been on the run to their gate. No time to look around. At least she didn't stink of vomit anymore.

She was not a drinker. There was never alcohol in her house—not officially. Her mum kept a special Port locked in the bottom drawer while her dad stayed dry. It wasn't until years later, the day after her mother's debilitating stroke, that he fell off the wagon again.

Agnes had never even tasted wine until a sleep-over at Niina's when they were seventeen. It had been a cheap and sour introduction to intoxication. She'd slept it off in Niina's bed after vomiting on her long pile wool rug. The very last time Agnes drank alcohol was when Niina had dragged her to South Hamlet's nightclub to usher in the summer. Niina, who'd worked in the bookshop every weekend for years, had been offered a full-time position. Agnes also had something worth celebrating. She wouldn't have to set her foot in school ever again.

The night started with them in a corner, sipping Sangria. When some funky favourite of Niina's swept her away, Agnes stayed, thinking another Sangria would help her brave the dance floor, too. That second drink was her downfall. After that she let a handsome tourist introduce her to tequilas.

One minute she was sculling shots and sucking lemons. The next she was in the alleyway, behind overloaded rubbish bins, pressed up against a brick wall. She had no memory of walking outside with him, no memory of saying yes. She never said no, never uttered a word. There was only the dull thumping bass from inside the nightclub and a spinning world. After, when trying to wiggle the skirt down and pull her undies up, she toppled over. There was no hand offered as she struggled to get to her feet. The handsome tourist lit a cigarette as she shambled away with a limp, heading for the canal and the long walk home.

Someone tapped her and she jolted. 'Agnes?'

'Apple cider from now on.' Her words came out sharp.

'Oh, sure.'

'Sorry, I was miles away—your thumbs, can I see the damage?'

He held out broad palms. 'These rugged tools are used to haul ropes and pull against the forces of nature. Your nails are pretty harmless.' He winked.

Agnes couldn't help but blush and tuck her hands away.

'Don't know if you remember.' Guy offered a crooked smile. 'I sail other people's yachts.'

He'd done all the talking while she'd been concentrating on her fringe and her nails and what on earth she was doing, and why did she make it such a big thing?

'I live right next to a canal,' she said. 'Göta Kanal. Doubt you've heard of it, but it cuts across Sweden from east to west. Still water, and narrow. Not so much sailing really.'

Guy gave her a surprised look. 'I have heard. Connected with a Swede in Brazil. Just been to see him. His company picks up groups in Stockholm, sails them around the

19

Archipelago and through the locks to one of your lakes, drops them there, and picks up a new group. Then does the reverse. And you're right. Not much sailing.' He combed his fingers through his beard. 'It put me off a bit, but I'm seriously considering the offer. 'And you don't sail?'

'I've never been on a boat.'

Guy cocked an eyebrow. 'Fair dinkum?'

'I head butted a yacht once when I was four.'

'Might need to hear that story.'

'Apparently, I wandered up to the canal embankment on my own, fell in the lock, onto a sailing boat, and sort of bounced off the deck before landing in the surging water. Would have drowned, if not for one sailor. Arm in a sling for six weeks, and a considerable concussion. Fifteen stitches.' Agnes brushed her fringe aside though he would have already seen. It may be the third thing you noticed, but you couldn't miss it.

Guy reached over, hesitated, then touched her forehead with his fingers, felt along the worm light as a feather. He brushed her fine hair across again. 'It's not that noticeable,' he said. 'But fringe suits you.' He dropped his hand back in his lap, his eyes fixed on hers. 'Good thing you have no memory of the almost drowning.'

She nodded.

The memory of almost drowning was in her dreams most nights, and vivid. The waddle home along the canal, the night she gave up her virginity to some nameless brute, ended up longer than expected when she tripped over and lost her balance.

It still haunted her—the fear, the cold, the sinking, the sound of silence underneath, swallowing water, splashing and fumbling for anything to save her, and nothing but liquid, her head bobbing above and below the surface, being swallowed up in the Swedish summer night. Somehow and suddenly her hands had found the grassy edge. She'd not been able to pull herself up but held on while the path, the water, and the sky reeled.

Time had stretched out endlessly. Then finally voices. Hands of strangers dragged her out. With chattering teeth, Agnes pretended her house was down the next road and ran off. She never told anyone, not even Niina. It was too pathetic.

'Are you all right?' Guy was patting her knee again. 'Adrenaline, alcohol, and another language—no wonder you're spaced out.' Then he nodded to the front. 'Food's on the way.'

The background noise rushed in, the hum of the engines, people talking, a baby's cry. As the two of them straightened up in their seats and released their tables, Agnes snuck a sideways glance at Guy. She was a yellow–fleece–pudge with a scar and funny dialect who'd vomited all over him, and *he*'d not asked to sit somewhere else.

3

twenty-seven days ago

'Big day tomorrow,' said Guy.

Together, they'd gone to collect their luggage. His duffel bag had tumbled out early, and they were waiting for Agnes's suitcase. The surrounding fellow travellers were steadily dispersing as their luggage arrived. Guy's words brought home what she'd been suppressing—the cocoon she'd nested in was about to release her. After close to thirty hours with him, swapping meals, dozing with his knees against her body or her head on his shoulder, exchanging bits about themselves, Guy seemed like someone she'd known for years. He'd made travelling easy. Now she'd be on her own.

Sharing a cab into the city made sense. Her destination was a hotel near Wynyard, while Guy would continue to Circular Quay. He'd be visiting friends in Manly for the weekend before heading up the coast.

'I was thinking,' he said. 'Why don't you come out for a bite?'

'Tonight?' The thought was comforting. 'Thanks, but I need an early night.'

'Casual drinks with some mates of mine. They don't bite, and I promise to have you home before you turn into a pumpkin.'

Mates of Guy surely meant jargon and jokes. She wouldn't be able to keep up. It would be a night of bewildered smiles, and too many people always made her words come out jumbled or not at all.

'Ferry leaves from Circular Quay, close to your hotel.'

No way would she step on some boat in Sydney harbour, not for anyone. A quiet evening—preparing for tomorrow, making sure she'd know where to go, book a cab—that was her.

'Say yes?'

'I have to make up bear names and write tags.'

'Come on, Agnes.' He elbowed her gently. 'It's your first time in Australia, and thought we'd already decided on names.'

It was true. They had. Strangely, Guy had shown a genuine interest in her bear-making. He'd listened to her describing the journey from design to execution to a finished creature without his eyes glazing over. She'd told him the history of teddy bears, and the story of her father's bear, the story of her parents. Only Niina had heard that one.

'How about we'll take the ferry over,' said Guy. 'Plenty of good places to eat only walking distance from your hotel. Perfect.'

'Maybe,' she said. 'But I wonder where my suitcase is.'

The conveyor opening had stopped spitting out luggage. A few remaining travellers were picking off their bags and walking off. Agnes and Guy gave it another five minutes before accepting that her giant suitcase was missing in action.

'We do apologise. Something's gone wrong somewhere,' said the lady at the help desk.

'Miss Andersson has an important expo this weekend.' There was a change to Guy's voice. Agnes imagined him at the helm ordering around his crew. 'Haul the sail.' Something along those lines.

'I'm sorry, sir. We will, of course, track down the suitcase and have it sent to your hotel, Miss Andersson.'

'Agnes will need it by tomorrow.'

His tone of voice filled her with hope. They'd take this seriously. It wasn't some tedious-tourist-complaint but an Australian-skipper-of-yachts command. The woman made note of Agnes's hotel details, promising they would contact the hotel as soon as they knew.

Guy asked Agnes to wait and took off, returning ten minutes later with a pre-paid phone card. He helped her activate it. She left her new mobile number so the airline could reach her directly, and Guy offered his number as a backup.

The cab trip into town was sombre. Guy tried to cheer her up. 'They'll sort it,' he kept saying. Agnes stared out the window watching suburban Sydney moving past outside, the endless traffic, the low buildings, the long streets hosting shop after shop, office after office, massive advertisement signs, one tackier than the other. Her skin was grimy, her scalp itchy, and an enormous lump of dough had settled in her gut. She pulled the hood over her head, then leaned into Guy's solid shoulder and dozed off.

'Agnes,' said Guy softly.

She sat up, disorientated. 'Where are we?'

'At your hotel.'

She released her seatbelt, found her wallet in her bag, and handed Guy two twenty-dollar bills.

He accepted one. 'This is plenty.'

The taxi driver got out to lift her cabin bag from the boot.

After so much time with Guy, it was weird to think she wouldn't see him again. The cab's dark windows softened the light from outside and dimmed the details of his face.

But she'd seen him in stark fluorescent light, and up close. Agnes knew well the fine wrinkles when he smiled, and his hazel-coloured irises with flecks of brown, the warmth in his eyes.

'I'm sorry, but I won't come out tonight,' she said. 'The luggage—I'm worried.'

'We'd do our best to cheer you up,' he said.

As much as Agnes hated the thought of getting out and having to face the rest on her own, she declined. All that mattered were the bears. 'I want to be here when it arrives. I will probably ring the airline again. 'I need my bag before tomorrow.'

'I understand.' Guy reached out and touched her tracky-dack-knee.

'Thanks,' said Agnes. 'For everything.'

The driver had left her cabin bag on the paving outside her door. He was back in the driver's seat. 'Time to go,' he said.

'Give us a minute,' said Guy with his skipper's voice.

She swallowed. 'I owe you—'

'Nonsense, you made the trip a lot of fun.' He took her hand in his.

'I'm in a hurry,' said the driver.

Agnes withdrew. 'Better go.'

Guy held his phone up. 'Any time, okay? If you need a chat. It's nice to know at least one person on this patch of land.'

The lump in her throat made her 'thanks' a whisper.

'Keep me posted on that suitcase. I bet they'll sort it. After you've had a shower and your bears restored, you might change your mind about tonight.'

'I have another booking,' said the driver.

Guy sighed and shook his head. 'Chin up,' he said.

Then she was out the door. Agnes watched the cab leave the kerb and disappear into the traffic. She stood there long after she'd lost sight of them—a yellow track-suited foreigner with a cabin bag handle in a tight grip, significantly smaller than usual in the shadows of the tall buildings around her.

Once Agnes had settled in her room, showered, and was freed of that awful tracksuit, she ordered food to her room and brought her bear photos out. As she and Guy had been brainstorming names, she'd written them on the back of each photo. All she had to do was transfer the information about each, and their name, to the swing tags. And then there was only worry left.

Agnes went to bed hoping, wishing, willing a knock on the door, at some ungodly hour by a suitcase delivery. Instead, she came alive in accordance with her internal clock set to Swedish time and stayed wide awake through the ungodly hours, watching endless re-runs of seventies cop shows and homegrown comedies that she didn't find funny, mentally kicking herself for having packed her new, four-hundred pages book purchase, in the vanished suitcase.

4
five days ago

Thomas had picked some new hot spot in Old Town. The stone-walled cellar with dripping candle chandeliers and brocade-upholstered chairs oozed charm with soft jazz and warm spices. He was being romantic. It didn't surprise Agnes when the velvet box came out minutes after sitting down. A fool, she was. A fool.

When he was waiting for her at arrivals, wearing the clothes he wore on the video clip from two days ago, she should have known he was taking up where he'd left off. She should have texted him before flying out of Sydney to make sure he *wouldn't* meet her at the airport.

To her defence, she'd been too upset to bother with her Swedish SIM card. It was still floating around in her bag. And she'd not in her wildest dreams imagined he'd meet her. When he did, his arms around her had both annoyed and comforted. She'd wanted to cry, let out all the bottled-up emotions held in for forty-eight long hours. There was so much inside, all jumbled. Confusion. Anger. Regret. Agnes supposed she'd hoped being held by him would return her to something she'd lost.

It didn't.

Then she'd let him talk her into this, coming out for dinner. Maybe it was a need for familiarity. She could have insisted on taking the bus home. But no, she'd pulled a crumpled top out of her suitcase, dry shampooed her hair, and added basic make-up. Gosh, next to him, she was dishevelled—inside and out. During the drive here and all his questions about the trip, she'd kept the lies and half-truths going. Short answers. All hazy now. *Now* was hazy.

'See if I can open it this time,' he said sliding the box closer to her.

Her head hummed from hours of movie dialogue, the thrum of aircraft engines, and her own thoughts which had not shut down since what happened on Felicity. If someone had stomped on her head and rubbed sand in her eyes, she couldn't possibly feel worse. Her heart ached as if inflamed—as if every disappointed cell in her body had dumped its toxic waste right there and given it a new density.

Talk about melancholic drivel.

This time he managed to open the box. 'I hope you like it.'

Agnes focused on the pinpricks of white brilliance, trying to sort through what she felt. She should not have agreed to this, should've taken the bus. She wasn't ready. Didn't matter though, did it? She was here. Agnes held out her hand, wondering if the ring would even fit.

It didn't.

'Fluid retention. You should see my calves. Look how tight this is.' She showed him her other hand with his original ring. She'd forgotten to take it off, though she'd experienced the same swelling, flying to Australia. The finger was a fat sausage around the once gold-plated metal.

'All the flying I've done, and never.' Thomas slotted it back into the velvet.

Agnes reached for the box, offering him a kind giggle. 'Don't worry. By tomorrow it'll fit.' She held the box close so she could take in the ring. 'It's pretty.' Was she relieved? Would it be easier to break it off with him if the ring never made it onto her finger? And was that what she wanted? There were no silver balls rolling into their slots, giving her a sense of arrival after her one bewildering detour. What her disarrayed mind needed was sleep. She tried the ring on her pinky. It managed halfway. Thomas laughed.

The champagne arrived. A waitress uncorked for them, congratulated them, and filled their glasses before disappearing again.

'To us and diminishing fluids.' He leaned in, and they met in a kiss over the table.

She made it swift, pretending the stretch was too far for her neck. When her lips touched his, she remembered Guy's.

Thomas smelled of her Christmas gift, *Pursuit* by Don Diego. Agnes had an urge to touch his shaven jaw. She didn't act on it.

They reposed in their seats. Away from the immediate light, it was easier to face him, her energetic and persuasive man. His short crop of hair was blow-dried and textured, his blue eyes intense on her while he sipped his bubbly.

If Thomas looked hard enough, surely he'd see the betrayal imbued on her irises and tattooed on her skin—the weight of another man, her palms on another man's buttocks, another man's tongue in her mouth. There was a fault in the linen weave where her fork rested, a stitched mend. Agnes touched the undulation with her fingers.

'So ... about the wedding.' Thomas dropped the glass back on the table.

'Wedding?'

He hesitated. 'I've ... booked a celebrant.'

'You've set a date?'

Thomas licked his bottom lip, back and forth, half-open mouth. 'I've had time to ponder. I want you to hear me out.'

He'd been sick, yet he'd been thinking of her while she'd been busy making a fool of herself, merely thinking of him in brief spurts.

'We'll keep it small and intimate. I know you wouldn't want anything glitzy.'

'When?'

'We've waited long enough. Time to do what's good for *us*.'

This was Thomas, the insurance man. This was him persuading a client to take the company's life, home and personal accidents package, plus all the extras.

No, that was something Niina would say. That was unfair. He'd missed her.

'South Hamlet,' he said. 'Your place, family, a few friends, nice and chilled.'

'A summer wedding?'

'Found a great deal on the Greek Isles—for the honeymoon. Spring's the best time over there. You'll love it.'

'Next Spring?'

'Not next ...'

Agnes drew her fingertips across the linen, landing her hands in her lap.

'I know it's madness. Totally.' His tone softened. 'Isn't that exactly what we need? Greece is booked and paid for,' he said, so softly she could barely hear him.

'When Thomas? When?'

He looked her straight in the eyes, again hesitated. 'Thursday,' he said finally. 'This one coming.' Then he picked up his glass again, on edge.

She sat stunned, watched him drink, waited until he put the glass down. 'Five days from now?'

'I kind of imagined you'd be all for it.'

'It's ... sudden.'

'Says the girl who once wanted to elope. Come on, Agnes, let's go the whole hog mad. I've got a place sorted for tonight, around the corner. A mate's Airbnb. Dennis—you've met him. Overlooks the water, the city, the royal castle. He's had it refurbished. Wait till you see the bed.' Thomas winked at her. 'Swollen limbs or not, I can't wait to see the rest of your tan.'

His words fed the jitter in her stomach. Of course, he had organised a place to stay. As Niina often said. Daft as a brush.

'Why do you shake your head?'

'I ... I need to go home. I'll reimburse you for any cost.'

He laughed contemptuously. 'You're not serious? I had to twist his arm for it. Dennis had a date tonight. He was going to use it himself. You and I, it's been what, a month? And we just got engaged.'

It had barely been forty-eight hours since Guy. It was too fresh.

Thomas shook his head in disbelief. 'You expect me to put you on the bus after this?'

Squinting, she nodded.

'Why Ness?'

She dropped her gaze and stared into her lap, at the ring still tight on her little finger. 'I'm sorry. I'm exhausted.'

'You'll sleep like a baby in that bed. Tomorrow we'll go find you a dress.'

'I already have one.' The heat behind her eyelids was intense. There was no plausible excuse for a two-hour bus ride this late. But go to bed with him? No. She needed to find her bearings, process in peace. He'd gone out of his way, and she was both deceitful and an idiot for putting him, and herself, in this situation.

'Even better,' he said. 'We'll have a lazy Sunday. Tomorrow we could brunch with my mum and—'

'I'm taking the bus.' Her words came loud and sharply blunt. Agnes sunk into her seat and clasped her hands, exhaled. 'It's the jet lag,' she said. 'I feel off.'

He considered her, licking his bottom lip.

Awkward silence.

To her relief, the waiter arrived with their entrees—delicate towers of seafood and black caviar sprinkled across white porcelain.

'What is going on?' said Thomas, once they were alone again. 'You're not yourself.'

'You know what could be romantic? We wait. It'll make it more special.'

'Extreme, don't you—?'

'And getting engaged and married all in the same week aren't?'

Thomas looked at her wide-eyed.

'I know you had a plan,' she said. 'However, it's overwhelming—a wedding in five days? I need to go home tonight.' She longed to crawl into bed. Her bed. Alone.

'All right. Forget it.' He picked up his fork, scooped up the decorative sprig of dill, and placed it on the side of the plate. 'Should I drive you to the bus stop right now or can you manage our engagement dinner?'

She let his sharp words wash over her without as much as raising an eyebrow.

He ate while she picked up caviar eggs with her fingertips. It looked delicious, but she lacked appetite. 'You can have mine,' she said after he'd finished his plate, then watched him work his way through the main as well, while she settled for a pot of chamomile tea.

She tried to return them to small talk but found she had nothing to say, and no energy to keep up the pretence about the bus tour. Her Australia trip had been a fiasco—except for facing her one fear, something she'd never explained properly to Thomas, to begin with. She couldn't bring that up now even if she wanted to. She also didn't want to.

Thomas thawed, found his default plus mode—a Thomas trait she loved—and turned his annoyance into enthusiasm over the wedding. He named the people he'd invite, his parents, his closest friends and their partners. No kids except for Pernilla, of course. Asked who she'd invite. Niina. He'd had the foresight to book enough rooms at the Hamlet Guesthouse. Had he organised catering? No. Could she do it? After all, it was her hometown.

With such short notice, they would have to settle for simple. Not that she'd let that trouble her—*if* she moved ahead with this. A smorgasbord with finger food was fine and their local baker would whip a cake up if she wanted nothing too outlandish. That didn't trouble her either. An unassuming wedding was perfectly fine.

Niina wouldn't approve—that troubled her, and her own confusion. What she needed was to sleep, find the Agnes she was three days ago but without the witless Guy-crush roadblock. That Agnes would see clarity.

By the time she stepped inside the door, it was almost midnight, and Agnes was shivering from exhaustion and sitting in air-con air for hours. The window lamp's glow, the warmth from the elements, and the house scent welcomed her with a bitter 'home sweet home' reminding her of loss and aloneness. The wall pegs seemed sad and deserted. She hung her jacket on one, her scarf on the next, then her handbag, and a boot on each of the other.

It was probably because she'd been gone for almost a month, this uncertain gut feeling, the sense of something foreign among the old and intimate. She locked the door. Then she walked through the house, flicking on lights.

The kitchen, dining and lounge room looked how she'd left them. So did the glass veranda. The panes, like mirrors against the black outside, displayed three Agnes, three frazzled reflections. She alone suffered the itchy scalp and the pull from the elastic snared into her sun-bleached mess.

Her mum's office was immaculate—neater than Agnes remembered. Cold prickled at the back of her neck. 'Get over yourself,' she said in a loud voice. 'You've forgotten how you left it.' She'd been pretty frantic, nervous about flying, nervous she'd forget to pack something. Agnes closed the door. Then she remembered the phone, walked back in and took it off the hook. If Olga spotted her lights on from across the canal, she'd ring in the morning. And what Agnes needed was to sleep.

She continued upstairs to check. As the rooms lit up, as the house came alive, her unease faded. Nothing was out of place. Her jewellery box was on its spot on the small shelf by her bed. She lifted the lid and yes, her parents' wedding bands and the few gold trinkets of hers were still there. Her bed was too neat, she thought. The throw pillows lay scattered differently from how she normally did. *I could have done that.* Agnes checked the guest room again. Nothing out of place. She must have done that.

She climbed the stairs to the attic, switched on the light bulbs hanging from the sloped ceiling, and inhaled. There it was, the aroma of metal, wood and fibre, of beeswax candles she burned when shaping noses, of browning essence from staining their fur, and her scent too—her sweat from the arduous work of stuffing the bears' hollow costumes, filling limbs with wood wool, and giving bodies shape. She'd spent some intense weeks here, in the lead-up to the expo. Agnes walked around her space, touching the sturdy oak table, the sewing machine, the empty shelves with one lonely bear in a slouching position, his ears in his lap, and no eyes.

'Poor little sod. I'll get you sorted this week—promise.'

The mere thought of replicating all the bears she'd lost ... By default, she never made the same bear twice, but this time she'd have to. Collectors had made their picks.

Your suitcase has not disappeared into outer space, Agnes. You'll get it back.

Guy. Where had he come from? She had no intention of having him in her head. Niina was already taking up enough room.

She would ring the airline again. They were predictably pleasant on the phone, but nothing happened. Tomorrow or the next day—after she'd slept—she'd threaten with the ombudsman. She needed her bears returned. Losing the hand-made ones was awful enough. Her dad's vintage Steiff was irreplaceable.

Leaving Villa Solus lit up like a late-night shopping mall, Agnes fetched Thomas's ring box and placed it on the rim of the bathtub. While running hot water, she took a shower to wash off her hours of travelling, using half a bottle of conditioner to persuade the stubborn elastic without losing too much hair. Agnes thought of her last two showers in Australia, the before and after Guy. Anticipation and physical longing. The memory pulled like grief, like drowning.

Once she finally stepped into the silky heat, Agnes sunk her head below the surface and screamed. She came up for breath, then under again, kept at it until her voice wore out. There were no tears, only water dripping down her face. After all, Guy didn't deserve tears. Agnes leaned back, closed her eyes, and breathed in ... and out ... in ... and out. She exhaled Australia and inhaled Sweden. Out with the holiday ... in with her normal life ... out with Guy ... in with Thomas.

After lathering up her finger with soap, she pulled the old ring off. With wet hands, she slid it into the box. Next to the engagement ring, the blue gemstones looked pretty shabby.

She lay back and rested her head on the hard edge, thought of their first time. They went for a drive out into the forest. She suggested it, thinking it was about time she put her introduction to sex behind her. After that, they went for forest drives each time he came by on his way south. When the weather cooled, Thomas persuaded his boss that South Hamlet was the obvious layover on his business trips south. He'd book the motel outside town and she'd stay until the mornings. Their first 18 months had been the best. She was in love.

Then she finally agreed for him to meet her parents, and the trouble started—her sneaking behind their back, pretending it was over, he talking her out of eloping, sure that her parents would get over it. And then the stroke, which made her mum impossible.

Reconnecting with Thomas this time around had been different. There was a new freedom but also a desperate need in her. When he showed up on her porch the week after her father's funeral, exhausted with grief and guilt she'd slid into an embrace without uttering a word. He stayed the night.

Her lovemaking had been fierce, a hunger to be filled, be consumed, be seen and vanish into him, into a different life.

And now she could have it all. Thomas had a point. Why wait? For what? It was their turn now. Greece would undo Australia. Greece would connect her to him, again.

'You know what, Mum, he keeps coming back.' Her words resonated between the tiled walls. 'You were wrong about him. Why shouldn't I say yes? And this time you don't get to interfere.'

Later—long after she woke up shivering again, after she'd layered up in fleece, watered plants, gone through the mail, and drunk a litre of tea—Agnes went to use the downstairs guest toilet. And peculiarly, though she'd never leave the seat up, up it was.

5

twenty-six days ago

Agnes had at last dozed off when the wake-up call came from the reception. She dragged herself out of bed and into a long, hot shower. Drowsy, drained, and disappointed, she dressed in the silk shirt Niina had picked out, then forced make-up on her sad face, and caked too much foundation over her scar. Wiped too much off. Bungled the hair drying more than usual. Wet her fringe twice for another shot at it. Walked out the door a failure.

She asked the reception to ring her if the suitcase showed up. For the five minutes it took for the cab to drive her to the Rocks terminal, she slept like someone had knocked her out.

Agnes stepped out in a dream state. Enthusiastic collectors were already lining up. The queue stretched at least a hundred meters around the building. She excused herself to the front with her passport in hand and was greeted by an usher who gave her a bag with a welcome note, the layout of the place, a name tag, a bottle of water, and mints.

They had allocated her a table right at the entrance. An excellent spot for sure. She'd worked hard at home on how to display, had searched through all her bear mags, to see how other artists did it. But here she was with nothing. The beautiful velvet cloth she'd bought was in the suitcase, too. The bears were all wrapped up in it. Agnes explained the situation, and after encouraging pats on the shoulder, the main organiser was called upon. Wendy, a boisterous woman, reminded her of Niina a little—except blonde, and three decades her senior.

'You should give this table to someone else,' said Agnes. 'It will look empty.'

'Dear Agnes, this is your table and don't worry, the bears will show up. We can find you a tablecloth, and we have a flag somewhere for you, so our collectors can see you're an international visitor. Yellow cross on blue?'

'I beg your pardon?'

'Your flag?'

When Agnes nodded, the woman sighed with relief. 'We get all muddled, Sweden, Switzerland. Anyway, we'll get that to you. Now don't worry. It will work out.'

Agnes showed her the photos. 'It's all I have.'

'Oh, come here, pet,' said Wendy. 'You need a bear hug, pun intended.' That idiom was the same in Swedish, and funny enough, it was definitely something Niina would say.

'Thank you,' said Agnes. It was all she could do to not run off into the ladies. Then they needed Wendy somewhere else.

White and ironed linen for the table was delivered, and a complimentary Swiss flag. Agnes hid the flag pole under the table, hung the name tag around her neck, and started organising her photos with corresponding swing tags the best she could. She also had a three-year-old article about her from a UK magazine. Despite looking after her mum, despite her father's drinking, she'd achieved some success that year.

The enormous hall was loud with chatter. Artists were busy at their allocated tables with the last finishing touches. After she'd set up, Agnes took a quick walk along the aisles. There were bears the size of half an inch up to over a meter, bears in elaborate velvet and chiffon costumes, bears with fat toes, long necks, or big teeth. There were no limitations to the artists' imagination. All meticulously made, all exquisitely presented. Not all to her taste, but there would be buyers. Beauty lay in the eyes of the collectors.

Too shy to walk up and say hello to other artists, she kept her distance but smiled as well as she could muster. They smiled back with enthusiasm on their faces. One called, 'Can't wait for the mad rush. Have a good one.'

Back at her table, she rang the hotel—no suitcase as yet. Then it was time for the show to open. Agnes held back the heat in her eyes. She could do this for a few hours. And the suitcase would show up, she told herself.

All who entered had to pass by her table. Some checked out the article, some checked out her photos and made friendly comments, and occasionally a person knew who she was from her online presence. Most said they'd come back for a proper look as soon as the bears arrived.

Agnes kept her new SIM card in. When Guy rang mid-morning, she faked pragmatism. He said he'd ring the airline and abuse them for her. When he rang later to confirm he'd done exactly that, and to ask how she was holding up, she didn't mention her twenty-minute toilet break. She'd forgotten to bring make-up and looked pretty washed out. Her scar seemed louder than usual. She was prepared to blame it on lack of sleep if anyone commented. No one did.

Late afternoon, some of the more serious collectors came back for a closer look at her photos, all carrying bags with the day's adopted bears. One lady was interested in a kangaroo and wondered if she could leave her contact details. After that, Agnes lay open her notebook for anyone else mildly interested. She should have thought of that first thing.

'Chin up,' said Wendy before she walked out. 'Tomorrow's a new day.'

Agnes had a cab waiting that she'd organised that morning. She didn't want to walk, in case she'd get the streets wrong.

She'd secretly hoped that the hotel personnel had got confused, or forgotten to ring her, and her suitcase would be waiting for her. No such luck.

Guy texted, wondering if she was up for drinks. She said no. She was tired and defeated, and damn tired. She changed over her SIM card. There was no text from Thomas. Too sick, poor guy. She'd not bothered telling him about her lost luggage and kept her message concise and carefree. There was nothing he could do about it, anyway.

She ordered food, had a shower, and crawled into bed exhausted only to wake up an hour later bright-eyed, ready for a night of crap television.

6
twenty-five days ago

On the Sunday, Agnes was that tired she paid the cab driver to drive her around The Rocks, an extra fifteen minutes so she could have a nap. Somnolent didn't even come close, she thought, stepping out of the cab. Before Agnes did anything else, she went to the free cafeteria section for a triple-strength coffee.

Wendy touched her on the shoulder. 'Got your bears? Thought we'd better put you in the spotlight today.'

Agnes shook her head, fixing her gaze on the brooch Wendy was wearing, a felted teddy bear the size of a thumb.

'Oh, I see. Gee, that's a shame, real shame.' Wendy's hand came up and stroked along Agnes's arm. 'Your bears are gorgeous.' She let her hand rest on Agnes's shoulder.

'Thank you.'

'We always show off our international guests.'

Instead of looking up, meeting the older woman's gaze, Agnes stretched for the nearest cookie, withdrawing from Wendy's hand. 'I'm fine—'

'We'll do it anyway.'

'I'd rather—'

'And you don't need to do anything, pet.'

That was not quite accurate. Ten minutes later, she had to stand next to Wendy who, with mic in one hand and bear mag in the other, spoke about Miss Andersson's years in the trade.

'Why don't you hold up some of your photos,' whispered Wendy.

It seemed so pointless, but Agnes did as told. She had to lock her elbows in so as not to shake too much. Wendy said something about the bears gone walkabout, which brought some laughs, but then she spoke seriously. After that, there were groans of condolences as the crowd understood the disastrous mishap. And Agnes had to fight back the tears and resist running off to the ladies.

The rest of the day was a blur. Guy rang, offered to come over the water to show her the Opera house in the evening. She sounded drunk to her own ears, thanked him, but insisted she needed to sleep. People kept coming over to say hello, say how sorry they were, and add their contact details for when the bears returned. Some offered to put a deposit to secure their choice of bear, but Agnes didn't dare accept any money.

When the other artists started packing up. Agnes collected her things and sneaked out, thinking she'd apologise to Wendy and her team via email once she could hold a sentence together. She'd forgotten to book a cab, so she set out for the hotel by foot. Naturally, she confused herself. Ended up walking two extra blocks and arrived at the entrance when she least expected it.

Agnes didn't bother with her lost suitcase, shower, or dinner. She lay down on the bed, shoes and all. She woke up at 11 pm and spent another night in front of mediocre TV.

7

twenty-four days ago

'What do you mean, you booked it?'

'I thought you should see a bit while you're there.'

Thomas had just informed her he was not on the mend. In fact, he would probably need another week before he'd be going anywhere. To make amends, he'd organised a guided bus tour up to the Great Barrier Reef. He'd meant well and made the effort despite being sick, but after her failure of a weekend, Agnes had trouble feeling gracious. She had no trouble feeling regret. She regretted not taking Guy up on his offer to see the Opera house. Yes, she'd been half dead, but more than that, she'd thought of Thomas and how he'd be in Sydney by Tuesday and how the two of them would experience the Sydney icons together. It was Monday, and Agnes had spent the better part of the day sleeping, crying, and waiting on the phone. She was getting better at talking to Australian Airways employees, but there was still no clue as to where her suitcase might be. Now this.

'You're cutting out. Thomas? Hello? Thomas?' With that, Agnes hit the red button. An absolute first in her life—acting out a mobile dysfunction.

She wasn't a cusser by nature. Even when she'd stitch two pieces the wrong way and have to unpick them, or screw on limbs back to front, she'd rarely go any further than flipping heck. But walking around the room, she swore at the heavy drapes, the locked windows with views of brick walls, the scrawny Aussie comedian on TV, and her phone—the stand-in for Thomas. 'Being squashed in with however many strangers for 240-something hours, having to share sceneries and social evenings with said strangers, whose only common denominator is visiting the barrier reef, is not my damn cup of piss-weak whatever.' She threw 'Thomas' on the bed.'

She stood still and breathed, chewed on a non-existent nail and stared at nothing.

After a minute or two, she picked up the phone again, changed the SIM card over and sent Guy a text asking if he by any chance was in the mood to do something touristy. Then she lay down on the crumpled bedsheets and closed her eyes, imagining her suitcase being handled by proficient staff, Half an hour it took for Guy to text her back.

> Decided to drive home
> :-/   Three hours out of
> Sydney. Sorry :-(

Agnes got up and walked around the room. Regret burrowed into her skin like leeches. Guy had been a twinkle in an otherwise dark sky during the weekend. And now he'd gone on his merry way. Now she really was alone. And she'd be alone for at least a week in Sydney, or longer, if Thomas didn't beat this thing, and she didn't go on the damn bus tour. She didn't want to sit cramped with someone she didn't know. Guy had been fine. She'd been lucky. But everything else about this trip had been total crap. She'd be home now if she'd followed her own heart instead of having Niina in her head and Thomas in her ear. And so would all her bears.

Home.

She collapsed on the bed and sat hunched for ages, biting her nails, staring at the carpet pattern, following the brown swirls around with her toe. She was being a child, she was.

She opened the itinerary Thomas had emailed her. The bus would travel along the coast, making frequent stops along the way. She read through the towns and tourist attractions. One name caught her attention—Coffs Harbour. That's where Guy lived. Two hours stop at the Big Banana. What if he would be happy to meet up with her there? There was a restaurant and she could shout him lunch as a thank-you.

No, she was farcical. She was the exhausting Swede, Guy's good samaritan project. And he'd be over that. Wouldn't he? But what if he was happy to meet up? Then the bus trip seemed more exciting. She didn't have to ring. She could text. He could say thanks, but no thanks.

I think you've got a thing for this guy.

'Niina, can you leave me alone for once?' screamed Agnes at the wall. Then she threw the phone on the bed, glared at it. She could fly home. There was that.

Yep, you could. That would be such an Agnes thing to do.'

'Oh, shut up already.'

Go back to the same old, same old. Be the boring, predictable homebody you are.

She wouldn't hear the end of it—had to go. She wouldn't make it on any boat up there to actually see the reef, but Agnes wasn't big on cities. Between staying in Sydney and going on the bus tour, the latter was the winner, if only just. And if she felt led that way, she'd text Guy later.

Of course, you will.

The Coast to Coast bus tour would leave early the next morning, so Agnes still had an afternoon and an evening, and she *had* slept. After she saw the receptionist about her suitcase, to make sure they had her Australian mobile number. She asked for a map and ventured out into the buzzing afternoon. Agnes could feel the leeches dropping off.

8
three days ago

One of South Hamlet's oldest shops had always been Agnes's favourite, long before Niina became the manager, long before she knew Niina. Agnes loved everything about The Book Nook—the green double doors, the shonky shelves cramped with anything from the latest bestsellers to leather-bound classics, and the redolence of old grass, vanilla, and musty wood. This was her childhood, where she'd spent her pocket money.

Agnes sneaked in with the ring tucked away in her jeans. She perched on *her* stool at the corner of the counter while Niina served a customer. Here, hidden behind the card stand, she'd over the years marvelled at her friend's ability to inform and suggest, charm and defuse customers—and agitate. Niina was herself at all times. 'I only piss off the rude ones,' she'd say. Overall Niina was liked, or so it seemed, because business was flourishing. The owner who had bookshops all over, rarely showed up, and Niina reigned supreme.

This was where Agnes had sat when she received the call her mum had suffered a stroke. Niina had been on her first day of the massive autumn sale. They'd set up extra tables in the street, re-arranged the shop, and had just opened the door. When Niina heard the news, she'd rushed everyone out, packed up, locked up, and gone with Agnes to the hospital.

This was where she'd sat when she met Thomas for the first time. She'd looked up from a book, to see who the baritone belonged to, and straightaway, self-conscious, hoped to God Niina wouldn't bring her into any chit-chat. Thomas, a well-groomed Viking in a suit under a trench coat, was buying a booklet about South Hamlet and a map of the town. Niina was her normal self. Nothing could intimidate that girl. Agnes had stayed quiet with her head down, waiting for him to leave. The Viking was taking up a lot of space, demanding attention. It seemed the entire wonky bookshop held its breath for this man. *She* certainly did. At twenty-two, she found men fine from a distance and was content with fictional ones.

'Earth to Agnes,' said Niina. She ruffled her short hair before leaning on the counter. 'Caught up on sleep yet?'

'Feel like a zombie.'

'Can't believe how tanned you are. For a zombie, you look amazing. Just so you know.'

'I don't feel amazing.'

'Ah, well, you get that. So what's what?' She offered an inquisitive Niina look—lifting one perfectly shaped eyebrow, her dark eyes glinting. 'I want all the smutty details.'

'What makes you think there are any?'

She laughed. 'I know how to read between the lines.'

'You've got another customer,' whispered Agnes.

While Niina served, Agnes pulled the ring out of her jeans pocket and slid it on her finger, keeping a hand over it.

As soon as the customer was out the door, Niina was at her again. 'What happened? You liked the guy. Give me something, woman.'

'There's nothing much to—'

'You got laid.' She whistled. 'I read you like a book, darling. Pun naturally intended.'

Agnes regretted the ring.

Niina tapped the counter. 'Come on Agnes. There's no one here. So what happened?'

'I think ... I think he played me.'

'What? You go all that way, to meet a douchebag? What's wrong with our local ones?'

It was sort of good to have Niina make light of it. 'You could come over tonight,' said Agnes. 'Found you a couple of things.' Telling Niina what happened might make her laugh about it.

'Are you going glassy on me?' said Niina.

'I'm jet lagged, is all,' said Agnes, not wanting a hug, not now, not here.

'So, finished with Thomas then?'

Agnes thumbed the ring. There would be an avalanche. Tonight? Or now? Now would give Niina a few hours to digest.

'Thomas picked me up at the airport, took me out for dinner and ...'

'What?' The smile Niina had carried since Agnes walked in slackened.

Without another thought, Agnes held out her hand.

Niina stared at her. 'Is this what I think it is?'

Agnes nodded.

Niina's chubby fingers took hold of her hand for a close inspection. 'One for each miserable year, is it?'

'That's unfair.'

'Didn't think you were that keen on diamonds.'

'I never said—'

'Yes, you did.' She dropped Agnes's hand the way you let go of a slimy fish.

Three boxes were piled on top of each other next to Agnes. Niina picked up one and slammed it on the counter. 'Where's the flipping knife?' She found it and slit the tape open in one quick movement, dropped the knife, and started unpacking all the books, piling them on the counter. She chucked the empty box on the floor. 'You can flatten them for me,' she said before picking up the next box, repeating the procedure.

After she'd opened the last one, she handed over the knife. 'It's my fault,' she said while she went through the books, counting them and ticking them off against the invoices. 'I'd known—no, not known—I'd known *of* him for a whole two minutes. And why did I introduce you? Because he wanted some of South Hamlet's famous ice cream. For crying out loud, I'd just sold him a bloody map. Why didn't I let him get on his merry way?'

It had mortified Agnes when Niina dragged her into the conversation with Thomas.

'My friend can show you, can't you, Agnes?'

They'd walked up to the canal with her bike and his monologue between them, her eyes fixed on the cobblestones. He'd ignored her protests, bought her a Banana Split, and pursued his questions until she started talking. It had thrilled Niina that he wanted to meet up again.

'You used to help me dress up for dates with him,' said Agnes.

'Don't remind me. I regret that too.'

Agnes crouched by the first box and sliced forcefully through the binding tape. 'You don't know him the way I—'

'I know him well enough.'

She didn't, just like Agnes's parents had never known him. While Niina's thrill over Thomas had faded bit by bit, her mum didn't like him from his first hello. She never told Agnes why. She never told you why about anything. Agnes's dad had followed her mum because that's what he did, but at least he'd come up with reasons. 'All city and smooth talking—typical salesman.' Thomas had that persona around other people and, sadly, often with her, too. But there was another side to him.

'You're right,' said Niina. 'How could I get to know him? Coming and going like a frigging delivery man. Not even that. He was like your bi-monthly subscription—yeah, yeah, I know, travelling the frigging country with his frigging insurances. But what about weekends? There was always something aloof about him.'

'He had his little girl. He had commitments.'

'If you ask me. He wasn't there for you.'

She wasn't asking. But he would have been, if not for her mum, who lost her speech after the stroke but not her temper nor her dislike for him. 'He's been there for me since dad passed,' she said.

There was no response. Niina was going through the books on the counter, pretending to read the backs. Niina wasn't reading anything. She was thinking.

Was Niina jealous? Had she felt left out since Thomas had re-entered Agnes's life? Agnes should have organised some dinners. She had neglected Niina over Easter. There wasn't a lot of love lost on his behalf, either. He didn't get their friendship, saw that Niina was her total opposite, but not how that was why it worked.

'I can't put this off. We need to talk now,' said Niina. Yes, she had been thinking. Those words were the top of some deep Niina iceberg. Two women were laughing outside, about to walk in. Niina rushed over to the doorway with impressive speed. For her size, she was surprisingly agile. 'Sorry, quick lunch break,' she said to them. 'Will open in ten.' She closed the door and flipped the sign on the glass. She stayed on the spot and put her hands on her hips.

Agnes stood up, flattened the first box, and threw it through the door into Niina's back office. 'Not in the mood,' she said.

'Don't care. He's not right for you. This on-and-off-for-years business—'

'You do actually know why.'

Niina wobbled her head. 'What if Nils and Irene had good reason to be protective of their only child? If they didn't think him good enough. What does that tell ya?'

Agnes shook her head. Seemingly, her parents had adored Niina. They were on their best behaviour when she visited. Niina had never understood what it was like to be their daughter. Because Niina was a colourful, larger than life, Picasso, while Agnes was an amateur pencil drawing. Thomas—not good enough—wasn't it.

'You fell for a man on the other side of the world. What does that tell ya?'

'I made a mistake. People make mistakes.' Niina had made plenty. Agnes glared at her. She kept her opinions about Niina's life choices to herself. Niina never paid her the same favour. Was their friendship even a good one? Was it toxic? Had she been too blind all these years to notice?

'I suggest between now and the wedding—what have you got? A year? Longer? Go spend some time with him in Stockholm, meet his friends, his family. You've never done that. And has he even met Olga? Didn't think so.'

Agnes dropped the knife on the counter, then launched the boxes through the doorway to the back room. Niina could do them herself. She put her jacket on.

'There's nothing wrong with, try before you buy,' said Niina. And ... I don't want to say it ... you always take this the wrong way—'

'Don't say it then.' There was the familiar rush of heat to Agnes's head, the shortness of breath, the frustration.

'What if I'm right?'

'What if you're right? You and mum.' Agnes had to force the words out. 'Him, love me for me? No. Not possible.'

'Agnes ...'

'Because as we all know. I'm not loveable.'

'I know it's not like millions or anything but you do have a solid trust fund.'

'That'll do,' said Agnes.

'You take it the wrong way. I didn't mean—'

'Whatever.' Agnes shoved her hands in her pockets and tried to breathe out, but the air was trapped. 'We're getting married on Thursday.'

Niina laughed. 'You are kidding me, right? Well, one needs to be an effing hummingbird to keep up with you.'

'We fly to Greece on Saturday.'

'For how long?'

'Two weeks.'

'And what about Olga? She's been asking about you.'

'She's been fine. You said.' There was the guilt like a sledgehammer. How had she not thought of Olga?

Niina shrugged. 'I didn't want to ruin your holiday. A bit of an incident one evening. Had to drive around and see her. She was going on about how you'd drowned.'

'She gets confused.' It was too late to change Greece. How had she not thought of Olga?

'Not wrong,' said Niina. 'Kept telling me how sorry she was.'

'I'll organise respite care. There's one lady she accepts—'

'I can do it.'

'No, it's fine. I'll find—'

'Don't be ridiculous. If you end up going to Greece. I'll look after her.'

'I'll have a talk to her. I'll go see her—'

'I told her you won't be home until Thursday. Thought you'd need a few days to recover,' said Niina. 'Turns out, you don't. You're ready to dive in. And by the way, I'm giving dinner a miss.'

The relief, of not having to deal with Niina in a few hours. But there was also disappointment. She wanted to show Niina the tops she'd bought her. And she wanted to tell her all that had happened. Then again, what was the point? She wanted to say so much, how Niina didn't understand anything, how she wanted Niina there at the wedding to be her family, her maid of honour, how she wanted her to be happy for her. 'Okay,' was all Agnes said.

'Go home,' said Niina. 'Sleep your way back to sanity.' She turned the sign again and opened the door. The women greeted her and walked past Agnes with a nod before disappearing into the nooks and crannies.

The upset was ebbing, her head cooling, the tightness in her chest easing. She was able to breathe out. Agnes started towards the door, then stopped. 'I need to ask you something.'

'What now?' Niina was flicking through pages, back and forth, her mind busy with all her opinions.

'It's not a problem. It's ...'

'What?'

'While I was away ... did you bring a bloke over to my place? I don't mind. You know that.' Niina's flat above the bookshop was tiny.

'I watered your plants, brought in your mail twice, and turned up the thermostat for your homecoming. That's it. Been out dancing on the weekends. Why?'

'Toilet seat was up. I assumed you'd brought a date or something.'

'I bet you did that last time you cleaned it.'

She must have.

9
two days ago

Coercing her body to the Swedish time zone proved harder than Agnes had expected. The phone didn't land back on its hook until Wednesday midday, when she finally found the energy to deal with Australian Airways again, and the rest of the world. The latter would include Thomas and Olga, possibly even Niina.

The airline was in the end represented by a man whose name went in one ear and out the other. Agnes had lost count on how many times she'd sat and waited with that artificial music in her ear. This time it took less than forty minutes to get through, and she was only re-connected twice. When the man at the other end let her know they had found the suitcase, she assumed he'd made a mistake. He checked her name again.

'We had no luck with your first number of contact,' he said.

'That was my pre-paid, while in Australia.'

'Right,' said the man, sounding clueless. 'We had another mobile number in Australia.'

'But I rang. And I gave you my home number here in Sweden and my address.'

It was quiet for a minute. 'I don't have any details of that here.'

'Well, I spoke to someone, a woman. That was ...' What day was that? What day was it today? 'It was last Friday,' she said. 'I spoke to someone.'

'Did you, by any chance, take their name?'

'No, why would I?'

'It's always helpful.'

Agnes sighed, loud enough for him to hear. 'Never mind,' she said. 'I'm on the phone with you now. You'll get my address again. And I expect it to be freighted back A S A P. That's important cargo, you understand. And I've been waiting an awfully long time.'

'Miss Andersson. It's already been despatched.'

'It has?'

'I believe so.'

'Believing isn't exactly good enough, is it? Double check please.'

There was a moment's pause and then, 'Yes, we have definitely despatched it.'

'And to where?'

'One of my colleagues spoke to a Mr Ventura—'

Nothing more than his surname coming from a stranger's voice over the phone, and still there was a tug inside, the memory of his hands in her hair, his breath in her ear, his peculiar scent of salty air, sunblock, and Felicity. When they rang him, did he feel the smallest sting of guilt, of remorse?

'Was it sent to Sweden?' she said, feeling sick with fury, with embarrassment. She should have confronted Guy.

'One minute, please.'

While the man put her on hold again. Agnes prayed, hoped, wished, and begged that he'd made a mistake, that they still had her suitcase or that somehow they'd sent it to her home address.

He was back. It sounded like he was fiddling with papers, possibly preparing himself for aggression. 'So, we spoke to a Mr. Guy Ventura. You had left his sister's address with us and so that's where we sent it. We wanted to deliver as expedient as possible, Miss Andersson.'

'Did you now?'

'On behalf of Australian Airways, I do apol—'

'Expediency is not something I'd accuse your airline of,' Agnes interrupted, with a niggling that she was over the top. She couldn't help herself. He was the stand-in for the company. Tough luck. 'Your company managed to lose my merchandise on the way to my business exhibition.'

'Did you take out any insurance?' he asked with the voice of a man who knows his trump card.

She had. For herself, in case she'd need a hospital for any reason, not for her bears, and not for her beautiful suitcase. It had never occurred to her they'd misplace them. 'This is not about money,' said Agnes. 'It's about the inconvenience and the worry.'

'Again, I apologise, but it would have been better if you'd given us your home address in Sweden to begin with.' He'd found his momentum. 'If you had, Miss Andersson, your suitcase may well have arrived by now.'

'I had merchandise to sell while—Never mind.' Agnes sighed. 'So you have delivered my suitcase to Coffs Harbour?'

'Yes, to the sister of Mr Ventura, a Holly—'

'Fine.' Agnes sighed again, even louder. Well, Guy had money allocated for freight and her address. She would not ring him or his sister.

'If there's anything else we can do for you today?' said the man.

Agnes could think of a thing or two, but she kept them to herself.

She sat with the phone in her hand after, undecided about dropping the receiver back or leaving it off the hook for the rest of the day. She dropped it back.

Agnes didn't even have time to get out of her mother's chair before the phone rang. She thought, Olga for sure, but it was Thomas.

'Finally,' he said. 'How come you're not answering your mobile?'

'I lost my phone card, remember?' It wasn't exactly a lie. Agnes had not put it in the phone because she'd not been in the mood for Thomas or Niina, the two people who texted her. She was pretty sure which little pocket she'd put it in, but not bothered to search. So it kind of was lost. 'I bet I'll find it in my luggage, but I've been sleeping, and not even unpacked.' That was the absolute truth.

'I just wanted to run a few things by you.'

Agnes rested her eyelids while Thomas talked and talked. About their vows—should they go with the standard? 'Sure,' she said. About South Hamlet's Guesthouse—should they cover for his mum? 'Of course,' she said. And his uncle? 'Of course,' she said. And what about the best man? 'Sure.' And by the way, his daughter was opting out. 'Okay.' That was all she had. Pernilla needed a bit more time. 'Fine.'

'You sound tired,' he said.

Agnes exhaled. Should she say let's stop this? Stop. She could put an end to this right now. She could.

'Don't worry Ness. I've not invited many people, promise. I thought we'd have a party later, for midsummer. Friends can come and camp on our back lawn.'

Her dad would hate it. And where did *our* back lawn come from? Our?

'You go sleep. And what can I do? Should I order the food? Give me the name of the business and I'll ring from here. How hard can it be right?'

She groaned inwardly. It was at the tip of her tongue. *I can't do this. I don't know what I want.* Why couldn't she just let the words out, set them free? *Because I'm jet-lagged. I can't be trusted. I'll say it and then I'll regret it.* 'It's all under control.' She'd seen Patrick the day before, paid him, told him to create whatever he wanted. It had taken all of ten minutes. 'I invited him,' she said.

'You invited who?'

'The deli-man?'

'Okay ...?'

It couldn't just be Thomas's family and Thomas's friends. And Niina wanted to meet Patrick. He was four weeks new to town, and lo-and-behold, Niina hadn't devoured the man yet. He was going to be the distraction for the day. 'I think he can hold his own,' said Agnes.

'I beg your pardon?'

'Don't mind me,' she said. 'Thinking out loud is all.' Shivers tingled down her spine. That was the title of the song she and Guy danced to. There he was, smiling at her, checking his sails, checking the horizon, the two of them flying across the water. She'd thought good of him, only good.

'Agnes? Are you there?'

'I'm inviting my neighbour as well,' she said.

'Not the strange one across the—?'

'Not strange, Thomas. Unwell.' What was with this new disagreeability? *I'm becoming my mum.* The suitcase bothered her. As did Guy, the wedding, Thomas, the song, Tanya. She needed to sleep. 'Got to go. I'll call you when I find the SIM card.' She hung up. Just like that, she hung up. Then she took the receiver straight off and left it on the desk, and sat in her mother's chair, looking vacantly out the window, listening to the ringtone.

They'd found her suitcase. It was on a detour via Holly's, but it would return. Guy would surely organise the freight back. Her bears were not lost. *You'll get your bears back.* Guy's words from another time when she'd thought she'd met a man she could trust.

10
yesterday

After having called Olga without her picking up, Agnes wandered up to the canal with her duty-free bag and the intention of sitting on her father's bench until her neighbour would spot her. The elderly woman spent most of her time in her sunroom painting, so it shouldn't take long. Unless, of course, Olga worried it was her imagination that played tricks on her.

Agnes's dad had secured the wooden seat on a concrete slab on the grass, five meters from the small pier that existed solely for Olga's rowing boat. As long as Agnes could remember, her dad had delivered his neighbour's groceries this way. Before stacking the boat, the two of them would sit here drinking coffee from a thermos, having a *chinny-wag* as her father called it.

After her mother's stroke, as his relapse into alcohol became a problem, Agnes took over the deliveries. She'd hang the bags on the wheelchair and push Irene up the short hill. Agnes would bring coffee. Olga and she would small talk while her mum was chewing on the biscuits they fed her, staring at the scenery, lost in her own world.

Agnes never ventured out on the pier when there was water in the canal. And after her father's death, she preferred the twenty-minute drive around to Olga's place. The last time Agnes had been up here, the canal had been its lowest with the water on the bottom, frozen, and the steep slopes, covered in snow. The winter landscape differed from the other seasons. The waterway that lay deep and mysterious from spring to autumn became a giant gutter, open and bare. There was nothing that could swallow you. At Easter, the canal had been full again. Thomas hadn't suggested walks. If he had, she would have found excuses. For that had been her—avoiding guilt, pampering her fears, staying in her comfort zone. She wouldn't do that anymore.

There was Olga, waving. Even from this far away, Agnes saw the excitement. She'd be out in minutes, rushing down to her boat. She may or may not be shocked to see Agnes up on the canal again. You could never be sure of Olga, what she remembered and what she'd forgotten. Since the tragedy, she'd become more uncertain of herself and others. It wasn't fair to leave Niina to monitor Olga for another two weeks, so soon after Agnes's trip away, but Thomas had not thought that far because that was Thomas. And come to think of it, neither had she.

Olga had enough voices and characters to deal with, so you didn't introduce new people into Olga's life unless it was necessary. Marrying Thomas made it necessary, but it could wait until after Greece. Contrary to what she'd led Thomas to believe, Olga would graciously decline the invitation.

From her dad's seat, Agnes watched the elderly woman row across the moss-green water, impressed with the strength in those arms, despite her age and petite frame. She was wearing a neon yellow life vest. She never used to, but good to see. Agnes tilted her face to the sun that had found a break in the clouds. She thought of her dad digging in the garden, taking cookies out of the oven, his radio blasting in the background, him kissing her mum's cheek—her dad when he was intoxicated with life.

One day, when Olga was in a good headspace, over a thermos of coffee, Agnes would ask about her mum and dad, about when they first met, ask if there had ever been a love story there at all.

The rowlocks clicked as Olga pulled the oars through the water, followed by the heavy drops as they lifted before they dipped in the water again. A beautiful rhythm. Then the oars landed in the boat as the dinghy hit the small pier with a thud, and Agnes opened her eyes.

Olga hauled the rope around the piling with a quick hand, tied a bowline before moving to the side of her seat, then grabbed the sill, pulling the boat close. Her knobbly fingers held tight to the plank. Agnes walked onto the pier, crouched, and put her feet in the boat to give Olga respite from hanging on. The surrounding water was still, dark, and thick. It was easy to imagine sinking. But she was okay. A little nervous flutter, but she was okay. Tanya to thank for that. Such a strange blend of dislike and gratitude for one person.

Olga, in her funny little beret over her fine silver grey and her pink cheeks, beamed and clapped her hands. 'Look at you?'

Agnes reached over and gave her a padded hug. She'd always preferred Olga's scent of coffee, chocolate, and turps, to her mother's. It was always smoke and dry paper. After the stroke, her mother's miasma made Agnes think of an old chest with dirty laundry.

'You've not come to the pier for a while.'

'I haven't. But I will from now on. And not today, and not tomorrow, but soon, we'll have coffee on dad's bench.'

Olga nodded and touched Agnes's cheek with icy fingers, coarse with dried paint. 'I don't mind rowing, from mine to yours. I never minded that. But I don't walk any longer.' She nodded towards South Hamlet. 'They tell me I shouldn't.'

'Okay,' said Agnes. It was usually easier to go with it, and then sidetrack. Agnes handed over the bag. 'Chocolates,' she said. 'All the way from Australia.'

'Koalas?' said Olga, looking deep into the bag.

She loved chocolates more than Agnes if that was possible. No point in buying trinkets since they'd end up in the garbage, with Olga claiming *they* told her to throw them out. Clothes she'd splatter with paint within hours, so Agnes kept supplying hand-me-downs. Sweets were practical and appreciated while she spent hours and hours in her art room.

'I'm getting married,' said Agnes. 'Tomorrow.'

'You are?' Olga had taken out the different boxes and piled them next to her. 'I didn't know,' she said, carefully returning them to the paper bag. 'Did I forget?'

'No. It's all quite sudden. And I wonder if you would like to come? At ours, small, but there will be other people, of course.'

Olga shook her head. 'I'm sorry, Agnes. I don't think so.'

'It's fine.'

'You'll show me photos?'

'Of course.'

'And who's the lucky man?'

'You shall make his acquaintance after our honeymoon.'

'That's what you deserve, dear, a holiday in the sun.' Olga frowned at her, confused. 'You went to Australia, didn't you?' she said.

Agnes nodded.

'The week after Easter?'

'That's right. But tomorrow I'm getting married.'

'I didn't tell her,' said Olga to herself, or a voice in her head, perhaps. 'I must tell her.' She turned to Agnes. 'I saw your lights on?'

Dang. 'Well ... I had to sleep for a couple of days.'

'I saw lights sometimes,' said Olga again. 'While you were away. Came from the kitchen, and Irene's room I think, and upstairs too.'

'I bought these special lamps that come on and off, randomly,' lied Agnes.

'Clever girl,' said Olga.

Half an hour later, Agnes sat in her mother's chair by the computer's screen having checked her accounts again. She kept her passwords in the notebook in the drawer, hidden under a heap of papers, which was stupid. Yet, there was no money missing. There had been little available. Her allowance was delivered once a fortnight. Not even she could dip her hand into the trust fund at random. The most anyone could have stolen was a few thousand, but there were no transfers or withdrawals, except for her own.

Seeing the splurges in Coffs, forced images of Guy. Tanya followed. Agnes flicked both of them out of her mind and closed her banking.

She glared at the desktop screen. The folders belonged to her mother and her accountancy, another procrastination. After Greece, she'd deal with it. The trash bin was completely empty. She had no recollection of doing that. Just for the heck of it, she checked the search history. It had been erased—all of it. Someone visiting her house while she was away to clean up her rubbish? That was nonsensical. The week before she left for Australia had been utter madness, with all the finishing touches and the packing. She'd obviously done this herself, and shouldn't let dear Olga's imagination run wild with her.

11

twenty-three days ago

On the Coast to Coast bus, Agnes had the misfortune to be seated next to a talker, an exuberant woman in a turban-like entanglement of coloured curls and scarves, in layers upon layers of skirts, and sleeves like butterfly wings, a personification of an artist's palette, a disorderly bundle of rainbow rayon, bad breath and sweat.

Mind you, she'd come off a long flight. Agnes couldn't pronounce her name at all, couldn't get her mouth around the syllables. The woman had a similar problem with English, which did not inhibit her need to express herself. Agnes's hopes of reading her brand new book went out the window like the mist over Sydney Harbour Bridge as they departed at sunrise.

Agnes sat with her back pressed to the window, listening and holding her breath until her nasal sensory cells had adjusted. It was the woman's first time in Australia. She wanted to see Uluru and kangaroo and didgeridoo. Agnes, nodding and smiling, contributed an 'aha' here and there, or an 'okay'. Every time Agnes said, 'okay', the woman repeated it with enthusiasm. She didn't mind that Agnes said very little else.

The rest of the bus was full. Most passengers seemed to travel in pairs or in groups. They spoke with consideration of their fellow travellers. Their conversations were a gentle chatter, the odd and subdued laugh blending with the motor beneath them. Agnes's companion was the loud one on this trip without a speck of self-awareness. It was ironic that they had teamed her up with the quiet one.

At their first stop for breakfast in Newcastle, Miss Butterfly spread her sleeves around the others, giving Agnes an opportunity to sit down in peace with her new romance. But she had trouble concentrating, kept reading the first page of the first chapter over and over, not registering. It wasn't the English that stood in the way but the anticipation to catch up with Guy, if only for two hours.

Standing at the bottom step of the Opera House on Monday evening, she'd braved it and sent him a text asking if he wanted to meet up. His response came within seconds.

Typical :-(Working

Immediately, the week ahead lost colour. Ten minutes later, she received another text.

Time and place :-D Meet
you there

She'd run up the stairs to the Opera house entrance and sat on the top step among other excited visitors, watching the sun colour the sky pink.

The hours after Newcastle dragged on. Her companion alternated between asleep and awake, afflicting her fellow passengers with irregular snoring or rambling, while Agnes sat cramped between butterfly thighs and window armrest. By the time the bus rolled into the car park at the Big Banana in Coffs Harbour, Agnes was desperate for a break from the padded swaddle of joy.

Guy was waiting in shorts and a T-shirt, hair damp and sleek, his curls combed out tucked behind his ears, his beard shorter and neater. A big grin on his face showed he was happy to see her. As he pulled her into a hug, all the shyness dissolved and she allowed her body to fuse with his chest for the shortest time, resting her face into his neck that smelled of soap.

'Two hours is all we've got,' she said. 'I've been told in no uncertain terms by our guide that I must be back in time.'

'Let's not waste it,' said Guy. 'But first—' He kept one arm around her and held his phone up. 'Say cheese.'

'I'm not photogenic,' she said, catching herself brushing the fringe. He'd seen it. It didn't matter. *Oh, what the heck.* She relaxed and said cheese a few times while he snapped.

He showed her as they walked towards his car, three in instant succession.

'I look idiotic—'

'Happy is the word, Agnes. And that's a beautiful smile.'

In all three, he wasn't looking at the camera; he was looking at her while she gazed up wide-eyed, showing most of her teeth. The hair, meticulously blow-dried at five that morning, lay sleek and flat from the detrimental humidity. The breeze lifted the fringe to one side, and her mascara had smudged since Newcastle. She didn't like what she saw but had to admit, she did look happy.

Guy drove a station wagon of some sort, cramped with stuff—a surfboard, flippers, fishing rods, something harpoon-like, a plastic box with a pile of towels and whatnot. Sand spread through the carpet and there was a smell of silt.

'Sorry about the mess.'

It didn't bother her, only brought home the experience of visiting a strange place. She admired the surroundings, the trees, people's houses that looked so different from the ones at home. Though brown brick seemed rather popular, there were plenty of innovative creations—unusual angles, corrugated iron, and expansive glass. Not like at home, where they were conservative, staying true to the heritage of vertical wood panels and moderately sized windows with pretty flowers in pots and curtains from IKEA.

They didn't travel for long before Guy drove into a car park facing the ocean. She'd suggested lunch, and he'd insisted on a picnic. She couldn't be more thankful.

He lifted out a cooling bag and handed her a couple of worse-for-wear towels. She trailed after him down to and along the beach. With each step she took, delicious sand found its way in between sandals and soles, only to dash out in front again. The ocean glittered, and the waves made a whooshing sound as they broke and came rushing up the pebbles and sand. before receding, and meeting the next rush of water. Agnes thought she could smell the salt.

They spread the towels under an enormous tree that cast the shade behind them. A Pandanus he told her. He brought out chilled apple cider and bought sandwiches. Agnes couldn't believe how beautiful it all was, how perfect. The sun was high and stark. The sky was cerulean blue without a single cloud. She pulled up the long cotton dress she'd bought the day before and took off her sandals. Then she stretched out two white legs, dug her feet into the sand, and put her face to the bright light.

'You need sunnies,' said Guy.

'Not at all,' she said. The warmth caressed her eyelids in the most delightful way.

He poured her a glass. 'Cheers and welcome to Coffs.'

Agnes drank and thanked her lucky stars, the universe, God, and with some demurral, Thomas. Then she quickly tucked him away among the undies in her cabin bag, closed the lid and returned to enjoying how wonderful it was. She, Agnes Andersson, was in Australia, on a beautiful beach with a newfound friend. This was a holiday.

They didn't discuss the missing bears or the expo flop. They'd already covered both in the weekend's phone conversations and texts. Instead, she asked Guy about the town, about the surrounding vegetation, about the handful of people surfing out from where they sat, the person waving at them. Guy waved back.

'That's Tanya.'

'Good friend?'

'We go way back.'

'She's good at that, at surfing.'

'Done it all her life. Good at anything physical.'

To sit out there emerged in moving water, so small, at the mercy of the power of the Pacific. What was it like to have that kind of confidence? 'What about sharks?' she said. 'You have them, don't you?'

Guy shrugged. 'You don't think about that. Not much.'

Tanya caught a wave. With great admiration, Agnes watched her go down what Guy called the face of the wave, do a bottom turn and come up again, do a snap off the top, sending spray out behind her and then down for another go. After disappearing into the wave, she came back up and lay down on the board. Pushed by white water, she was coming back to shore.

'You need protection,' said Guy. 'I'll see if I can find a pair of sunnies in my car, or a hat.'

Agnes realised that half an hour had already passed. Why was it that time knew to drag when something boring or sad was going on in your life, but as soon as you dared to enjoy yourself, it picked up speed?

'G'day.'

The bronzed woman stood in front of her, the board under an arm, her trim legs glistening with wet, and her upper body squeezed into a tight, long-sleeved top, shading Agnes from the sun.

'Hello,' said Agnes, putting a hand over her forehead, sounding like the foreigner she was.

Tanya put the board away in the grass behind them. Then she came and sat down next to her, in Guy's spot. With some effort, she pulled her top off. She was all muscles, toned arms and legs, even a faint six-pack in a bright-coloured bikini that covered very little.

'I'm Tanya,' she said. 'You're the Swiss woman, yeah?'

So Guy had mentioned her. 'Swedish,' she corrected. 'I'm Agnes.'

Tanya squeezed the excess water out of her long hair, flicked it behind her, and sat back, stretching her legs out next to Agnes's. The difference was remarkable. Agnes's knees were unshapely and embarrassingly white. Tanya's were sinewy and tanned. Though she guessed Tanya was older than her, the opposite was more believable.

Guy was back. 'Sorry about the scratches,' he said, handing over a pair of sunglasses before sitting down on the other side. Agnes wished he'd sat down next to her. She could barely see him.

'Haven't got a spare glass?'

'Didn't expect an imposter, did I.' Guy leaned across and filled up Agnes's.

Once he'd poured his own, Tanya snatched it out of his hand and held it up to Agnes. 'Cheers to your holiday,' she said. 'Heard you're on a tour, heading for the barrier reef.'

'Yes.' Agnes couldn't think of anything to add to that.

'How do you like it so far?'

'It's so nice.' Nice? Was that all she could come up with?

'Should go for a swim. Water's like a bath.'

'I didn't bring my bathing suit.'

'Go feel it,' she said. 'You can't come to Coffs and not even stick your toes in the water.'

Didn't Tanya have to be somewhere, go home for lunch or go back to work or get some dry clothes on? Agnes thought the breeze was a little cool herself.

'Don't worry,' said Guy, taking back his glass. 'We'll get to it. Just chilling for a bit. You know that thing where you enjoy being in the moment without being active? Should try it.'

'What's on your wish list, then?'

'I'd love to see dolphins,' said Agnes.

Tanya laughed. 'You just missed them. Here an hour ago. But I meant you Guy, what do you want as a welcome-back gift?'

'Nothing,' said Guy.

'I'll think of something.' She nudged him with her shoulder. 'And it'll be tomorrow night.'

'What will?'

'Your welcome back do,' she said and smacked him on his thigh, leaving her hand there.

'A party for you?' asked Agnes, leaning forward, trying to get eye contact with Guy.

He picked up Tanya's hand, placed it back on her own thigh, leaned forward and shook his head at Agnes. 'It's just an excuse for her to get drunk and get her hairy legs on the dance—'

'Yeah right.' Tanya gave him a sudden push that sent him sideways, landing him on his elbow in the sand. 'He's full of shit,' she said to Agnes. 'Loves it when we fuss over him.'

Agnes smiled weakly.

Guy handed the glass to Tanya again, stood and held his hand out to Agnes. 'She's right, we should go for a walk.' He pulled her up, then said, 'See you later.'

Tanya emptied the glass into the sand. 'Tomorrow night. We'll all be there.'

'Very nice meeting you,' said Agnes.

'You too. Happy travels.'

'She can be full on,' said Guy, as they walked down to the water.

They strolled along the water's edge, Guy with his hands loosely in his jeans pockets, she with hers busily holding up the hem of her maxi dress. She was acutely aware of Guy's body next to her, his steady walk, his hand that kept leaving its pocket to hold his flying hair down.

It was the first time in her life walking along a beach, the first time experiencing waves. Her bare feet sinking in the cool sand, the constant moving back and forth, the patterns created by the sunlight, the clarity, being able to see the bottom that stretched out to sea—it was such a contrast to the still and dark of the canal. At home, the underneath lay hidden. Here it lay bare. Here it was easy to breathe.

By the time they returned to their picnic spot, it was time to pack up. Agnes took one last look at the long stretch of beach and waves before trudging after Guy in the hot sand, her heart heavy with the upcoming goodbye.

Guy walked with her to the bus. The other passengers were already seated, some of them blaring at her from their windows. The driver had started the motor and the tour guide was waiting outside with her passenger list in hand.

'There you are, Miss Andersson. I've been wondering if it was time to send out a search party,' her tone sharp with disapproval. 'We were supposed to be on the road seven minutes ago.'

Guy's firm hug around her was quick. Before she knew it, Agnes was on her seat, next to the butterfly woman, her face bright with excitement, the one person on the bus who couldn't care less about seven minutes. Agnes had an inkling she'd have lots to tell her about the two hours at the Big Banana. Guy waited below the window, looking up. The driver and Miss Tour Guide were having a conversation over the running motor.

Panic was rising inside. Two hours had flown by and now she had days and days ahead of her, on the road, with all these strangers, and her annoying seat-neighbour.

'You have man?' asked butterfly woman, who had gained the smell of cheese on top of her inherent odours.

'Friend,' said Agnes, not taking her eyes off Guy. He was moving his lips, trying to tell her something. She waved to him, wishing the rest of the world would stop dead so she could get out and enjoy more hours on the beach.

'Nice man.' Butterfly woman stretched across to see better and waved to Guy.

Agnes nodded while rolling up the bag strap tight, tight.

Guy pulled his phone out of his jeans pocket, began texting. There was the familiar ping. Agnes released the strap and fumbled around in her bag. Found the phone. It was one word.

Stay

Guy stood looking up at her, nodding and grinning.

'What he say?'

The doors shut and the bus began moving. From the front, the tour guide apologised for the delay. Agnes's mind buzzed with Guy's request. *Stay*. She looked at her screen, then Guy, who was walking now, to keep up. He was nodding. Then he stopped and her view of him disappeared as the bus left the parking area.

'He wants you stay?'

'I'm supposed to visit the barrier reef,' said Agnes, her gaze on the palm trees gliding past, wanting badly to be out there. Thomas crawled out from underneath her undies and into her mind. Sick at home, and he'd still booked her on this tour—a considerate gesture. But then there was Guy, a man without hang-ups about women, a man who obviously had friends who were women. Would it bother Thomas if she had a holiday here instead? Apart from Niina, there wasn't much of a social life at home, and Guy had popped up out of nowhere offering friendship. She knew him. She didn't know the tourists seated around her.

'Forget reef,' said butterfly woman. 'If he my man—'

'Not my man. A friend.'

'If he my friend, I stay.'

'You would?' Agnes turned her head away from the window to look at her.

'Yes.'

'Too late,' said Agnes. And it was. The bus driver was ready to turn onto the highway as soon as there was a gap in the traffic.

'No,' said Butterfly woman with a loud whisper. Behind all the thick mascara and crackled foundation, green eyes twinkled at Agnes. 'See.' She picked up Agnes's hand and pressed it gently on Agnes's chest. 'Don't listen head. Listen heart.'

The ticking underneath Agnes's palm seemed so loud, so furious, booming in her ears.

'See heart.'

'Okay. I stay.' The voice didn't sound like hers.

'Okay.' The Butterfly was out of her seat. 'Stop bus!' she called. 'Stop bus! Anness stay! Stop bus!'

Agnes grabbed her handbag and cardigan. She gave her cheerleader a big kiss on the cheek before scrambling past her and up to the driver, ignoring the huffing from some passengers, and jumping over a few feet. 'Please stop,' she said.

Tour guide woman, who sat in the single seat right at the front, shook her head at her. 'No, it's O H and S. Safety rules, you hear me? You must sit down.'

'My journey ends here.'

'Go back to your seat. We're not some public transport service.'

Agnes stepped past her and addressed the driver. 'You need to let me out. Now.'

He ignored her, keeping his eyes on the busy highway where the cars were flying past.

'I'm getting off. You can't force me to stay. I'm free to do as I choose. And I choose to stay. You hear me? It'll take all of ten seconds. Let. Me. Out.' Was she being rude and unreasonable? She was. She, mousy Agnes from South Hamlet, was misbehaving.

'I won't go looking for your bag,' he said. 'No, time for—'

'I don't care!'

'You've already delayed us enough,' said the tour guide.

But the driver, who'd started rolling, stopped and opened the doors. The cars behind him showed their annoyance with honking horns.

'Thanks!' she called as she jumped out.

Agnes couldn't see Guy but started running towards the car park. She caught up with him as he clicked the lock on his car. And what came over her? It was not like anything she'd ever done before. She half jumped and placed her hands on his shoulders, slamming her handbag into his back. Doubt came like lightning. What if she'd misunderstood him? Too late.

Guy flung around. Then he laughed and hugged her, lifting her off the ground. 'You, Agnes from Sweden, are one big surprise.'

12
today

Agnes always imagined her wedding day under a bright summer sky, a garden in full bloom, and vows exchanged underneath the honeysuckle with—against all odds—her parents' blessing. Here it is in early May with low thick clouds and a northerly bite. No tulips this year, only a few yellow Narcissus flowers, and the honeysuckle is nothing but sinews wound tight around the trellis. Not a single budding leaf. And no parents.

'Not too late to pull the plug,' says Niina.

'I'm not pulling any plug.'

They're standing on the lawn, bare feet on damp grass, dressed in satin and wrapped in blankets against the crisp morning, Agnes with her cocoa, and her unease, while Niina sucks the living daylight out of her minty cigarette. There's bird twitter, and there's an outboard motor in the distance heading towards South Hamlet.

'They've promised rain,' says Niina.

'I don't care.'

'Might be a sign.' Niina lifts her chin up, pouts her lips before releasing the smoke meditatively.

What if receiving so many presents is the sole reason she gave Agnes a break last night? She'd better not start up again. Mind you, Niina needs nicotine, with its complementary toxins, to distribute through her blood before she's fully human.

'You could have waited a few months,' she says. 'He should move in for a bit. Do a test run for crying out loud.'

Agnes drinks the last mouthful. It's too sugary and too thick. Thomas has stayed over a fair bit since her dad's funeral. 'What needs testing? I already know he leaves the toilet seat up, the coffee jar open, and sucks at washing up. I can live with that.'

'You'll end up in Stockholm. He's such a city slick.'

Agnes glances at Niina's profile—her puffy cheeks, her black hair standing out in short tufts, her determined, generous lips. When Niina Bogati arrived at South Hamlet High, she made a name for herself on the first day. Got sent to the principal's office before the morning break. She'd come from a foster home in Gothenburg, had moved across the land for a fresh start. The new family wasn't evil or anything. She was miserably hard work, was all—her words. The day she turned sixteen, she moved into a small flat above the old bookshop. She's still there.

Niina is everything Agnes isn't—loud, tall, and confident. Their peers admired her even if they didn't particularly want to hang with her. She moved between groups with the ease of someone who was and is, in herself, enough.

Their friendship is a fluke. If Agnes hadn't braved that first school dance in year nine, if Niina—already an avid smoker—hadn't walked outside for a cigarette, their friendship may never have happened. When the school bully shoved Agnes behind the hedge for his own private touch-up, Niina heard muffled protests in the dark autumn night. She found them, pulled him off and punched him just like that. 'I was permanently on the lookout for someone to punch in them days,' she's told Agnes. The bully didn't come to school for an entire week. That was the beginning of an unlikely alliance.

A sailboat glides past on the canal, a mere stone's throw away, yet all they see from here below the embankment is the mast as it moves past the Andersson pier, straight into the lock. The thought of Guy comes and goes in a split second. It'll probably be like this for a while; yachts will remind her of him.

'I have to live my own life,' says Agnes.

'Yours, not his,' says Niina, tapping her cig, flicking the ash off.

'This makes sense.'

'Makes no sense to me. It's bat-shit-crazy.'

'Okay.' Agnes sighs. 'So I'm not boring for once. Thought you'd like that.'

'You're just rushing into this because of what happened.'

'Not true.'

'You should realise there are other—'

'I don't want other men.'

'You wanted that guy.'

'Surely the Aussie wanker, as you so accurately named him, proves me right.'

Niina holds her tongue. She flicks the ash off again, then holds up what's left of her precious cig, considers it, maybe calculates if a couple of small puffs are in preference to a long hard drag to finish it off.

'Niina, you have to stop this. I mean it.'

Niina doesn't throw back something smart. She draws in the last on her cigarette stump.

There's a quiet moment between them and a faint clink from the old lock gate.

'I'll shut up,' she says finally. 'If you wanna marry the guy, marry the guy.' She casts a glance at a non-existent watch on the wrist. 'I'll let you enjoy what freedom you have left, which is eight hours, give or take.'

'Niina.'

She laughs. 'I'm joking.'

'It's not funny. And I do have a list of things.'

'Stitching bears—is that on the list?'

Agnes doesn't bother answering.

'Don't worry, Agnes, I'm at your service. Gotta doll myself up a bit, of course.' Niina drops her butt in Agnes's empty cup, then squeezes her with a generous arm, blowing the last smoke away from them with little effect. The smoke still finds its way up Agnes's nostrils.

'I wouldn't go, you know, overboard,' says Agnes.

'Meaning?'

'It's just ... I think Patrick is a down-to-earth sort of man.'

'Meaning?'

'And he's old school. Well mannered.'

'Meaning?'

That's when they hear screeching tyres on the gravel at the front of the house. Agnes knows one person who drives like that. 'Here's Thomas,' she says. First time he's been early for something.

'There go your hours of freedom.'

'Do you mind?'

'Oh, touchy.'

'It is wearing a little thin.'

'It bugs you that he's here,' says Niina. 'As it should.'

'I'm fine. He can set up chairs and move furniture. We'll make use of him,' says Agnes. She'll find a new angle. Their Sunday dinner has a hazy weirdness over it and they've only had random phone talks during the week. Spending a few hours together before everyone arrives could be beneficial, give her a chance to ease back into what they had before she messed it all up. And then it hits her, again, like the old alarm clock her mother used with the striker battering the bells. She's a step closer.

'Yes, Agnes, it is happening,' says Niina, who does read her like a well-thumbed book.

'Wedding jitters,' says Agnes. 'To be expected.'

'Your poor nails,' says Niina, taking hold of her hand.

'And your poor lungs.' Agnes pulls out of the grip.

Niina lifts one eyebrow.

'If you think you're trying to please my parents, Niina. Stop. I've had it up to here. Guy was a fling, a sidestep sure, but unlike you, I don't need to go through a pile of men before I settle for someone.'

As if surrendering, Niina lifts her hands up, and the blanket corners with them. Then she gets the all too familiar Niina twinkle in her eyes. 'All I'm saying is, *if* it's the wedding cake you're worried about, being expensive and all, don't worry. It's freezable and we can munch on it until Christmas.' She laughs, nudging Agnes with her generous hip. 'Lighten up woman.' She takes the mug from her. 'We'd better not let the groom wait.' With that, she walks back to the house.

Agnes follows. On the steps up to the glass veranda, she stops to contemplate her dad's garden. Despite the previous season's neglect, there's new life preparing to blossom. The birch trees are on the verge of opening their leaves, the perennials will eventually flower, and nature is about to explode with colour. Summer is on the way even if she can't see it yet.

She must have left the front door unlocked because Thomas meets them in the kitchen. It annoys her he didn't ring the bell, that he couldn't wait. Agnes reprimands herself. He'll soon live here, and have his own key.

Thomas is unshaven and unkempt in a crumpled shirt and chinos. He pulls her into a hug. The b.o. is at the level where it could serve as a weapon. His bad breath is a concoction of alcohol, smoke, and garlic. And spearmint to cover it up, she's pretty sure. It's not working. What has his buck's night entailed? And him driving—is that even legal?

Agnes has never regarded the kitchen as anything but spacious, with its eleven-foot ceilings, the wide window along one bench, and plenty of room to get around their table and chairs. She's never found her dad's cookbooks and appliances, potted plants, and collection of coloured glass bottles along the benches encroaching. Now, her kitchen is suddenly confined and cluttered.

She wiggles out of Thomas's embrace, pulling her blanket off. 'A shower, perhaps?' she says.

'Ouch,' says Thomas.

Niina takes both blankets and hangs them over a chair. 'Good night?' she asks, before turning her back to them. She's going to try opening the window.

'You know it's stuck,' says Agnes, which Niina ignores. 'And mind the bird feeder.'

'Too stuffy in here.' Niina pushes with both hands on the window frame, and her generous backside sends waves through the satin. On her third attempt, the window flies open. It bumps the bird feeder, then flings straight back, hitting it again on the way back. Niina swears at the top of her voice. It's likely both volume and selection of words have less to do with jammed fingers, and more to do with the presence of Thomas. Niina shakes one hand while securing the latch. Cool air finds its way in, and she re-wraps her robe and ties the belt in a tight knot. 'Flipping heck, I broke a nail.' She holds up her longest finger.

Agnes can't tell if it's truly broken or if she's just using the opportunity.

'You're too early,' says Niina to Thomas.

Agnes glares at her. Not that she notices. According to Niina, that should have been Agnes's line and since she didn't use it—open season.

Thomas ignores her remark. 'I'll shower in a minute. Wouldn't mind a coffee first.' He pulls out a chair. 'And a bite to eat.'

'I certainly need a strong one,' says Niina.

'I'll make it.'

'No, Agnes,' says Niina. 'Big day ahead. You sit.'

'I won't be in your way,' says Thomas. 'I might crash for a few hours.'

Thomas, asleep, will work better for them. 'I'll need you later,' says Agnes. 'To rearrange the furniture.'

'You've got more than that to do,' says Niina.

There's a bang in the driveway—a car door.

'Pernilla,' says Thomas.

'I thought you said she wasn't—'

'Change of plans. She was at some party, way south, spent the cab money I gave her, and no night bus apparently. Rang me early this morning to be picked up. It was halfway to yours, so made sense to keep going.'

The front door slams next, and shoes get kicked off in the hallway. Then she's in the doorway—Thomas's beloved from a failed relationship, the daughter Agnes has never met. Not because she hasn't wanted to. Because Pernilla hasn't. Another layer of aversion conjoins her already unfriendly kitchen. Agnes's fingers brush through her fringe.

Pernilla is tall for her age with streaked and straightened hair to her shoulders. Her stalk legs have been poured into a pair of skinny jeans. A snug, low-cut top reveals the flesh of tiny breasts being pushed up and in. Last night's makeup has taken liberties. At her age, Agnes hid her body under big T-shirts. She spent her time sewing bears, reading books, or baking muffins. At her age, she'd not even tried lip gloss.

She walks over to the girl. 'Pleased to meet you at last. This is Niina.' Agnes gestures.

Pernilla looks at her outstretched hand, as if it's riddled with leprosy, then glances past her, and it's possible Thomas gives her a sign, because she takes it with an uncommitted looseness—all of one second. There's a trace of cheap floral perfume before her long fingers let go of Agnes's grip, limp and cool. Thomas's daughter loathes her.

Or she's just tired from a party.

'You drink coffee?' Niina asks.

'Don't touch percolated.'

Niina gives Agnes a look—enormous eyes as if she wants to pop them out, and the tip of her tongue touching her top lip, just so.

'Can I have a shower?' says Pernilla.

'Upstairs.' Agnes waves for her to follow, self-conscious in all her satin. She shows the girl where everything is, from towels to tampons—doesn't know why. Pernilla hovers behind her with her phone in one hand. They don't talk. Agnes stops in the doorway, wanting to say something, but where would she begin? The entire wedding idea seems stupid now. Pernilla is leaning against the sink, texting someone.

'I'm glad you're here,' says Agnes finally. 'I know it's kind of—'

'So last minute,' says Pernilla without interrupting her flow with the fingers.

'Yes.'

In response, there's the tapping sound from the girl's texting. Agnes can't think of anything else to say, so she leaves, closing the door quietly.

In the kitchen, Niina has brewed coffee and produced the breakfast they were going to eat in peace, before the busy day ahead.

Thomas helps himself to croissants. 'Perfect timing,' he says.

Another Niina-look across the table. Agnes grimaces apologetically to let her know how sorry she is. Niina shakes her head.

The phone rings in the office.

'Olga,' they say in unison, which makes Thomas look up from his phone.

Niina offers, but Agnes goes.

She writes a list of what Olga needs. 'Meet you at the pier in an hour,' she says. 'Keep an eye out for me.'

'You have a visitor?' Olga asks. 'I saw a car.'

'That's the groom. Wedding today. You remember?'

Olga pretends she does, though it's obvious she's forgotten. Agnes has been wondering for a while if she's developing dementia.

'Give *me* the list. I'll do it,' says Niina when Agnes returns to the kitchen. 'Saves you wasting time driving. Oh, that's right, you're done with all that. Who'd have thought.'

'Who'd have thought what?' says Thomas mindlessly.

'Tell you later,' says Agnes.

'I hope our dear Olga will not ring every half hour. Might be worth taking the phone off the hook,' says Niina. 'I mean, does anyone else use your landline?'

Agnes shakes her head. 'I've had it off all week. And yeah, I just did.'

'Good to see some agency,' says Niina. 'Who's this new, Agnes? Treading actual water. Taking phones off hooks. And getting married.' She smiles widely for the first two accolades but pulls a face on the third statement, without Thomas noticing.

'I'm gonna get a move on,' says Agnes.

'A wedding doesn't execute itself,' says Niina, aiming at Thomas. 'You got to eat, Agnes.'

'Not hungry.'

'Don't want your croissant?' Thomas looks at her, hopeful and oblivious to what's going on around him.

Agnes moves it to his plate. 'I'll have a piece of fruit later,' she says.

'I'm off as well.' Niina quickly butters the last croissant.

'I thought you—'

'Remember? My hair. Don't worry. I'll be back midday.'

She leaves, and Agnes hears her rummaging upstairs, changing, gathering her things. Within minutes, she pops her head in through the doorway and blows Agnes a kiss, ignoring Thomas, who ignores her back. Leaving, she slams the front door.

Then the shower finally starts up, the copper pipes reverberating.

Thomas swallows the last bit of his croissant. 'If Pernilla wasn't here ...' He flicks his gaze at the ceiling. 'I'd have my way with you.' He licks jam off his fingers. 'I know, I know. We're being romantic.'

'I have to go,' she says. It's possible she misjudged the Saturday night situation. It's possible if she'd stayed the night, got the sex out of the way, there'd be no awkward tension now. Then again, the self-conscious sentiment is hers. He's oblivious to anything except his, more than likely, erection. It's like a bit of gravel in your left shoe, the sharp prick each step you take. She's the left foot, Thomas the right one—can't feel a thing.

'Tonight,' says Thomas, giving her a light tap on the bum as she walks past.

Agnes is dressed and back in the kitchen. Thomas is still on his phone. The shower upstairs is still going.

'You'll wash up?' she asks.

'Where are you going?'

'Getting some groceries and meds, for Olga. Won't be long. You'll wash up?'

He nods.

Agnes lingers, folding her piece of paper, again and again, until it's a tiny hard square. She pushes it into a pocket of her jeans. 'I want to say something.' She relaxes her shoulders.

'Sure.'

'Could you?' She waits. He's absorbed. 'Thomas. The phone.'

He finally looks at her, places the phone on the table, keeps his hand on it as if it'll escape otherwise, away from his reach. 'Yeah,' he says.

'It's about Pernilla,' she says quietly. 'Your daughter doesn't want to be here.'

'Know that. Think it's worked out the best way, though. After all, it's her dad's wedding.'

'Maybe we should, I don't know. Cool it a bit.'

'Cool it?'

Agnes perches herself on the edge of the chair opposite. 'It's the first time she's met me. And this ... the wedding ... seems unfair.'

'To whom?'

'Both of us, actually.'

Thomas licks his lips. 'Why is it unfair? I don't get it?'

'Do you really want to live here?' she says. 'In little South Hamlet?'

Thomas looks over at her father's glass bottles, keeps licking his bottom lip. 'Yes, Agnes,' he says. 'Do we have to go over this again? I'm going to rent the flat out for a while—Airbnb.' He turns back to her, fixes his eyes on hers. 'Is that what this is about? You're worried about that?'

'Niina thinks—'

'What's she got to do with anything?' His tongue keeps going back and forth over his bottom lip. 'Thought you said this was about Pernilla?'

'Oh, it is. It would have been nice if she was all for it. If she—'

'Why is it about what other people want? First, your parents rule and reign. And now you think my daughter should have that power?'

'I think it's about being considerate. All we have to do is cancel the celebrant, keep the party as an engagement one. Take it down a notch. Let her get used to the idea.'

'No, Agnes. Enough. I'm fed up waiting. Pernilla will come around. You'll see. I'll have a word with her. If she's going to be shitty all day, she can stay in the spare bedroom for all I care. Or once Mum gets here, we can send Pernilla over to the guesthouse.'

'I don't like that thought.'

'Why not? She's a spoiled brat. Her choice, if she wants to join the rest of us or sit in a bed with her phone. I'm not putting this off for anyone. Don't let her get to you.'

Agnes realises she's moved her elbows to the table, leaned in, and now has all fingers more or less in her mouth. She straightens up.

'It'll be brilliant.' Thomas sends her the smile that dazzled her so long ago. Still does.

13
today

An hour later, Agnes hands Olga a box of groceries. 'Will you be fine to lift it out later?'

Olga shakes her head in disbelief that Agnes should even ask. She opens the chemist bag placed on top of the eggs. 'I need my pills.' She presses one out and swallows it without water. Then she hands Agnes the airport bag. Olga has replaced the chocolates with a painting. 'For the wedding couple,' she says.

It's an unwrapped piece of textured paper attached to a masonite board. Agnes gently pulls it out while Olga waits keenly with her hands clasped.

She's used pale blues and greens, made them bleed into each other. There's a lot of white space. Agnes sees a vortex of snow and ice, but also a swirling mist blown across the sky. Most of all, she sees sails on a wild ocean. 'It's beautiful,' she says. 'So lucid.' She guides the painting back into the bag. Then she gives Olga a long hug. 'I will treasure this.'

'Shame about the weather, dear, on your wedding day and all.' Olga wipes her face. 'So sorry, I can't be there. I'm letting everyone down. Irene and Nils ...' She looks at Agnes with suddenly wide eyes and flared nostrils. 'Your poor, poor dad,' she says. 'I ... I ... am so so sorry, I—'

'It's fine. I'm fine,' says Agnes though it isn't, never will be. Like the scar on her forehead, the guilt will fade but also become part of her. 'I understand you can't be there, but if you change your mind, just come.'

'Agnes!'

Both Olga and Agnes lift their heads to the trombone voice. Thomas is standing on the embankment, fifty metres away, waving. Hopefully, Pernilla hasn't flooded the bathroom.

'Who's that dear?'

'That's the lucky man. How about I introduce you?'

It's not the best of circumstances, not the best day for Olga, but Thomas strides towards them. His long legs cover twice the space to Agnes's. It reminds her of the two of them, moving through the forest—she, half running behind him—on their way to their *hot spot* with blankets and condoms.

Agnes lifts her feet out of Olga's boat. As she stands, Olga reaches for the ropes.

'Thomas would love to meet you.'

Ignoring Agnes, Olga's fingers pull at the knot she's made.

'Please, wait,' Agnes walks to meet Thomas. He's showered, his hair lay sleek, and he's changed into a clean T-shirt. He's shaved. Would he consider giving that up? A short stubble would suit him. In her head Niina laughs at this, ready with a smart remark. Agnes has changed her mind, that's all. Smooth chin is overrated.

'I'd like you to meet—' She hears the oars hitting the water and swings around. Sure enough, Olga's already rowing away.

'Poor Olga,' she says. 'Having a bad day.'

'It's Pernilla,' says Thomas. 'She's got nothing to wear.'

Pernilla has dried her hair and reapplied mascara. She looks tired but clean, her jeans merely tired. She's wearing a fresh top, casual, and in Agnes's opinion, at least two sizes too small.

'She needs a dress,' says Thomas.

He's slumping against the kitchen sink with his fingers stuck into his pants pockets. Agnes is slouching in the opening to the lounge room with the paper bag in her arms, while Pernilla stands in the middle of the doorway to the hall tapping on her phone. An obtuse triangle, her mum would have called it.

'I was hoping you'd take her.' Thomas gives Agnes that boyish, pleading look of his—the raised eyebrows, pulling in his lips with his teeth. 'You know South Hamlet. And you're a girl. I'm just a stupid dad.'

Surely Agnes is just the stupid girlfriend that her stupid dad's going to marry at today's stupid wedding. It makes her smile a little. After all, Pernilla is just a stupid teenager.

'I had a late night, barely got a few hours sleep before Pernilla rang,' says Thomas.

'So what?' says Pernilla. 'It's not as if *I've* slept.'

Where has she been, this fourteen-year-old, in her misguided attempt for cleavage and inflated make-up? Being picked up at five or six in the morning. No wonder she's in a foul mood. Agnes should get this over and done with quickly. Then Pernilla can sleep in the guest room, and wake up to the friendlier version of herself. In case there is one.

'I'll take you downtown,' says Agnes.

Without looking up from her phone, the girl says to her father, 'You drive me.'

'Agnes has offered. Show some gratitude.'

'I need money.'

'Agnes will use her card if you find anything.' He glances over at her. 'I'll transfer to your account. Do you mind?'

'No,' she says. Does she? Yes, a little, but it isn't about the money. It's about him taking it for granted. If the guest house was open for check-ins at this hour, she'd send the tired father and his surly daughter on their merry way.

When Pernilla goes to put her shoes on, Thomas draws Agnes close. 'I'm sorry, babe. And thanks for covering. Bit in the red at the moment. I mean ... you know, with Greece, and the rings. But I'll fix you up, promise.'

'Okay,' she says.

He kisses her neck. 'If she takes a nap later—'

'Thomas, your family is coming in a few hours. I have stuff to do.' She puts a hand on his chest and pecks his cheek. 'You'd better let me go. I'm on a mission *you* assigned me.'

'Are we going or what?' The sharp words from Pernilla.

'Get some sleep,' says Agnes to Thomas.

He follows them out into the hallway before climbing the stairs, leaving her with his offspring.

'I think there's one boutique you'll like,' says Agnes. 'The local girls shop there.' She did as well, before she left for Australia, thanks to Niina. And from now on, she'll not shop anywhere else. No need to inform Pernilla about that minor detail.

'There's North Hamlet. Isn't there? With a proper shopping centre,' says Pernilla.

'I don't really have time today.'

'Whatev.'

'Why don't we give Annie's a chance? If there's nothing there, then maybe.' Agnes regrets the words as soon as they're out.

Annie herself serves them, in high boots and a fitted jersey dress—scarlet red. She has the wow factor, as Niina calls it, and legs to die for. The last time they were here, Agnes was her old awkward self. She's different now. Something has shifted, though she can't put her finger on it exactly. The tan helps.

'How was your trip?' says Annie.

I got laid and played. 'Good, thanks.'

Annie has not long come out of a divorce. Her second marriage. Another one who doesn't know how to pick them is Niina's take on it.

'I hope the expo was brilliant. Niina raves about your bears.'

'She does?'

'All the time, and I want to buy one for my niece as a keepsake.' Annie smiles. 'I know they're not toys. Can I have a look once you're back from your honeymoon? Oh sorry, I wasn't meant to know that, was I?'

'It's not a secret. It's the reason we're here. The groom's daughter needs a dress.'

'I'll have just the thing,' says Annie. 'Take a seat.'

Agnes reclines in the lounge provided outside the change room while Annie leads Pernilla around the shop, picking out clothes, suggesting this and that, gathering various garments, completely ignoring the girl's bored persona.

After Thomas finally confessed he had a little girl, he often talked about her. She was clever at reading, brilliant at anything sporty, and naturally the cutest eight-year-old to walk the earth. 'You'll have to meet her one day,' he said. But the two times Agnes visited Stockholm, Liese found an excuse to keep Pernilla away. Since Thomas came back into her life, it has been mainly negative comments. 'Puberty,' he says with a sigh.

Well, puberty is not a walk in the park. Your own body betrays you, forces new shapes on you, makes you plump, and pimply, hippy and cumbersome, makes the boys notice you, makes them want to touch. Though Pernilla seems to embrace it. Then again, why wouldn't she? With her petite figure. She gets it from her mum. Agnes has seen a photo of Liese. Tall. Brunette. Stunning.

I like your curves—the voice of Guy in her head. She shakes him off.

Pernilla's in the changing room and Annie's on standby, murmuring to her, giving advice, making positive comments, encouraging her to show Agnes. The girl does, reluctantly. She opens the curtains, rotates once robot-like, before closing the curtain again. Agnes gets to see each outfit for all of three seconds. But she smiles and offers a thumb. Pernilla looks good in most of the dresses she tries on.

What does Thomas see in her? Agnes has probed in the past. Why not Liese? Liese drives him bonkers—his words. Tanya is like Liese, but a smaller version. Agnes believed Guy, yet was wrong about him. She's had trouble believing Thomas, and he wants to tie the knot. She obviously doesn't get men.

'Let's go to town.' Pernilla hovers over her, phone in hand like a weapon.

'But you looked lovely, in all of them.' The thought of driving in, finding a car park, going through hundreds of shops, and probably still finding nothing, then driving home to deal with the rest of the day—there is no way.

'I didn't like any of them,' says Pernilla.

Annie has left most of the dresses hanging in the changing room while returning a couple of definite rejections to their racks. She's giving them space, but she can hear them. It's a small boutique.

'What about the halter-neck one? That plummy colour is gorgeous on you.'

'Nah,' says Pernilla.

'Or the turquoise?'

Pernilla wrinkles her nose, shaking her head.

This is going to cost. Agnes steels herself. 'Sorry, but there's no town.'

'But you said, you'll drive me.'

'You can pick whichever dress. Pick two if you like. Pick three.'

'You said—'

'I know. Can't be helped.'

Pernilla walks back in to the dressing room. She comes out with the one Agnes thought was a little brash. 'I'll have the black one then,' says Pernilla. 'You don't like it, do you?' There's an obnoxious delight in her tone of voice?

'Yes, I do,' lies Agnes easily.

Annie's at their side to take the hanger from Pernilla. 'Excellent choice,' she says.

She's possibly lying, too. Needs the sale. Agnes can appreciate that.

'You said two.' Pernilla dashes back into the change room, fetches the turquoise one. 'Actually, three you said.'

'I did.'

'Can I have jeans as my third choice? Please.' Her voice is sweet, and she smiles. The transformation is remarkable. Her eyes sparkle. Her upper teeth show. She's pretty.

'Why not?' Agnes, to her shame, didn't think to buy anything for the girl as a gift from Australia. So indeed, why not?

A pair of bleached threadbare jeans land on top of the dresses.

Then Agnes surprises everyone, including herself. 'We'll have the halter neck one as well.'

As she finishes the transaction. Pernilla says to Annie in a voice that could melt butter.

'Where can we buy shoes?'

14

twenty-three days ago

In the car, Agnes paid absolutely no attention to north or south, didn't ask where they were going. She was too much in awe with her brave leap into an adventure. True, he'd suggested it and a woman in giant bell sleeves had cheered her on, but it was she who'd run through that bus with all eyes on her. She had ordered the driver to stop. Life seemed a new place to be, full of possibilities, fragrant, flavoured, intensely sweet.

The one negative was her cabin bag. She and Niina had gone shopping the previous week. She had new jeans in there, never worn T-shirts and a one-piece bathing suit she'd bought in Sydney, which had looked quite okay on her. Now both her suitcases were on the loose. And her new book. She'd forgotten it in the rush. Would the tour guide, or the driver, be willing to send her book and bag down to Coffs? Not likely. Well, so be it. This was still the best decision of her life. This was finally living, finally doing something exciting. Niina would love it.

They were back by the water. Guy parked by a huddle of shops placed between the ocean and a marina. There was a long road on top of a break wall that led all the way out to a peninsula, a high green hill that rose out of the sea.

'Mutton Bird Island,' said Guy. 'I'll take you up there another day.'

People were walking back and forth along the break wall, clustering on the restaurant balcony, and spreading out between boutiques and cafes. The place held the same components as the canal hub at South Hamlet—water, boats, visitors, food, and nature. Yet the contrast was spectacular. But then, how could you compare the brackish Baltic, tamed and channelled, to the Pacific Ocean, over-salted and roaming wild between continents?

'Where are we going?'

'To meet a special lady.' Guy gestured with an arm. 'This way.'

They joined the other walkers on the tarmac along the many meters thick wall. The giant stones and concrete blocks must have been placed strategically by heavy machinery. But they looked as if they'd randomly tumbled on top of each other in a long, messy line. The waves kept pounding hard against them. When a wave hit, water sprayed up in the air, hovered, suspended for a second, then fell with a splash before being pulled between crevices back into the ocean. Seagulls squealed and swooped and carried on, fighting over anything edible to their beady eyes.

The seaweed breeze prickled Agnes's skin and the blue above was more expansive than any sky she'd ever seen.

South Hamlet Canal was picturesque. This she found breathtaking.

Guy veered off, down a ramp to the side of the break wall and waited. He took her hand as if it was the most natural thing in the world and they continued along a pier towards the marina. Here they were protected by the wind and the water was calm. Pontoons, connected to the main pier, stretched out into the bay where yachts and motorboats of various sizes docked side by side in their berths. Agnes did the usual, avoided looking into the water and focused on something else. At home, it was the trees. Here she set her eyes on the masts swaying against the backdrop of feathery clouds.

'This bothers you more than breaking waves?' asked Guy.

'It's a stupid fear,' she said.

'I have a fear of needles. Don't tell anyone.' He squeezed her hand. 'It's shallow water.'

Guy stopped at a closed metal gate. Still holding on to her, he pulled out a key and opened it, led her through, then causally stepped onto the pontoon. It was a small step. Reluctantly, she followed. The pontoon was steady, but her legs stiffened and her heartbeat sped up. The edge of the pontoon was as close to the water's edge as the path along the canal at home, but the path along the canal was wider, and it was land. Here they were, in fact, floating on water. That thought alone terrified. She tightened the grip on Guy's hand.

'You're perfectly safe,' he said.

'So are blood tests.'

This wasn't the impenetrable brown water in the canal. You could see through the deep green to the bottom, the ridges in the sand. Yet she imagined her father floating to the surface. She took a deep breath and concentrated on the boats, squinting, feeling beyond silly.

'What do you want to do?' Guy came closer and lay his arm around her back. 'Go back?'

Agnes sensed relief waiting, ready to wash over her as soon as she'd be back on the pier, but she didn't want to give in—not today. 'You want me to meet someone,' she said in a pathetic voice.

'It doesn't matter. Another time.'

'It matters.' She'd been curling all her toes in. Determined, she released them, and took a step, hanging on to Guy like a little old lady.

'It's not far,' he said.

Guy led her slowly along the absolute centre, towards the end of the pontoon. He stopped at the stern of a sailboat. Wooden letters screwed into the fibreglass spelled FELICITY. The yacht wasn't particularly long or big. She was mostly white, but her low cabin displayed natural timber with small, round windows.

'My humble home,' said Guy, giving a sweeping gesture.

How had she not seen that one coming? Of course, he lived on a boat.

'All year round?' she asked, hoping there would be a nice motel nearby where she could sleep.

'Well, I travel too much. But when I'm home, Felicity's it. She's an Alan Payne Sloop, built in the fifties, gets up around eight knots, stable and heels beautifully. Never mind,' he said and laughed. 'Getting carried away.'

Agnes's blank face had nothing to do with a distaste for boat designs or nautical technicalities—not even the surrounding water. It dawned on her how she'd not considered the sleeping arrangements, and in fact, what sleeping meant. What if by jumping off the bus when Guy asked her to stay, she'd basically agreed to have sex with him? Why hadn't she thought of that until now?

Because you are socially inept.

His arm around her back and his hand on her waist suddenly seemed too intimate. There was nothing but a flimsy cotton dress and a thin cardigan between his fingers and her skin. Fool, she was. For all the romance read, all the digested books of men and women getting involved with each other, she'd learned precious little.

'I reckon you'll be fine once we're aboard,' said Guy.

Had he planned this?

'Are you okay? You're white in the face.

'I need to go shopping,' she said.

'Right now?'

What if there was more to Guy than she could see? What if he had a certain manipulative cunningness, had set her up from the beginning, had spotted her long before he'd said that corny thing, whatever it was? He'd sucked her in, dropped his bag, interfered with the controlling boyfriend, been caring and charming. All along he'd been hauling her in. No, that was farfetched. Besides, she'd contacted him. He'd tried really hard in Sydney though.

'You're freaking out, aren't you?' Guy tightened his grip on her.

'I'd like to go shopping now.'

'You're only one step away.'

He pulled the boat closer and placed a foot on the seat by the tiller. Agnes could feel his attempt to help her take that one step. Her feet planted themselves right next to his remaining foot and used all her willpower to keep her there.

Humour, she thought. To diffuse. 'Unlike Felicity,' she said, 'I'm unstable and don't heel well.'

Guy laughed. 'I could lift you aboard.'

She shook her head fervently. 'Must go shopping.' She needed to get off this stupid pontoon. She needed to work out how to continue, where to sleep, and what to do tomorrow. There would have to be another bus she could catch.

Guy put his hands on her shoulders. Then he looked at her feet. 'You know what you need? Shoes with grip.'

He turned her around and guided her back. As soon as she was through the gate, Agnes stepped away from him. He pulled the gate shut and reached for her hand, but she took another step back.

'I need a moment,' she said.

'You look like you've seen a ghost. I didn't mean to—'

'Let's just go.' She waved her hand. 'You first.'

'Are you okay?'

'Can we please just go.'

He led the way, took his phone out, and made a call.

Agnes followed a step behind, shaken by this new revelation about what she'd done. She'd thought it was a good idea to stay with a man she didn't know in a country she'd never been? If something happened, she couldn't just walk home along a canal. This had truly been a hare-brained decision.

'Why don't you ever pick up the phone? I'll be over later. Bringing someone. You'll like her. And can we stay the night?'

'I'll stay in a motel,' said Agnes as soon as he hung up.

'You're not staying in a shitty motel.'

'Who said anything about shitty?'

He turned to her and put a hand on her arm. 'Hey, I know that freaked you out. I'm sorry. My bad.' He pushed his sunnies up and came closer. 'I'm an idiot. Agnes, I honestly didn't know it would frighten you like this.'

If he knew what circled around in her head. Was her imagination taking it all a bit too far? She forced herself to look straight at him. There was that smile. It was just Guy. Her body sighed, letting the adrenaline fizzle out. It was Guy, for goodness' sake.

'I asked you to stay. You're my guest, so not alone in a motel room, at least not tonight. We can look around tomorrow if you really don't like my family.'

'Your family?'

'Thought you should meet Holly.'

'Holly?'

'My eldest sister. She doesn't bite either. Can be bossy, but we pay no attention to that. I think you'll like her.'

'Did you make the bus driver stop?' Guy's eight-year-old niece looked up at Agnes, her bottom teeth gently biting her top lip, her eyes enormous. 'And he kept your bag? And now you have to buy all new stuff?'

'Not shoes,' said Agnes. 'See.' She pointed at her feet.

Ruby checked Agnes's new top-of-the-range canvas sneakers. 'Noice,' she said, exaggerating her Australian accent.

Guy had stopped at a warehouse store that sold anything sport, fishing or boat related, his regular local hangout no doubt. Enough handshakes and backslaps to make any politician envious. By the time they'd escaped, it had been too late for any further shopping.

Guy's sister seemed to find this annoying. Or maybe she was just tired.

They'd arrived on her doorstep as she and her teenage son were heading out the door. Brisk pleasantries. Then Holly ordered Guy to take Nathan to footy training. And since the Swedish tourist hadn't thought to bring luggage, Agnes should come with her to pick up Ruby from ballet. With any luck, they'd find a few basics at the supermarket.

'You need a toothbrush?' asked Ruby. 'You want me to go get one for you?'

'Yes, please.'

And off she went, twiggy legs in ballet tights, hooded jacket hanging off her shoulders, her hair in a tight bun on her head, swinging Agnes's basket. She'd insisted on carrying it.

'My brother will find himself demoted to second place this evening,' said Holly. 'Not a minor feat, considering apart from him dropping in for an hour last night, we haven't seen Guy for over a year and Ruby is his biggest fan.'

'I'm sorry to barge in like this.'

'As long as you don't mind sleeping in a messy guest room.' Holly pushed the trolley over to her. Then she walked off and Agnes trailed after.

In faded jeans that sat on her hips, her brother's straight shoulders and the same curly hair, Holly looked like a smaller version of Guy. She carried a certain self-possessed suaveness. She stopped at rows of pasta sauces.

'So Guy told me you don't sail. Hard to believe.' She handed Agnes two large jars. 'Nathan's turn to cook, and he handles up to three ingredients, four if push comes to shove. Hope you don't mind plain food?'

'I don't mind.' Agnes put the jars at the bottom of the trolley. 'And I'm what we in Sweden call a land crab.'

'But you live by a canal, only meters from the water. You're surrounded by boats. Believe me, we've heard all about it. The archipelago is basically your backyard.'

'I wouldn't say that. It's another mile.'

'My brother seems to think otherwise.' Holly set off again, and Agnes pushed the trolley behind her, wondering why his sister was so bristly. She was nothing like Guy. 'Are you gluten-free or anything?' Holly asked as they reached the pasta.

'Not at all.'

There was a curt nod of acceptance. 'You know ...' She picked up a package of spaghetti. 'He's travelled for years. Time to drop the anchor for good.' She took another two packages and handed them over. 'He's always like this when he comes home, finds it hard to settle, but Mick has work for him here and plenty of it.'

Agnes smiled and nodded. Did Holly expect her to comment?

Holly stretched a hand into the trolley and lined the packets in a neat row. 'We're a big family,' she said. 'The others live on the land three hours from here—Mum and Dad, our sisters with their families. We all miss him.'

'Of course,' said Agnes.

'His friends, too. And Tanya.' Holly looked at her and there was so much of Guy in her eyes. 'You met her today, didn't you? She said she ran into you on the beach. You know they—' Holly was interrupted mid-sentence as Ruby came to an abrupt halt beside them.

'Is this a good one?' Ruby held up her find—a pink brush with sparkles and odd angles to the multi-coloured bristles.

'Darling that's not for adults. Go find the ones mum usually buys.'

'It's fine. I quite like it,' said Agnes.

Ruby held up the basket to show her the rest of the gained treasures—red hair clips, gold nail polish, a brush, and a collection of hair elastic in bright neons.

'I doubt Agnes needs all that,' said Holly. 'Put them back, please.'

Ruby looked disappointed at her mum, and then at Agnes, pleading.

'Actually, I can use these,' said Agnes. 'Maybe you can find me four more nail polishes in your favourite colours, and I need toothpaste?'

Ruby beamed at her before skipping away.

'You know how to make yourself popular,' said Holly cooly.

Contrary to Guy's assumption, his sister didn't like her being there, or even at all. In the car, Holly had informed her it was fair that Guy took Nathan to training since Mick had to deliver a boat to Brisbane, the job Guy had promised to do, but got out of thanks to *her* visiting. She was annoyed with her brother, but more so with Agnes.

They continued along the aisles, Agnes pushing while Holly picked up jars and packets. 'Tanya and Guy have a long history,' she said. 'I assume you know they were a couple for many years?'

He hadn't. Why did Holly?

'He met her when he and I first came to Coffs. They started off as surfing buddies but later got serious. They've got this kind of soul mate thing going on. Something glues them.'

Light feet behind them announced Ruby again. Agnes thought she could detect a small tube of toothpaste in the basket as colourful as the expanded range of small glass bottles.

'Darling, can you get me a bag of mushrooms?'

Ruby frowned at her mum. 'It's getting heavy.'

'There's nothing much in there,' said Holly. 'Thought you were stronger than that.'

'Mu-u-m.'

'Come on. Off you go. Make sure you fill the bag up.'

'I hate mushrooms in bolognese,' said Ruby before she stomped off.

Holly kept strolling ahead. 'I don't know if Guy told you, and I'm sure it seems a little odd, you being Swedish and all, but we don't let him bring women to our home and sleep with them. We're not, you know, religious or anything. Not a good look, that's all. Our kids never take their eyes off their uncle so ...'

Being Swedish and all?

'It's old school, I know, but that's how we are.'

'We're only friends,' said Agnes, glancing at Holly's profile, her lips held tight. 'I'm going back to Sydney at the end of next week, to meet up with Thomas, my partner.'

'Does Guy know this?'

'Yes.'

Holly looked at her for a few seconds before taking over the reins and striding off, leaving Agnes dumbfounded. What was this about? How had Holly misunderstood? It seemed she was speaking on Tanya's behalf, letting her know Guy was off-limits. Seriously? Agnes was obviously no threat, not that she'd even think of him that way.

'Here you go,' said Holly when Agnes caught up to her in the next aisle. 'Undies and socks. Cheap brands, but at least you've got something.'

Agnes started searching along the rows and rows of hooks for the right size and style, having trouble making sense of it.

'Thomas, doesn't mind you willy-nilly jump off a bus last minute to spend a week with another bloke?'

Agnes kept picking up ankle socks and crew socks, unable to decide, unable to think about socks. 'He doesn't,' she said. Would he? It was easier to let him believe she was on a bus tour, but maybe she ought to tell him where she was.

'You're going to miss out on the barrier reef to have an entire week in Coffs Harbour? Such an impromptu thing to do.'

Agnes shrugged. 'Guy asked me to stay. We made good friends on the flight over.'

'He said.'

'And who wants to sit cramped on a bus with a heap of strangers?'

Holly said nothing.

'You have so many beaches here.' Agnes grabbed the white ankle socks and moved on to undies. Did she want hi, lo, bikini, g-string, boy leg? What colour? And size, where was the size? 'You live in a beautiful place.'

'That we do.'

Agnes found a decent in-between cut but pretended to be still looking, not wanting to face Holly. 'I wanted to book into a motel for tonight. I still can if—'

'No, you're staying with us, but I don't beat around the bush. That's just who I am. And I don't want to see Guy get hurt.'

'Get hurt?' Agnes snatched the undies box from the hook and took off down the aisle—a most unusual initiative for her. A tremble had started in her hands and she was hot all over, but in particular, her head was cooking. She continued around the next corner on shaky legs, and then along the next aisle. Guy's sister came after. At this higher speed, the trolley produced irregular thumps. It clicked away as if pushed across the cobblestones of the little old streets at home.

'Wait,' called Holly. 'Agnes, stop!'

Agnes slowed. Of course, she slowed. She was being childish, and so was Holly—two women at either end of their thirties. Guy's sister caught up to her and Agnes stopped, overheating in her cardigan. Only minutes ago, she'd been cold.

Holly touched her arm. 'I got carried away. It's just that I'm protective of him.'

'I have a man in my life already. We're ... engaged.' Agnes kept her eyes on the boxes of undies and socks in her hands, and her chewed nails fought the urge to put a finger in her mouth. They sort of were engaged. Or they sort of used to be.

'Look, it's not you, Agnes, okay? It's a lot of things. My brother has been overseas for a long time. He meets some Swedish man in Brazil. It's been all about the archipelago ever since. Then he meets you. He thinks you showing up ...' Holly sighed. 'He's keen to go up north for a bit. Guy's "for a bit" usually turns out longer than he plans. Last time he initially went for a month. It turned into fourteen of them. We don't want to lose him again.'

Agnes shook her head, still staring at her box of undies.

'My brother got involved with a woman last year. She was the reason he left for the States. Turned out, she was married. There. I've said it.'

'Mum, is that enough?' Ruby had caught up with them.

'That's great, honey. Well, done. Now we need cheese.'

'My legs are tired.' Ruby handed Agnes the basket and jumped up on the front of the trolley, gripping the sides. She glared at her mother with great ferocity, done being told what errands to run.

'Ruby, this thing is already going every which way. You're making it even more unbalanced.'

'I don't mind pushing,' said Agnes, holding out her basket to Holly. 'Can I buy some dessert for us all?'

Holly let go of the trolley and accepted the basket. 'Ice cream is always a winner,' she said. 'Meet you at the checkout. I'll get the cheese.'

It was such a relief to have a few minutes alone with Ruby's happy, freckled face smiling at her. Despite suggesting it, Agnes didn't want to go to a motel. She looked forward to Ruby painting her nails and arranging her hair, which the girl had suggested enthusiastically. Agnes had spent next to no time with children, not even when she was one herself. It wasn't as if friends had come with her home after school wanting to play beauty salon. To the weird Anderssons? Never.

Once Holly joined them at the checkout, and Ruby was out of earshot, Holly whispered to her. 'Don't tell Guy about, you know, what I told you.'

'I won't.'

'And don't charm him.'

'Charm him?'

'Don't give my brother a reason to misread.'

Agnes shook her head. 'That's not who I am,' she said.

Dinners growing up were sombre events. Her dad would make an effort, ask her about the school day. Mostly, Agnes would shrug and focus on her food. Occasionally she'd make something up, just to cheer him up or break the monotony. Her mum, who'd been cooped up in her office, seemed more bothered than anything to socialise with the two of them. When Niina came for dinner, she took charge of the conversation. Niina on the fourth chair made them seem a little brighter and a lot less weird. 'She adds to the equation, Irene, doesn't she?' her dad would say.

Dinner with Guy's sister and her family was like having five Niinas around the table. Nathan and Ruby carried a strong familiarity with their mum and uncle—more or less curly hair, shades of dark, with golden highlights from time spent in the sun. Mick was the odd one out with a shaved head, and only Ruby had inherited her father's freckles. Olive skin was the order of the day, as was laughter and friendly bantering. Agnes's freshly sunburnt arms stood out. So did her quietness—to begin with.

She ate, watched, and listened, conscious of Holly's glances while unable to keep up with the well-entrenched idiosyncrasies. The others would all break out in laughter and she'd smile and wonder what was so funny. Each time Guy wanted to explain, but Agnes waved him off, told him she was fine, because—despite Holly—she was.

When Mick asked her a question about Sweden, silence fell over the table. Self-conscious, she answered, and that was the end of her hiding behind the food. Nathan and Ruby were curious about what on earth young people did in such a chilly place. In particular, Nathan spoke fast, and Guy or Mick repeated his questions slowly and properly. Pronouncing a word wrong or getting stuck became a signal for everyone to rush in and help with suggestions and much laughter. Instead of shutting her up completely, it made Agnes feel part of it. As she'd discovered during the long flight talking to Guy, conversing in English provided the perfect excuse to be less fluent. With no pressure, she found it easier to express herself.

Guy's sister kept glancing at her as if there was something to figure out about her, but there were moments when Holly relaxed and joined in with her own questions.

When the children cleared the table, she said to Guy, 'I assume you'll be sleeping on Felicity, so I'll drop Agnes down in the morning.'

'Actually, I'll stay the night,' said Guy.

'Nathan will take the lounge,' said Mick. 'Remind me to hide the game controller, honey.'

'Don't fuss. I'll take the lounge,' said Guy.

'May as well,' said Holly. 'We know you won't last.'

After dinner, Agnes escaped with Ruby to her purple bedroom. She hoped it would make Holly happy to chat with her brother without the untrustworthy woman from Sweden around. Agnes was grateful to not have Holly's suspicious eyes on her, deciphering her every smile, every word she said, how she said it, if she laughed, how she laughed, how she spoke, moved her hands or sneezed.

Ruby, on her own, was easier to understand. She was a sweet and happy soul, twittered away about this and that while they painted each others' toenails. And she braided Agnes's hair with a superb touch while Agnes closed her eyes, enjoying the slight heat on her skin from the day's sun.

When it was Ruby's bedtime, Agnes followed her lead. Holly handed her a towel and a T-shirt of hers to sleep in. As she lay tucked into eucalyptus-scented sheets with the background laughter of Holly and the men from the living room, she pondered the sharp and unexpected turn her life had taken. She was in a town that stretched along beach after beach. And she'd met a man who lived on a boat. Water surrounded her. A different kind—glittering, energising, and see-through to the sandy bottom. An opportunity had landed itself. There was a reason she was here. In her dreamy state, setting sails seemed a fitting analogy. She was going to spend her time on the beach and get used to the waves. Her first ever holiday had finally arrived. Next week she'd meet up with Thomas, a new sort of woman.

15
today

Once back at Villa Solus, Agnes gets out of the car without waiting for a thank you, leaving Pernilla tapping on her phone. Buckets filled with cornflowers, baby's breath, and white miniature roses wait on the porch, and a large box filled with ivy—delivered by the local florist.

'Maybe you could help me with the decorations?' suggests Agnes once Pernilla catches up with her.

'I'm no good at stuff like that,' says Pernilla with a yawn as she walks past.

Agnes gets busy carrying the delivery into the kitchen. She wipes the benches, stacks the dishwasher, and clears the kitchen table before laying out a plastic cover, scissors, strings, and ribbons. It's already after eleven. Niina was right. The florist could have done this. But this is the bit Agnes loves. Once Niina shows up, they'll wake Thomas, to help them rearrange furniture, and organise the house. There's no need to stress. She's going to enjoy this time of quiet.

Agnes creates an understated wedding bouquet first and puts it in a vase with water. Then she lines up the ivy on the table and ponders how to attach small clusters of flowers along the stem. She's always found working with her hands calming. Drafting a pattern, sewing, embroidering, or binding flowers—it's all therapeutic. Agnes focuses on the gentle flow of arranging the blues and whites, and humming, loses herself in the serenity of doing. Suddenly Pernilla is in the doorway. Agnes quietens. Edginess replaces the serenity. What happened to I need to sleep?

'Would you like to make one?'

Pernilla shrugs but sidles up next to her.

'They're like miniature posies. It's easy. Start with a rose, then some baby's breath, then a cornflower like this.'

To her surprise, Pernilla picks them up. Her fingers are like her legs, long and slim.

'A little white, a little blue. Keep it small,' says Agnes.

It's both painful and heart-warming to watch the girl. She fiddles too much, doesn't trust her own judgement. Agnes waits, not wanting to seem too fast.

'Now we tie, like this.'

Pernilla follows her lead.

Agnes slows down and takes her time so they'll finish the decorations at the same time. Pernilla's creation is not as wispy as hers, but she's done a good job, and Agnes tells her so. 'We're going to fasten them to the garlands,' she says. 'I can do that if you like.' She expects Pernilla to leave when the girl picks another rose and starts up again.

Agnes moves over to the opposite side to give them both room to move. They work to the sound of breathing, and the muted rustle as they pick through the flowers. Then, from Agnes's bedroom above, a snore. They both pretend not to hear it. A minute later, Thomas does it again, and they both giggle. The snoring continues for a few more minutes before he turns over.

'He won't pay you back for the stuff.' Pernilla says. 'He has no money.'

'It's not important,' says Agnes.

'You don't care?'

'I'm going to marry your father. We'll be sharing everything. So no, I don't mind.'

'Huh.' Pernilla doesn't look up.

'But since we're not married yet, it can be a gift from me.'

Again, Agnes doesn't expect a thank you. Again, none is produced.

'You're good at this,' says Agnes. Pernilla's fingers have got used to the fiddly of it. They have both improved.

'Is this your house?'

'Used to be my parents, but yeah.'

'Dad said you make teddy bears. Don't you have a proper job?'

'If you mean going to an office? No.'

'Huh.'

It's clear Pernilla has more questions. The conversation feels paper thin. Pernilla and she are finally meeting, talking, and able to get to know each other on their own terms. She'll let the girl take the lead. Such a shame they didn't meet years ago, but at least they have now, and if she's sensitive to where Thomas's daughter is at, this could be the start of a friendship.

'Mum works in an office,' she says.

'Does she like her job?'

'Nah, hates it.'

From what Thomas has told her, Liese lands in the half-empty glass camp. 'I'm lucky,' she says. 'Love what I do. Started when I was about your age.'

Pernilla furrows her thin eyebrows and glares as if Agnes has just told her she stole the crown jewels.

'For something to do. Taught myself.'

'You're weird.'

Agnes shrugs.

'Do you make good money?'

So this is about the money? 'Yes, and no,' she says.

'Mum can't make ends meet.'

Agnes would prefer to steer their dialogue in some other direction, but can't think of what to say. What could she ask her? Thomas's daughter has given up soccer, tennis, and swimming. It's all about boys and music. Agnes knows nothing about the latest hits, the ones that are hot or sick or whatever in Pernilla's world.

'Mum's not getting any alimony, cause dad snakes his way out of it. He's selfish.'

'That's a little harsh. Don't you think?'

'He is. And it's my money.'

Agnes doesn't point out that inaccuracy. She doesn't want to talk about finances or Thomas's misgivings. She knows next to nothing of what's gone on between Pernilla's parents. He claims Liese causes trouble when she can. Rarely gives details. Agnes hasn't asked for them. That's because, she realises, she's been self-absorbed. The morning's crawling sensation through her entrails is back. Or is it hunger? A bit of both?

'Dad says you're going to Greece.' Pernilla is on a roll now. Her hands move faster and less efficiently. It's painful to watch. 'Two weeks,' she says. 'At a five-star resort with daily cruises around other islands.' The girl, who knows more than Agnes about the upcoming trip, holds the bunch up. She's only used cornflowers. 'Dad's never taken me on a holiday like that.' She begins tying a string around the poor stalks with erratic fingers.

Agnes wants to take her hands and hold them still.

'You paying for that as well?' She's trying to tie the knot, but the string won't cooperate. She shakes the flowers.

'Pernilla?'

'Stuff it.' She throws the flowers on the table, picks up her phone, and barges out of the kitchen, leaving Agnes standing with a half-made bouquet in her hands.

Before Agnes has figured out her next move, Pernilla has put her shoes on and is out the front door. There is the sound of tramping across the pebbled path, around to the back, then through the back-gate. Agnes lays down her half-finished piece. What is she meant to do with this? Thomas has taken up his snoring again. She could go wake him up. His daughter needs him. But if she wakes him, the father-daughter collision could get out of hand. Agnes grabs a jumper off the hook and sticks her feet in her clogs.

As soon as Agnes reaches the canal embankment, she sees Pernilla, head dropped, walking towards South Hamlet, towards the lock. Agnes mentally kicks herself for not calling on Thomas. His daughter's surface animosity hints at a depth that demands more than half an hour on a busy wedding day. And frankly, Agnes doesn't really have even half an hour.

Agnes has also not been near the lock since that day. She's wanted to bring a bunch of her dad's favourite flowers, have her own private ceremony and sit in quiet, allowing grief—and whatever emotions will come—to wash over her. She meant to do it as soon as she came home, but the week ran away. Facing it today isn't part of the plan. But Pernilla needs someone to care, so Agnes pursues her.

The girl stops at the lock where the gates have closed. A woman on the other side has secured the boat through the solid iron rings attached to the old quay. She's holding on, concerned. A man waits at the helm meters below in the lock chamber, surrounded by stone walls. When the gate valves open, as the water rushes in creating a surge, the woman who's taken a stand with her legs wide apart, ready to hold against the force, realises it's not that strenuous. She laughs with relief down to the man.

This is where they found him, in the middle of the lock. He would have fallen from the narrow bridge or the quay. The water level would have been at its peak, yet with half a meter up to the edge, and the stones unforgivingly slippery, it would have been impossible to pull himself out. If he'd been able to swim out of the chamber, and further along to where the grass reaches into the water, then maybe he'd stood a chance. As it was, her father was a poor swimmer sober, the water was freezing, and he was in his winter jacket and boots.

She was here among inquisitive locals when they dragged him out—a lump of soaked flesh and fabric. It shocked her. Deep down, she'd hoped. Suddenly, he was irreversibly gone. And it was her fault. A strange weight forced her to the ground, caved her knees, bent her over, forced the air out of her lungs, and pressed her face to the icy gravel. Though it's less sharp now, the guilt is still there.

'My dad never took me on a holiday either,' says Agnes, sidling next to Pernilla.

'Oh, goodie. We can be best friends.' With that, Pernilla takes off again. She walks across the spot where the divers laid his body.

Agnes walks around. 'It's a honeymoon,' she says. 'It's what people do when they get married.'

'Duh.'

'We could go on a holiday, the three of us. Later I mean.'

'Whatev.'

Agnes shuts up.

The sound of rushing water fades behind them, blending with the bird twitter from the medley of naked leaf trees that line the canal. Despite the cool weather, already wildflowers have begun flowering among the high grass on either side of the track. Cow parsley, red clover, wild pansies, and cowslips add specs of colour. The water mirrors the spruce-and-pine-clad Ramund Mountain where windflowers speckle the ground with white. Agnes takes in the beauty and pushes her father away. Listening to their syncopated footfall, she wonders what to do. She could turn around and walk back. Why doesn't she?

'I bet that's why he never married Mum. Not rich enough,' says Pernilla with nonchalance, eyes on both phone and path, kicking the gravel with the toes of her shoes as she walks.

'Is that what you think? That this is about—'

'You'll be moving in with Dad, then?'

'Actually, we're going to live in my—'

'He won't leave Stockholm for anyone, no offence.'

'None taken,' says Agnes. She's ashamed to admit, she's given no real thought to what this will be like for Pernilla, to not have her dad close by, not be able to drop in, ask for a lift somewhere, hang with Dad. 'You can come and stay whenever you—'

'He's a gambler, you know.'

Trying to shock, is she? Desperate to stop Agnes from becoming part of their lives? 'I know,' says Agnes. He's lost once or twice at Solvalla Trot, but he's not a committed gambler, not addicted. Is he? She's never seriously thought about his gambling. Is it a thing? It's true he's borrowed from her, but he pays her back, usually. She takes a deep breath. 'We should—'

'If he tells you he's quit, don't believe him. He lies, you know. I keep track.'

'What do you mean?'

'I put a tracker on his phone,' Pernilla says smugly. 'I don't care if you tell him. Might delete it anyway.'

'If you're worried about anything—'

'Worried.' She huffs at that. 'I'm used to him.'

I'm not doing this.

They're approaching the South Hamlet canal quay. Though it's early in the season and few visitors, the cafes, restaurants, and boutiques are open. There are two sailing boats, docked and deserted. Agnes pictures their interiors and the people who live on them. She pictures Guy momentarily before blocking him with the thought of her flowers home—her wilting flowers. 'I think we should get back?'

Pernilla shakes her head. 'I'm gonna check this place out.'

'We have a wedding—'

'I don't. You came running after me, not the other way around.'

And for what? She may be a decade and a half ahead of Pernilla, but Thomas's daughter usurps authority as if she's the older one. How does she do it, pour such venom out?

Pernilla halts. Her face is flushed. Due to cool air, or adrenaline and fury? Her certainty, her arrogant youth under her new thread-bare jeans and tight jacket, makes Agnes sorely aware of her lack of height, her pear shape of denim and knitted bulk—her lack of savvy.

'Another thing I bet you don't know about my dad.'

Agnes holds her breath. This girl sure carries a lot of hurt around.

'You met years ago, yeah? Like when I was just a kid.'

Agnes wants to walk away. She's an adult. Can do whatever she likes. Thomas should have this conversation with his daughter.

'When he was seeing you, Dad was still with Mum, still living with us.'

So, Agnes is to be the bitch who came between the parents. 'I didn't know to begin with.'

'You could have broken off with him once you did.'

She did. She walked out of that motel room in the middle of the night as soon as she found out.

It doesn't count when you take him back, Agnes—and within weeks.

Liese and Thomas have been long finished. Their relationship was a train wreck from the start.

That's his words, not hers.

Too bloody trusting, you are.

'Mum reckons he was seeing you while still living with us. Until she threw him out—the first time.'

Agnes nods, trying to find words, her own amid Niina's rhetoric.

'Dad and Mum started hanging out again last summer. He stayed over heaps and they'd go for dinner and stuff.'

She'd had her hands full then. Any free time went towards bear making. She'd bring her hand sewing downstairs to keep her mum company and monitor her father, make sure he didn't forget a cake in the oven or try to lift his wife onto the toilet while intoxicated. Thomas was long out of the picture. He texted her occasionally, wanting to meet up, but she kept telling him no. She had no claim on him. She'd thought they were finished for good, and assumed he'd move on—not back to Liese, though.

'Like I said, I keep tabs on my lying dad,' says Pernilla, now scrolling on her phone as if in search of something. 'I know when he started seeing you this time around.' Her hands tremble with anger. This is what she's been wanting to show her all along. She holds up the screen to Agnes with both hands to steady them. It's her phone's calendar, and it has capital letters written on different dates. 'SV means Solvalla,' she says. 'I know when he's out there for the races. You can guess what SH stands for. I didn't know what there was in South Hamlet, but I showed Mum. She knew. Dad and you were meeting up. And he and mum ...' Pernilla doesn't finish the sentence but scrolls past the weeks to show her the dates Thomas has visited in the last five months.

So that's what Pernilla holds against her and him. They've gone and done it again.

Pernilla closes the calendar. 'Don't worry, Mum's so totally over it, won't have a bar of him anymore. And now you know, I know,' she says with gritted teeth. She doesn't wait for Agnes to respond, but leaves her, waving the phone over her head. 'Tell him. I'll text when I need to be picked up.' She walks off towards town, keeping the same pace as before, her tiny butt jutting from side to side.

Has Liese put her up to this? Agnes has never met her, but Liese must hate her, and she has passed it on to her daughter. Thomas and Pernilla should go to counselling and have it out with each other. And later, Agnes will go too, if need be. Beneath the tough exterior, there's a girl who can tenderly make pretty flower bouquets.

Two minutes later, Agnes finds herself at The Strawberry Patch ordering a double choc with sprinkles, putting it on her tab. She gulps down the silky sweetness, considering her options—trudging along the canal, or walking to Niina's flat hoping to get a lift. There's a chance Niina hasn't left yet. But if she has, it will further delay the walk home. Agnes decides the risk of missing Niina isn't worth it.

She steps out of her clogs. They're not designed for long walks and the leather edges across the bridges of her feet have left red lines, itchy and sore. The grit's rather coarse under her bare feet, but she'll be able to run back over the grass on the sides of the path.

She soon regrets the double-choc which becomes a bopping dollop on top of the persistent nausea. Agnes longs for water to wash out the taste of sugar. Not even a minute and her wish is granted. Niina's rain arrives. Perfect.

It starts with a random droplet here and there, as if hesitating, as if testing her to see her reaction, or not sure if it will bother. And then it breaks loose. Drops heavy on her head, dribbles down her face, catches in her eyelashes, and follows hair strands to her neck. Water trickles down her back between her shoulder blades, prickling her skin with goosebumps.

Within minutes her hair's a wet cap, her jumper drooping heavy, and the t-shirt underneath clings to her body. Her jeans are soaked through, hugging her thighs, restricting and slowing her down. Really, she may as well walk. But she doesn't. Agnes keeps going furious with Pernilla for showing up when she doesn't want to be here, furious with Thomas for not being upfront with her, and herself for ... for being in this predicament. When she reaches the lock again, she stops at the spot. There she runs around in circles, dragging her bare soles through the gravel.

16

twenty-two days ago

Agnes got out of bed as the Coffs Harbour sky turned mauve with the rising sun. She had dreamed of suffocating, which meant she had slept, which meant her body clock had surrendered to Eastern standard time. The dreaming had been less vivid than usual, and each time she'd fallen asleep within minutes. So she felt reasonably rested. Wanting to take a walk on her own, Agnes tip-toed past the living room, so as not to wake Guy up. But Holly had been right about her brother. He wasn't there.

Holly's family lived in a hilly suburban area with the distant mountains as a backdrop. There wasn't much to look at except people's gardens and the lineup of bins along the street. Agnes didn't care. The cool morning air, the distant kookaburras laughing, the sun barely over the horizon illuminating the heaven with pink and orange—it was all bliss. There was only her and the scud of her new shoes on the paving. The solitude was delicious. So much so, the occasional dog walkers with their friendly good mornings annoyed her, though she was on *their* turf.

She slowed her steps to change the phone card. There was one message from Thomas. He'd sent her a sick face and a face with hearts attached. Agnes imagined him worn out from fever and coughing, had genuine empathy for him. At the same time, she was thankful for how it had made all this possible. She changed cards again to get into her online mail.

After considering the pros and cons regarding truth-telling, she sent Thomas an email. She described how she'd stayed the night in a nice resort in Byron Bay, how she'd met a friendly couple on the bus, and included a photo of the lighthouse she found online. It surprised her how easy it was—writing about her fictitious bus tour.

While she was at it, Agnes checked the schedule for the next couple of days, picked up a few more photos online, and stored them for later. No need to overdo it. Thomas knew she wasn't big on photography. He wouldn't expect much. She set the alarm on her phone so she wouldn't forget to send him another email the next day.

Did it matter to him where she was? No. If he thought she was on a bus sightseeing the North Coast, he'd sleep better. While he did that, she was going to face her fear. Thomas didn't grasp the extent of it. She'd never woken up from a nightmare when he stayed over. He knew of her accident as a child and that her father drowned, but really, he was clueless.

Two hours later, she was again in Holly's buzzing kitchen. Mum was packing lunch boxes while both children were scurrying in and out, looking for lost paraphernalia, mainly socks. There were good morning greetings aimed at Agnes and last-minute commandments between mother and children. Then Nathan and Ruby slammed the door, leaving Agnes on her own with Holly.

'I'd planned to take you shopping first thing,' she said chirpily. 'But after the wet April we've had and your first time Down Under, let's enjoy the sun instead. Guy suggested we meet him on the beach.'

'Actually, we're going to Felicity,' said Agnes.

'Oh,' said Holly, taken aback. 'Guy didn't think—'

'I spoke to him five minutes ago. Felicity it is. Then beach.' Agnes was excited. Right now she was. She'd never had a bucket list. But last night she'd started one. Felicity was at the top. Getting used to waves was on a good second, standing in the waves, at least knee-deep.

'Great,' said Holly. 'I've got a box full of swimmers and I've lots of shorts and T-shirts, casual dresses, whatever you want to borrow.'

If only she'd demanded the bus driver to get her bag out. Holly was taller and slimmer.

'Don't worry, Agnes, my weight goes up and down like some rollercoaster ride.' She waved for her to follow. 'We'll find you something.'

Holly had changed. Maybe she was a morning person. Or had Guy noticed the spikes and pulled her into line?

'Have a pick,' she said, emptying a large box onto hers and Mick's bed. Swimmers of every design and colour landed in a pile. She rummaged through. 'The top and bottom don't have to match, you know. Pick whatever fits. Here on the North Coast, no one cares.'

They arrived at the marina, in denim shorts and T-shirts with swimmers underneath—Agnes in a mismatched two-piece she didn't feel overly exposed in. Holly had also supplied her with a pair of better fitting and less scratched sunnies, a tote bag packed with sunblock, towel, jumper in case the wind picked up, and a rash vest—a nylon thing that bonded like second skin—that Agnes had no intention of wearing.

Holly, with a small esky in her arms, led the same way Guy had the day before. Agnes followed in her footsteps like a duckling to its mother. As they walked along the pier, the emotional Agnes conspired with the physical Agnes. Anxiety crept in through her feet, working its way upwards, intent on making her feel lousy about having to walk what? Less than ten meters from the gate. Pathetic.

This fear that ruled her right now was infuriating and plain silly, yet held her with an iron fist. It was the idea of sinking, of drawing water into her lungs, unable to reach the surface, unable to see. Swallowed by liquid.

Her fear had never met resistance from her parents. Living so close to the canal, it must have been practical to have a child who'd keep away from it. Especially since she played on her own, and they offered scant supervision. The night she almost drowned had fuelled it further. Her father's death changed her nightmares. She didn't drown alone anymore.

The small office in her brain, where logic ruled, kept informing her nerves—she wouldn't fall in, the pontoon wouldn't sink, and the water wouldn't rise. It didn't matter. Her nerves paid no attention. They were like headless chooks. Her legs were unbendable like metal poles. She hoped Guy would come to meet them.

'Got my own keys,' said Holly on cue.

Agnes reminded herself she was wearing proper shoes with rubber grip, making it impossible to skid. Holly held the gate up and ushered her through. On the other side, Agnes pretended to struggle a bit with her tote handles so Guy's sister could walk past her, but Holly waited.

'You go first.' Agnes's attempt to casual, sounded like she was choking.

Holly gave her a look, then whisked past her. Focusing on Holly's head, Agnes followed legs both stiff and jelly. She spotted Felicity. Thought she could see two heads sticking up. Agnes walked as close as possible without treading on Holly's heels. There was nothing to hold on to. No railing. No Guy. She desperately wanted and yet resisted the urge to place a hand on Holly's shoulder.

The second person in the boat was Tanya, luscious hair flying in the wind, white top taut over her bust, showing off golden brown skin. Holly greeted them while jumping aboard catlike, leaving Agnes stranded, unable to replicate her leap, unable to run, fixated, glued to the pontoon, cold sweat at the back of her neck.

'I told you to text me once you'd parked the car,' she heard Guy say.

How had Holly approached getting aboard? There was the guard rail to get over reaching the back seat and the other wires that connected to the mast. Could she hang on to that, pulling herself forward, or would it be safer to haul herself over the railing? Her body was trembling. Then there was Guy, reaching out, grabbing hold of her wrist.

'One foot up,' he whispered.

She did her best. Her legs were made of wood. If it hadn't been for Guy hanging on to her, the entire Agnes would have tipped sideways and bounced off a boat for the second time in her life. Sturdy—as if screwed into the boat like so many other things around them—with muscles like rocks, Guy held against her lack of balance. The Swedish landlubber found herself safe and sound, both feet on the cockpit floor.

Agnes collapsed on the teak-clad seat opposite Holly and Tanya, glad to lose sight of any water, conscious of her clumsiness. Holly had a face of suspicion and surprise. Tanya smiled. Sort of. Agnes brushed her fringe.

'Welcome aboard,' said Guy. He placed himself next to her, lay an arm around her shoulder. Agnes could feel the fear settling.

'Sorry about taking off,' he said. 'But there's nothing like the gentle roll of waves lulling you to sleep.'

Tanya's eyes bore into her. She and Holly, what a tag team.

'Did you just boil the kettle?' said Holly. She got up and stepped through the small opening into the boat. 'Give me a hand, Guy.'

Obediently, he followed his sister.

Agnes leaned back and gazed up into the sky. The subtle swaying of the mast, the gentle movement of the boat, was not unpleasant at all. Only the thought of the hull submerged in water was an image better off suppressed. She focused on all the smaller details on the boat, all the wires running between mast and deck, the ropes, the things that she had no names for. She was doing her best to listen in on Guy's and Holly's muffled conversation when Tanya spoke.

'This is a surprise,' she said. Between wind gusts, her dark mane fell in soft waves around her face, enough hair for a dozen women—the unfairness of it. 'What happened to seeing the barrier reef?' She spread her hands through her hair, airing it as if it needed airing. It needed nothing. It was perfect. She was perfect. She was also wearing shorts. Tanya's stretch denim covered half her trim thighs while Agnes's loosely fitted ones ended at her knees. They hadn't seemed so bad when she tried them on at Holly's. Now they made her feel dumpy.

'Change of plans,' she said, crossing her legs.

'You staying at Holly's?'

She nodded. 'And you?' Do you live close by?'

'We're neighbours.' Tanya pointed out on the pontoon. 'See that mast there?'

'You have a boat as well?'

'Used to. Now I boat-sit. Sydney owners that don't sail too often.'

'And if they want to?'

'I usually just stay with Guy.'

'And usually, I'm not even here.' Guy's head popped up. 'Strong, lots of milk,' he said, handing Agnes a cup.

'Sometimes he is,' said Tanya.

Guy's head came up again, this time holding out a cup for Tanya but looking at Agnes. 'I'll have to show you around down here after. More room than you think. Got a couple of sleeping quarters.' He disappeared again.

'I look after Felicity when Guy's away. After all, she used to be partly mine.'

'Really?'

Again, Guy was in the opening. 'That's all ancient now,' he said, handing them a plate each with Holly's sandwiches cut in triangles. 'I bought her out five years ago.'

'I didn't want to give Felicity up. Needed funds for my training, but.'

'For what?' asked Agnes. Then she ate her sandwiches while Tanya told her about all the courses she'd put herself through and where she now worked. She taught Zumba in a couple of gyms, aerobics, step, and spinning. No wonder she was so fit. The woman didn't keep still. Meanwhile, the siblings joined them. Holly took a seat opposite with Tanya. Guy sat down next to Agnes, spread his legs wide and relaxed. His thighs were hairier than Thomas's, which suited him, and bulkier. Next to them, Agnes seemed less chunky.

'I do personal training too,' said Tanya. 'Got a couple of celebrities in my stable. No names, of course. Sealed lips.'

'And she teaches swimming,' said Holly.

Guy kicked his sister's leg. It was subtle—him pretending to stretch his legs further—but Agnes noticed it.

'You teach adults, don't you?' said Holly.

'Sure, I do an aquarobics class.'

'And people who have a fear of water?' said Holly and received another kick. Guy had obviously said something. If Holly's purpose was to embarrass, she was succeeding. Agnes sipped her coffee, kept the mug on her lips, and tried not to look perturbed.

'I get the odd person who's totally scared of water. Weird but true.'

'You might give Agnes some—'

'Do you mind?' Guy kicked his sister a third time, not subtle at all.

'Seriously?' said Tanya. 'You don't swim?'

Agnes held the mug to her bottom lip. 'Not really.' She swallowed. 'I mean ...' She licked along the edge of the cup. 'No, I ... I actually have a bit of a fear. Idiotic, but true.'

'I'm pretty busy.'

'You're not *that* busy.'

'Holly, can you stop running other people's lives?'

'Oh, shut up, Guy. I'm being helpful.'

'Agnes has a few days and I've already planned day trips. We'll be busy.' Guy started naming places they were going to see. 'I've planned a couple of overnighters. I want to take Agnes up the coast.'

Tanya had been looking at her while Guy talked, weighing things up, perhaps. Now she smiled. 'I could give you lessons,' she said. 'How many days are you here? We could do morning or afternoon. I'd have to charge you, but.'

'You can't teach someone to swim in a week,' said Guy.

'Sometimes you can get surprising results.'

'Agnes is on holiday. I want it to be a week of fun, not anxiety.'

'You should give it a shot,' said Holly, looking intensely at her. 'Sounds like an opportunity.'

The three started bickering while Agnes watched, sipping her coffee.

Guy was not keen on the idea. It would muck up his travel plans. Holly was not keen on his travel plans. Mick could do with some help all week. Tanya enjoyed arguing for the sake of arguing, it seemed as if it energised her, or perhaps she shared Holly's point of view.

'Excuse me,' said Agnes a few times. They ignored her. Not even Guy paid attention. Finally, she raised her voice. 'Excuse me!' That stopped them in their tracks. They all quietened with expectant looks on their faces. It was so unusual for her to get that kind of reaction that Agnes lost her trail of thought.

'You were saying,' said Guy.

'I just want to know, would it be one-on-one lessons?'

'Sure, if you can do early arvo.' Tanya lifted her sunnies and cast an exaggerated glare at Guy and Holly. 'Contrary to what people think, I do actually work.'

'Is it worth it, do you think? I'm one of those weird ones. Pretty fearful.'

'We'll start from scratch. I'll give it my best shot if *you* will.'

'See Agnes, how—'

'Oy,' said Guy, kicking his sister again.

'Could we book in the lessons today for the rest of the time I'm here?' said Agnes. 'That way Guy can plan some trips?'

Tanya shrugged. 'I suggest at least an hour at a time, but preferably two. Up to you how committed you are, what results you want. Gotta be in it, to win it.'

'Would you mind?' said Agnes.

Guy smiled, shaking his head. 'It's your holiday.'

Holly was looking quite smug behind her mug.

'And you think even a week can be beneficial?' said Agnes.

'How do you feel about taking showers and having baths?' asked Tanya. 'I'm serious. There are people with real phobia and it can get that bad. I'm pretty sure you're not. You're on Felicity right now. I'll get you, if not swimming, at least treading water, I reckon. Love a challenge.'

There was something about the confidence with which she responded that encouraged Agnes. 'It's a deal,' she said, ignoring the jitter that nudged deep in her gut.

'Don't you want to know my hourly rate?'

'Sure,' said Agnes, though she couldn't care less.

Tanya wedged in between her and Guy with a phone in her hand. 'Righto, let's start today.' She put in her PIN code twice. The phone wouldn't open.

Guy got up. 'I bet it's mine,' he said and disappeared inside Felicity.

Tanya tried again, more numbers this time, and it worked. 'Buy yourself a new cover, would you?' she called out to Guy.

Holly leaned over to Agnes. 'It'll be the best thing, this,' she said. 'You'll see.'

'Found yours,' said Guy, landing next to Agnes. He and Tanya swapped phones. Then she checked her calendar. 'I can squeeze you in after lunch. How does two thirty sound?'

Agnes glanced at Guy. He looked disappointed, she thought. 'Okay, two thirty it is,' she said.

'Oh, shit!' Tanya jumped up. 'A class waiting. Gotta run. You can buy goggles at the pool. You'll need them.' She put her right hand out to Guy and they did some kind of complicated handshake routine. Holly received a kiss on the cheek, and Agnes, a wave. Tanya leapt off the boat like a gazelle in flight and took off to her own boat.

'Don't you have to be somewhere?' said Guy to Holly.

She zipped up her esky and collected her things. 'Good on you, Agnes,' she said. 'See you later, then.' The last thing before she walked off was, 'Guy, take her shopping. Will you?'

Guy picked up the cups and plates. 'Finally, some peace,' he said. 'Welcome to my abode. I'll give you the quick tour.'

He showed her all the nooks and crannies around the space beneath. The tiny opening was called a companionway. There was the galley right as you came down the ladder steps. The main cabin with a table in the middle and padded seats on either side, Guy called the salon. He showed her how he could easily make it into a place to sleep. After the salon, there was a toilet the size of an upright coffin on your left.

'Except,' said Guy, 'toilet is called head, left is called port, right is starboard.' Opposite was an equally sized shower that, wonder of wonder, was called a shower. Finally, at the front—the bow—was a triangular space, which was a bed and a compartment for the different sails Felicity needed to perform her best. It was like learning a new language. Guy gave her proper names for everything. Most of them went in one ear and promptly out the other.

After the tour, Agnes sat in the salon lounge watching Guy wash up the dishes and stow the crockery away. Felicity had obviously sailed past her glory days. The timber was not brand spanking new. The faded and torn upholstery needed replacing, as did the tiny curtains covering the porthole windows. But Felicity was tidy, which surprised Agnes. The inbuilt shelves were filled with books in neat rows, folded clothes, and other bits and pieces. The orderly boat in comparison with Guy's car, spoke volumes about what mattered to him.

When he was done, Guy sat in the seat opposite.

'I'm sorry about this afternoon's pool session,' said Agnes.

'You know what? It's a good thing. Don't tell Holly I said that.'

They sat in silence, smiling at each other, she, immersed in the smells, and the gentle movement, amazed at the strangeness of being on a sailing boat, *Guy's* sailing boat.

'You have an open invitation to sleep here,' he said.

His words sort of flew out and started bouncing around in Felicity's small space like a trapped bumblebee in a jar. He'd said sleep—nothing else. It was her thought of *nothing else* that buzzed. Her cheeks went all hot and flushed, and she was suddenly aware of her hands. Agnes tucked all fingers between her thighs.

'What I mean is you'd choose where you'd prefer, and I'd sleep in the place you didn't pick—I didn't mean—I just reckon you'd love it.' He gave her a sheepish look, then stood.

'Let's get cracking.' Guy collected his wallet and car keys. He leapt outside, barely using the ladder. Agnes followed one step at a time.

While he closed the hatch, she wondered why he was so keen on spending time with her. Did Holly have a point? Did Guy have that kind of interest in her? Yesterday, in a moment's confusion, she'd thought so, but she'd misunderstood him. Was there something going on between Tanya and him? Was she being dragged into some jealousy game?

17
today

Agnes is drenched by the time she reaches the back porch. She scrambles through the French doors, her wet feet skidding across the threshold. To her surprise, a woman sits in the cane lounge with coffee in hand. Agnes has never met her but the forehead, the shape around her eyes, and her long legs twined to the side let her know this is Thomas's mum. She's in pearls, a blouse, slacks and loafers—quite mother-in-law-like.

Agnes drops the clogs, and attempts to pull her wet flat fringe across her forehead while giving his mum a wave, before leaning over, hands on her knees, catching her breath. Is the rest of his family around too? Is it later than she thinks? And where is Thomas? Then she spots the cane table. Coffee has been served in the delicate china she and Niina cleaned and arranged on the sideboard, for the afternoon, for the wedding guests. And Thomas—assuming him the culprit—has also laid out, on a matching plate, a selection of the patisseries and handmade chocolates she ordered specially.

'You must be Agnes?' says his mother.

It sounds like, *Look what the cat dragged in.* Agnes scolds herself for thinking that. It's the Stockholm accent. Then she scolds herself for not using the front door. She finds a kind of Quasimodo stance, holding her soaked, clinging jumper from her body. 'Rain,' she says. *Yes, Britt-Marie can see that it's bucketing down.* Water is finding its way from the hem of her jeans and sleeves, onto the floorboards. And is that blood? She tilts one foot at a time. Yes, indeed. She's brutalised a couple of toes.

'Should I get you a towel?' Britt-Marie gets up without waiting for instructions and disappears.

A minute later, she returns with hand towels from the guest toilet—the new white ones Agnes bought specially—and spreads one on the floor at Agnes's feet. 'Now take off that sodden knit.' Britt-Marie waits. Once the jumper is off, she hands over the other towel. 'I'll drop it in the sink.' She carries the bundle at arm's length into the kitchen. When she comes back, his mum makes herself comfortable in the lounge again.

While drying her fringe and hair, Agnes sneaks glances, thinking of something to say.

Britt-Marie picks out a chocolate, places it on her tongue, and closes her Botox lips around it. She looks like a much older and thickened version of Pernilla. The granddaughter has missed out on the grandmother's beauty spot. There is something familiar about his mum. Agnes has seen her before. But where? She thinks back to her Stockholm visits years ago. Thomas had a few photos of his little girl, not his mum.

His mother licks the truffle off her front teeth. 'Thomas has gone to pick up Pernilla,' she says. 'He woke up to an empty house. All a little strange.'

So much for checking out South Hamlet. 'We went for a walk.' Agnes wraps the towel around her upper body, inspecting her feet spattered with dirt. The toes she dragged ache. Patches of polish are all that remain of her brightly coloured toenails—courtesy of Ruby. She needs to clean, file and paint in one colour, and she needs band-aids. They have to move furniture. Niina will look after the drinks and Patrick will bring the food, but she has to organise the kitchen before either of them arrive. And she has flowers to finish before that. Britt-Marie must leave.

'Strange to go for a walk when you have a wedding in less than five hours.'

And what about dropping in for a coffee and cake? She's known Thomas's mother all of three minutes and is already having an internal go at her? The woman fetched towels without being asked. 'Pernilla was a little upset,' she says.

'My granddaughter is finding all this, a bit, sudden. We all are.'

'The wedding?'

Britt-Marie lets out a condescending, 'What else?'

'No, it is sudden.' Helpful with fetching towels or not, Agnes has no mother-in-law time allocated before four this afternoon. What was Thomas thinking, offering his mother a fika? 'What is the time?' she asks.

'Half-past eleven,' says Britt-Marie. 'My husband and brother wanted to try out the local golf facilities, so we came early. Don't know how they keep playing in this weather, but they've not called to be picked up yet, so ...'

Half-past eleven is okay. Isn't it? Agnes has never had the best sense of time, born the complete opposite to her mother, who lived her daily life according to the clock's arms. It was the obvious thing to throw out after she passed. Her father spat the dummy when he discovered the light round patch on the kitchen wall.

'Why the hurry?' asks Britt-Marie. 'I've never even met you, Agnes.'

Have you asked your son? 'It's a long story,' she says.

His mother nods broodingly. 'Funny,' she says. 'You seem oddly familiar, somehow.'

'Did Thomas show you a photo, perhaps?'

Britt-Marie shakes her head slowly. 'He should've.'

He wouldn't have many. Agnes avoids having her photo taken. Guy sneaked a few, and she snapped a couple of him on the beach, innocent photos where he could be *Joe*. If Thomas found them. On the flight home, she deleted every single one.

'You own this house, Thomas tells me. And you sew bears?'

'It's a niche market.'

'So you can make a living on that?'

Agnes sighs inwardly. What is it with the women in this family? Does Britt-Marie want to make sure the girlfriend isn't after her son's hard-earned dollars? Agnes folds the towel again and again. 'There is ... ' she says, watching the inquisitive face of Thomas's mother. 'There's a family trust fund.' She regrets it immediately. Really, it's no one's business. She doesn't have to justify herself.

'Oh, I wasn't. I didn't mean to pry,' says Britt-Marie.

Is that right? Could have fooled me.

'So the two of you go back a few years?'

'Yes, we do.' Her skin's cooling. A hot shower would be heaven.

'He said you met when he separated from Liese the first time.'

'Yes, it's a while ago.'

'And he never mentioned you.'

That's not my fault. Surely? Agnes shrugs but says nothing.

'He mentioned your mum. You looked after her for years, he told me.'

'I did.'

Agnes catches herself biting a fingernail. Not that there's anything left to bite. The state of her nails is the worst they've been in months. She doesn't have to stand here, shivering. She should excuse herself and take the chocolates with her. Hide them.

'I'm sorry you've lost both parents. Very sorry about your father.'

'Thanks.'

Britt-Marie picks another hazelnut fudge.

'Would you like me to ring South Hamlet's Guest-house?' says Agnes. 'I can find out if your rooms are ready.'

'I didn't mean to disrupt your day. Thought you might need help, but you seem pretty relaxed about the whole thing.'

Thomas certainly is.

Britt-Marie leans towards her, tilting her head. 'How come you two didn't settle for an engagement party? What's the hurry? You've not even lived together yet?'

You and Niina should get along.

'What is the rush, Agnes?'

Agnes doesn't have to answer that because the front door opens and shuts. They're back. Agnes is wiping the floor as they walk in.

'So you've met,' says Thomas. 'Great.'

Agnes leaves the room without bothering to acknowledge him or his daughter.

The bathroom is in shambles. Pernilla has cluttered the vanity with make-up, flooded the floor, and opened every bottle or tube, from perfume to cracked-heel cream. Agnes won't clean it up again. This was to be the second option toilet. Thomas's guests can all share the downstairs one, as small and poky as it is.

Ten minutes later, with dry enough hair, dressed in bamboo pants and another loose-knit, Agnes is back in the kitchen to deal with the aftereffects of Thomas's efforts to serve fika—open containers, spilled milk on the stove, coffee package tipped over on the counter, letting its aroma go to waste. There's also *her* flower project on the table. She'll give Thomas and the others five minutes of courtesy. Then they have to leave. If the guesthouse isn't ready for them, there are lounges, in the foyer, to sit in, or they can sightsee—or sit in Britt-Marie's car for that matter.

Thomas is in the other cane armchair while Pernilla has stretched out on the two-seater with a pillow under her head. She has the phone resting on her chest and headphones in her ears.

Agnes carries her mother's footstool from the lounge room. You need to straddle it, resting your knees on the floor for it to be sturdy. With regret, she realises her head is now marginally higher than the coffee table. She's like a child visiting with the adults.

'The rental chairs should be here soon,' she says.

'I'll set them up,' says Thomas. 'Won't take a minute.'

'The ever-optimist,' says his mum, pouring herself another cup from the kettle.

'We'll just take it as it comes, won't we, babe?' Thomas looks down at her, touches her feet with his.

Babe has never been her favourite word. He forgets that, the way he forgets to seal the coffee. Thomas's long legs stretch out towards her. He's oblivious to her telepathic vibes, and her feet distancing themselves from his.

The questions she has for him are lining up. From why he didn't clean up the kitchen like he said he would, to Liese and his imputed gambling. It's clear Pernilla is doing her best to throw a spanner in. It's possible she's capable of blatant lies. But she has convinced Agnes there's truth in the mix. And there's something else, something slippery. This she's certain of—having to sit and play nice is making her skin crawl.

'Agnes.'

'Sorry, what?'

'How was Australia?' asks Britt-Marie. 'You had an expo?'

'Agnes sold out. Didn't bother bringing the suitcase with her home.'

She's forgotten that he doesn't know. At first, she didn't tell him because he was sick. Then she didn't tell him because he forgot to ask. When he picked her up at the airport, she gave him the exact story he's just passed on to his mum. The trip seemed such a failure. Lost bears and a broken heart. The ache had been so all-consuming, she'd not find the energy or the courage. If she'd started with the truth about her Sydney weekend, how would she have kept the rest from him? Sunday night was all about keeping up appearances. And these last few days, it has been all about the wedding.

Now she's thankful that he doesn't know. This is better. In their eyes, she's a success. Why not? There will be no more stupid lies, but this is an honest mistake. Isn't she entitled to be a fake success on her wedding day?

'I booked her on a coastal tour,' says Thomas.

Agnes puts on a smile. 'Niina will be here soon,' she says. 'I should actually get to the flowers.'

'Did you go to Byron Bay?' asks Britt-Marie.

'Sure,' says Agnes, pushing herself up from the footstool.

'At which resort did you stay? We were there last year.'

'I can't remember—so many resorts. I'm sorry, but I really have preparations to get on with.'

'Of course, you do,' says Britt-Marie. 'I'll wash this up—'

'Absolutely not. Thomas will do that,' says Agnes. He gives her a surprised look.

'I might leave Pernilla behind,' says his mum.

'No, take her with you,' says Thomas, leaning across to wake her.

Agnes grabs his arm. 'Leave her. If she wakes up, you can drive her over later. You're going to the guest house anyway. Remember? After you've helped me re-arrange.'

'I was going to claim your spare room to finally get some sleep.'

'Out of the question,' she says. He's taken aback. And she likes it.

18
twenty-two days ago

As Agnes walked through the gate to the pool and smelled the chlorine, old school carnival memories came rushing in, of her peers lining up enthusiastically by the pool-side, waiting their turn to dive in, to perform the incomprehensible task of racing each other from one end to the other. Sitting in the shade, away from the exertion and the cheering, alienated from the camaraderie, wasn't the worst. The breaks every two hours were—when it was time for one teacher to force a brief lesson on the losers while the abled ones watched.

She became quite efficient at hiding in the toilet block. She'd sit on top of a lid with her feet up and the door closed but not locked. It was only a couple of times anyone went half-heartedly looking. As she got older and the non-swimmers got younger and younger in comparison, Agnes stayed home. She pretended to go to school, but sneaked back inside, up to her attic. Her dad never noticed. And as far as she knew, there was never a note sent home. She crawled through the cracks with the teachers, not her classmates. Her absence, as well as her incompetence, fuelled their aversion to the weirdo.

To Agnes's surprise and relief, Coffs Harbour's swimming centre was almost empty around the two outdoor pools. In the large one, a handful of slow swimmers were gliding through the water. In the shallower one, a few young mothers played with their babies. The air was warm enough, like a decent Swedish summer day. The well-kept grass around the area was inviting and she would have loved to lie down to read or work on her tan, forget about the task at hand.

She was paying for a casual visitor's card and a pair of goggles when Tanya showed up ready in swimmers and rash-vest. Agnes was sure she spent her life in lycra.

'Hey Don,' she said to the man behind the counter. 'Can we borrow a pair of floats and a noodle, thanks?'

After a few jokes, they were off, Tanya with her backpack bouncing, a fast mover, Agnes hurrying after, regretting her decision. Tanya led the way to another pool, an indoor one. Again, a handful of people were taking up a couple of lanes. That was positive. However, here the water was not lit up.

'Maybe we should go outside?' suggested Agnes.

'The Aussie sun will roast you.'

'I know I'm pale, but I do tan.'

'You don't wanna get back to Switzerland with peeling skin.'

There was no point arguing. That much was obvious. Tanya claimed a table and chairs in a corner. Agnes wiggled out of Holly's shorts, self-conscious about the stark contrast in constitution and fitness between the two of them, and

wrapped Holly's towel around her before pulling Holly's
T-shirt off.

'Got a rash-vest?'

Holly lent me one.

'Well, put it on, woman. It'll keep you warmer. And
stop looking so freaked out.' She put her hands on Agnes's
shoulders. 'Slow and steady. I promise.'

Agnes nodded, shivering, though she wasn't cold yet.

'I'll show you what we're going to do, so you'll know the
steps before we do them.' Tanya pulled a thin folder out of her
bag. There were cartoon pictures with complimentary text.
'As you can see, I'm starting you with basics.' She sure was.
Step one was sitting on the edge of the pool, splashing feet.
'If you get to step two today. That's no worries. Okay?' Step
two was wading in the water.

'Shallow end?' asked Agnes.

'You bet.'

'And where will you be?'

'Right next to you.' Up close, Tanya wasn't much taller than
Agnes. The slim figure and straight posture gave an illusion
of height. She would have been one of the sporty and pretty
girls at school, self-assured and popular, the girl who offered
you a superior smile, whispered behind your back, only spoke
to you when you had something of value such as the correct
answer to a question or a bag of your dad's home baked
cinnamon buns. She would have been a winner, beating the
boys at freestyle, who would have loved her, anyway.

174

While they dangled their feet in the water. Tanya queried Agnes about her fear, if she knew where it originated. Agnes told her the usual toddler accident story. She wasn't here for a heart-to-heart.

'I've never thought to ask for professional help,' she said. 'You think you can fix this?'

'No. *I* can't. I'm only the facilitator. And remember, you're not up against me. You're up against you.'

'Is it slippery? I mean, the pool floor. It's not slippery, is it?'

'Fear is a funny thing,' said Tanya. 'Fear of any kind of unknown, and fear of the fear itself. All a bit complicated, really. You must face it head-on. I used to have a real spider phobia, not something I recommend, in this country. It bugged me like nothing else. I started small, the size of nits and worked my way up to huntsmen.'

'How long did that take?'

'Not important. My point is, I had friends cheering me on, but *I* had to do it. It was me on my own against the fear. I'll cheer you on, show you how. But with your fear, you are alone. One thing I promise. Beating the beast empowers you.'

Despite the water being twenty-five degrees, and wearing her rash vest, after an hour, Agnes was shivering from the cold. She'd been wading about without holding on to the poolside, the water at chest height. She'd touched the water's surface with her chin, and she'd taken long breaths and blown bubbles on the surface. The pool floor wasn't slippery, and as long as she kept herself in the moment, focusing on the task at hand, she was fine, more than fine. To her astonishment, she enjoyed the smooth resistance.

Agnes bought them both a hot chocolate at the pool's café. She couldn't stop smiling. She'd taken a practical step towards solving a problem—shifted the algorithm, as her mum would say. Tanya had surprised her. Her persona when Agnes first met her had been cool, if not suspicious. The entire time with her in the pool, she'd been positive and encouraging, a little pushy perhaps. They decided on times for the next five days and she paid for the session she'd finished, as well as the rest of them.

'You didn't need to pay in advance,' said Tanya, rolling the notes into a small bundle before squeezing it into her tiny wallet. 'Good thing Guy isn't here, or he'd get on his soapbox about giving me a stack of cash. Reckons it seeps through my fingers like sand. Gets a little protective.'

'He's very considerate,' said Agnes.

Studying her, Tanya relaxed into her chair with the mug in her lap. 'So what's your story?' she said. 'Got a bloke in Switzerland, I hear.'

'Sweden,' said Agnes, giggling. 'One of those long affairs.'

'Sounds like me and Guy. We met when he and Holly came here. He wanted to live on the coast, wanted to learn to surf. Best friends from day one. One thing led to another. Then Holly met Mick, who got Guy interested in sailing. I tagged along. We bought Felicity, thinking we'd do her up.'

'What happened?'

'The old girl was costing us. Guy started taking on sailing jobs while I was losing interest. Don't take me wrong, when the wind's up and there's swell and you must tack your way home—love that, but nah, I'm better on land where I can get around, change scenery whenever I want. Not one to sit still for too long.'

Apart from their mutual preference for land, Guy's ex was her opposite.

'We're still as close as ever, you know.' She twisted two fingers together and winked at her. 'Friends with benefits, if you know the term.'

Was that why he'd gone back to Felicity? Tanya had been there this morning. They'd got their phones muddled up. Agnes had an instant visual of the two of them, naked together. Her cheeks flushed hot and sparks of unease or irritation went through her. Why should she care? Agnes cleared her throat. 'How come you're not a couple?'

Tanya shrugged. 'Too independent. Both of us. Guy comes and goes like the northerly swell.' She gulped her drink, then eyed Agnes over the rim of the cup. 'I think he wants to take it up a notch, now he's back.' When Tanya placed the empty mug on the table, she had cocoa stains in the corners of her mouth and the cracks in her lips were dark lines. Less perfect.

So you've got yourself a crush.

So what if the two of them had a friends-with-benefits arrangement? She had Thomas. With shame, Agnes thought of him sweating and shivering in bed. He'd recover quickly, though. Next week they'd be in a nice resort. With a lot of hard work, she'd be able to surprise him by going into the pool. Not swimming, but she'd be in it, and she'd be tanned, and she'd tell him about her pretend bus tour. Or she'd come clean, explain how she wanted to surprise him with the whole overcoming-water-fear thing. Except, he wouldn't get it.

'Here's Guy.' Tanya leaned across. 'Have I got cocoa around my mouth?' Agnes pointed to her own lips, and Tanya dug out her water bottle for a quick splash.

'I've been texting you, Agnes.' Guy placed a hand on her shoulder. 'Been waiting in the car while you two—'

'We forgot about time. Thanks for the drink, Agnes. I need to get to the gym. No rest for the wicked.' She picked up her bag. 'So I'll see you tonight,' she said to Guy.

'Looks like we're going out, Agnes,' said Guy.

The look on Tanya's face.

'I'm booking into a motel,' said Agnes. 'Might have a quiet night.'

'Out of the question. You're coming,'

'You're not the boss over me,' said Agnes, winking at Tanya, who smiled.

'What if I plead? You're visiting Australia and I'm your host. Please?'

'I've nothing to wear, remember?'

'We go pretty casual. Where should we go? Tanya, can you recommend a shop?'

She shrugged. 'Really gotta run. You'll work it out.' She kissed Guy on the cheek. 'See you tonight then.' She waved to Agnes without really looking at her.

Guy took the empty seat while Agnes finished her chocolate. 'How are you two getting along?'

'Good, I think.'

Guy sat hunched with arms resting on his thighs, car keys dangling from his fingers. 'I'm glad. She can be … unpredictable.'

Tanya was missing when everyone met up at a busy Thai food place. The group, men and women between thirty and forty, had booked a long table. The cracking of jokes and the constant prattling among so many people made it impossible for Agnes to grasp what was being said. Luckily, Guy chose seats in one corner with Holly and Mick.

He'd not only patiently chauffeured Agnes around all the shops he could think of, but also come with her, complimented on anything she'd tried on, and come with his own suggestions—only suggestions since he was definitely not the boss over her.

They'd arrived back at Holly's just in time to get dressed and go. Guy's annoyance with his sister that morning had evaporated. And Holly herself seemed relaxed. She was keen to find out how the swimming lesson had gone. Holly had suggested they hold a seat for Tanya, but when half an hour had passed and someone wanted to claim it, she'd given in.

Tanya arrived late and loud, strutted in on wedges too high for comfort, in black skinnies and a skimpy top, all hair and panache, calling out to people she knew. When she realised Guy and the rest of them sat cramped at the other end, she waved them off while making snarling comments about not holding a seat for her. Tanya was best friends with everyone, so Agnes supposed it didn't matter that much where she sat, but Agnes caught her again and again, observing them.

After dinner, they moved on to next door—two bars, lots of mismatched tables and seats, lounges randomly throughout. A sibling-like duo in pigtails and man-bun were performing, she on guitar, he singing and playing mouthorgan. It was folksy. People talked while they played, but clapped and cheered wildly after each piece.

The large group spread out and mingled. There was a lot of backslapping and cheering and pulling Guy away, wanting to buy him a drink and hear the latest of his travels. To begin with, Guy insisted on introducing her to every person who wanted some of his time. But when she discovered that Holly and Mick had found a sofa with a little room left, Agnes asked if he'd mind much if she took a breather.

She watched the muso couple perform and nodded and smiled to people walking past whom Guy had introduced her to. It was fun to be out, to have a drink in her hand, being part of it without the alcohol and without having to converse with anyone. Holly, Mick, and she clinked glasses after each song, but talked little. It seemed they all enjoyed the ambience.

When the duo had finished and started packing up. Somewhere, a DJ started playing dance music. Tanya collapsed on the armrest next to her with an empty beer in her hand.

She put the bottle clumsily on the table and leaned in, sharing her yeasty breath with Agnes. 'Look at you,' she said in a loud voice. 'You scrub up all right.' She was beyond tipsy. 'Did you get that today?'

She fingered Agnes's new tunic, a silk weave knit in baby blue. Guy had pulled it out 'This one, I reckon,' he'd said. When he'd spotted the price and attempted to hang it on the rack again, she'd snatched it off him and, against his protests, brought it to the change room. It seemed to elongate her, make sense of her shape. The shop girl had commented, and later Holly, even Mick. She was going to visit that shop before she went home, buy herself a new wardrobe, and find a few gifts for Niina.

Agnes only smiled. It was pointless to talk. Too much ruckus.

'Have you seen Guy?'

Agnes shook her head.

'If you see him, send him to the dance floor.'

She gave a thumbs up.

Tanya stood, leaned in, and tried to drag Agnes with her. 'You come dance with me.'

Agnes held up her drink.

'Bring it.'

Agnes gave in and let Tanya pull her up. She could find a chair or a corner. With Tanya's sweaty arm around her shoulder, they walked to the back of the club, the pub, whatever it was. The dance floor was the size of Agnes's hallway at home and packed with people bouncing about, moving limbs how they saw fit. When Tanya tugged, Agnes slipped determinedly out of her grip and watched her swimming coach almost fall into the crowd before losing herself to the beat. Tanya was no Niina, but her body had the thing Agnes lacked—groove. At home on her own, Agnes could sort of dance. Nothing complicated, but at least in time.

In front of other people, it was as if she stuttered with her limbs.

'Why aren't you out there?' said Guy into Agnes's ear. His breath sent a shiver down her spine. He'd sneaked up behind and stood so close, his chest pressed on her back. She sensed the compact shape of him.

Again, Agnes held up her drink in response.

'In a bit then.'

Together they watched the sea of bodies while she held on to her cocktail, wishing she wasn't such a spineless bore.

Suddenly, Tanya was in front of them. 'Come on. Our song.' She reached for Guy's hand, and Agnes stepped aside so he could get past her, though he seemed unwilling. Maybe it was pretence, but Tanya had to pull and shove to get him on the floor.

Agnes watched the two of them—she shaking and shimmying, he moving around more controlled, often looking Agnes's way, waving for her to join them. Again and again, Tanya would grab him by the shoulders, trying to get hold of his hands. Again and again, he'd slip away. They kept disappearing into the crowd and coming out. It was like a cat-and-mouse dance. Meanwhile, Agnes hung near the wall aiming to look mesmerised by the music, showing her sad slush of soaked fruit and drowned peppermint leaf to any man who tried to invite her up for a dance.

Then Guy was back. 'Go find someone else,' he said, giving Tanya a gentle nudge, keeping his back to her until she disappeared into the dancing crowd again. He took the glass from Agnes's hand and placed on a wall ledge. 'Your turn.'

'No way.'

'Come on.' He found her wrists and started hauling her towards the floor with the biggest grin on his face, forcing people to step aside while moving his and her hands around in time with the music. Reluctantly, she submitted. He pulled her into the middle of the crowd where you couldn't possibly stand still for the other dancers bumping into you. Guy took some basic steps. He was tipsy, and he made her laugh. Agnes copied him. So what if she was out of sync? There were no eyes on her. No one cared. These people didn't know she was the odd Andersson offspring.

She had Guy to herself for a while before Tanya showed up. They danced with her constantly in the middle, vying for Guy's attention. Then a slow song came on. Agnes was not great with artists, but this one she knew, though she couldn't remember the title. The artist wasn't cool enough for Niina, who was mad about funky and upbeat and all of that, but Agnes had thought this song could be lovely for their wedding if she and Thomas ever got there. Niina had rolled her eyes at that.

Now the three of them stood like pillars while people around them were moving on and off, pairing up. She knew this was her cue to leave. Guy and Tanya were more than ex-lovers, more than friends with benefits. There was something going on between the two of them, she was sure of it. She was also sure that Guy was a true gentleman, who felt responsible for her having a good time. It was she who needed to step aside. Let the two of them have a moment.

Tanya zoned in on Guy. She swayed in time with the music, her tough exterior gone, her glazed eyes vulnerable, wanting him to reach for her. She ought to have what she wanted. Agnes ought to turn on her heel, but she didn't. She glanced at Guy. Their eyes locked, and she took the first step towards him, nervous yet knowing this dance was hers. In her periphery, Tanya flicked her hair and stormed off.

Guy pulled her to him, placed an arm at the small of her back, and drew her hand to his chest. Agnes closed her eyes and made her feet follow his. There was barely room to rock back and forth. You still had people bump into you, but all that, as well as Tanya and Thomas and Holly, faded away. There were only the two of them, their bodies moving in unison. She breathed in his cologne and the scent of Felicity—musty wood and fibreglass, turps and linseed oil. It was strangely similar to the smell of her craft room. Her lost bears surfaced, but she reminded herself they would be found. She let the worry drift away with the music.

Her guilt and confusion about what on earth she was doing blended seductively with the pleasure of being enclosed by muscular arms. Even though, deep down, Agnes knew she was being selfish and inconsiderate, she drowned all that, made it sink down into the deep while she remained floating in the moment. As the music faded into another slow one, they kept holding on, kept moving.

Too soon, far too soon, the DJ thought it appropriate to get on with upbeat music. People reshuffled around them. They slowed to a stop, but Guy held on to her. For a few seconds, she kept her eyes closed, wishing the moment to last. His hand found its way to her neck. He kissed her skin. Agnes opened her eyes and there, two meters away, was Holly glaring, shaking her head slow and subtle.

'Let's get out of here,' said Guy into her ear. He had a firm hand around her waist. He hadn't noticed his sister, or if he had, he couldn't care less.

She cared. And she stiffened. 'I need the ladies.' Agnes pushed away. Then she was off through the bopping bodies in the opposite direction to Holly and Mick, away from Guy. She hurried up the stairs to the next level, found the ladies, and burst through the door.

The three teenage girls glued to the long mirror didn't even look up. They were too busy blabbering while applying more make-up on their caked-up faces. She strode past them and locked herself in the one available toilet, slammed the lid shut and sat. The taste of curry, mint, and sugar in her mouth disgusted her.

You do know, you have to go back down there and face them. All of them. Holly.

She'd used Guy as a substitute for Thomas. Pathetic. And what was his game? There was no need to make Tanya jealous. Even Agnes could see that. And worst of all—the look on Holly's face? His sister's dislike made her feel small and false and rejected.

The teenagers soon left, and Agnes forced herself to get up and out. In the mirror, her ridiculous scar screamed louder than usual on her sunburnt forehead. Her fringe had come apart, and strands of hair poked out at odd angles from her French bun arrangement made with half a bottle of hairspray. She tried to re-pin. Her fidgeting merely produced the impression she'd stuck her thumb in a live socket, so she gave up, wet her palms and patted it down, fringe included. She cooled her flushed cheeks with water and thought about Tanya's words about fear.

Guy was waiting at the bottom of the stairs with a concerned look on his face.

'Call of nature,' she said. 'Sorry.'

They persevered for another hour, but the vibes had changed. Too many friends of Guy's had bought too many drinks for him, and it was showing. Agnes avoided Holly. Holly and Guy ignored each other. Mick hovered around his wife, looking bored.

When Holly decided it was time to leave, Agnes was both relieved and worried, worried that once home, she would take Agnes aside for a woman-to-woman chat. Mick offered to drop Guy at the marina, but he insisted on walking home and left them with a short good night. The drive back to the house was quiet. Agnes sat in the dark backseat, wishing she'd booked a motel.

Holly didn't have a word with her in private. She bickered with her husband instead, and Agnes sneaked off to bed.

19
today

While Thomas sees his mum off, Agnes carries the used crockery back to the kitchen, puts the sweets back in their containers, and in the fridge. As soon as Thomas closes the front door, she goes to meet him, pulls him into the office and closes the door, not wanting to risk Pernilla overhearing in case she wakes up.

'We need to talk,' she says.

Thomas beats her to the swivel chair, swings it around, dumps himself in it. 'Have a seat,' he says, patting the expansive desk.

When her mother was alive, neither Agnes nor her dad would ever dream of sitting in Irene's swivel chair. You also wouldn't dare to sit on top of her desk. Be it small, this was her kingdom. You had to knock and wait for a 'yes' before you entered. You said your piece, then you went on your way. But it's not her mum's old rules that restrain. Agnes is not in the mood. Instead, she keeps her distance staying just inside the door.

This is probably where her mum stood when she argued with Thomas that time. She was short too. Irene would have ordered him to sit in the visitor's chair while she remained standing, while she lectured him—tried to lecture him.

'What's up?' says Thomas.

They've never been in here together, she realises. The office isn't a room you visit for any other reason than to pay bills. It's small, boring, and somehow still smells of her mum. Agnes is really done with it, done with hanging on to her mother's stuff. The enormous desk that takes up half the room will have to go, along with both chairs, and the old computer. She could make this into a cosy TV room instead.

'You seem on edge,' he says.

Her pants lack pockets, so Agnes crosses her arms over her chest.

'I'm sorry about the kitchen,' he says. 'I was bone tired this morning.'

'Yeah, well ...' She doesn't have time for that, or the chocolates, or the crockery.

'What's with that serious face?' He's swivelling from side to side.

Will he understand the depth of unresolved issues that plague his daughter? Does he truly see her? Parents often don't. Agnes has no desire to create more friction between him and Pernilla, and it's going to be obvious where the information comes from. Yet she also cannot let this go. The best she can offer Pernilla is to play it down. 'There are a couple of things,' she says. 'No need to bring this up with her, but your daughter's upset—'

'Before you say anything, remember she runs her mother's errands. And she's fourteen going on twenty-four while stuck in her terrible twos.'

Agnes takes a deep breath, a breath that he notices. 'As I was saying, Pernilla was upset earlier. She seems to think you were seeing both me and her mum, claims you kept living with them for a couple of years after we met.'

A few seconds pass before he answers. 'I was upfront with you then. It was impossible to find rentals. Ancient history. Wouldn't you say?'

'You told me you were sharing with a mate.'

'Yeah. Dennis. Now and then I stayed over with them, for her sake, and if Dennis had something on.'

'Why didn't you tell me?'

'How could I, babe? I felt like shit about the whole arrangement. Could only get rentals further out in the suburbs. And I was not moving back to Mum's.'

'How often?'

He stops with the swivelling. 'I can't believe we're doing this.'

'Once a month? Every week?'

'How can you let Pernilla get under your skin like this?' he says, raising his voice. 'If you must know, I was there the weekends Dennis wanted me out and sometimes through the week when I wasn't travelling. I had no choice. And for your information, I slept in the lounge.'

Agnes isn't even sure why she cares or if she cares. It is old.

191

'And do you know the travelling I did in those days?' he says. 'It made no sense to pay for a flat. How often do you think I was home? It was work, work, and more work. The rest of it was about spending quality time with my little girl, and some more with my other girl, until her parents decided I wasn't good enough.'

Agnes ignores the stab. 'Did you get with her, with Liese after—?'

'After your mum told me to piss off?' His glare digs into her.'Yes, I ended up with Liese for a bit, sort of like a desperate rebound tragedy. You didn't want me, and she reeled me in. I'm sure you knew—'

'I mean, last year?'

He turns the chair to face her mum's desk, picks up a pen and starts clicking it in and out. 'Why are you doing this?' he says.

'I don't know what to think.'

'Pernilla is being self-centred and manipulative. You can see that, can't you?' He turns around to face her again. Finds a new calm. 'Look, I'll be totally honest with you. Yes, we were giving it one last shot. A foolish thing to do. When I came to see you after your father's funeral, it was a spur of the moment, you know that.'

He'd not said a word about Liese. Agnes had not thought to ask.

'I had to let her down gently,' says Thomas. 'We are finished with each other for good. I think she's met someone, actually.'

'She has. Pernilla told me.'

'Then what are we even doing here?' Thomas reaches for her. This time, he's quick. His hands find her waist and pull her in. She holds on to the chair's armrests, not touching him. 'What else?' He asks with a sigh.

'Are you gambling?'

'What's with the Spanish Inquisition today?'

'Is it a problem, something I should worry about?'

Thomas holds her out while pushing the chair backward, forcing her hands to let go of the armrests. 'You know I've gambled, and it's never been a problem,' he says. 'But today I'm getting married.' He looks at her earnestly. 'There are murky waters in my past, Agnes. But believe me, I'm done with all of it. I want to start again. I want to start for real with you, start a family at some stage. You know that.' He rolls towards her again, lifting her stiff arms, one over each of his shoulders.

She doesn't fight him, but she doesn't relax her arms either. She says, 'How *is* your money situation? Any debts?'

'Is that Pernilla?' he says, not taking his eyes off hers. 'Bet it's coming from Liese. I miss a couple of payments and it's all drama. Is that what this is about, money?'

He's close now, his blue eyes intent on hers. He's warm and solid and he smells good. Her arms are so brown compared to his cheeks. It's strange to be the one with the tan, and it's strange to be skin-to-skin with him. It's been a month. That last time isn't worth remembering, but the Easter weekend was good.

And this is what? Guy was exciting because he was different. Before him, it was always Thomas. *So this is what?* Good, she decides. *It's good.* Agnes allows her hands to glide along his shoulders. 'Money is right up at the top of what puts stress on a marriage,' she says. 'If you're in debt, I should know.'

'Nothing I can't handle.' He kisses her neck. His lips are soft, so soft.

'How much?' she says, much quieter. 'And to whom?'

'To a nobody.' Another slow kiss. 'And I will take care of it.'

'Is this nobody like, I don't know, a loan shark or whatever they call them?'

'Something like that.' He's kissing right behind her ear now, a tender spot.

She tilts her head, stretches her neck. 'Is he putting pressure on you?' she says, though she's losing track of what they're talking about, and thinking about what it will be like to have Thomas naked under her or on top of her. Their sex life is going to change a bit. Thomas does nothing slow, but he'll have to learn.

'I can handle a little pressure,' he says, spreading his legs, and pulling her in close.

'Your daughter dislikes—'

'I've not always treated her or her mum the best way. But she'll come around. Liese is happy now. When she's ready, Pernilla can come and stay.'

'She doesn't want to.'

'Give her time. She'll come around.' His hands slide up and down her back.

'We could make this her room?' Agnes can just imagine Pernilla shrugging her shoulders. But with time, maybe she will change. With time.

'I like that,' he says.

They should go upstairs. That's what she should have done on Sunday, stayed and faced it—her fear that he'd be a disappointment after Guy. You face your fears. Australia has, at least, taught her that. She was a fool on Sunday. Thomas has annoyed her since he arrived, but it's slipping away. Agnes feels it in her entire body, a longing to be naked with her groom, taste intimacy with him again. She kisses him back. 'Let's go upstairs,' she whispers.

Without a word, Thomas pushes himself out of the chair, sweeping her up in his arms. She holds hers around his neck.

'Pre-wedding fun?' he says.

When she nods, he kisses her lightly on the lips.

There's no time for lovemaking, but Agnes can't care less. She needs closure from Guy. How has she not seen that until now? She desperately needs to break the spell. Agnes laughs in Thomas' arms. 'I can walk myself there.'

But Thomas is already opening the door. 'I need a practice run,' he says.

Thomas carries her out of the office as Niina walks through the front door. There they are in her snug foyer, Niina in a royal blue bouffant gown, black hair fortified with matching highlights, and an impressive cake box in her arms, and Thomas with Agnes in his arms, and a tight crotch.

Beyond embarrassed, Agnes releases the grip around his neck, signalling for him to let her down. He does with a sigh. Agnes is disappointed, too. She's finally understood how Guy has claimed space between them. This would have been a quick way back.

'Sorry, if I'm interrupting anything,' says Niina, marching past them, a plus size taffeta girl on very chunky, very high gladiator sandals with impressive cleavage, and not one bit sorry.

'She can't barge in like this,' Thomas whispers with such force, he spits in Agnes's ear.

'Niina? Part of the furniture,' she whispers back. 'You know, the eclectic element.'

Thomas ignores her attempt to humour him. 'That has to change,' he says.

Boundaries for Niina? Only her mum managed that. When her mum wanted Niina to go home, she'd tell her straight and not take a no for an answer. If she didn't want her to visit for a week, she'd tell her. In Irene, Niina saw a worthy opponent.

After the stroke, Niina got her way all the time. In all fairness, her visits were mostly received with gratitude. Niina would joke with Nils and entertain Irene with monologues. Despite running her own business, she made time to take Irene for walks, giving Agnes a break. After Nils died, if it wasn't for Niina—though Agnes often craved it—the quiet would have drowned her. Admittedly, at times, her best intentions rub the wrong way, but overall, Niina has been a help more than a hindrance.

'You'll have to tell her,' says Thomas in her ear.

Agnes places a hand on his chest. 'After today, it'll change naturally, you'll see.' And she realises that's fine with her. She and Niina will have their regular movie nights and dinners when Thomas is on his business trips, which will be most weeks. 'Let's have a look at our cake,' she says, tugging for him to come with her.

He lets go of her hand. 'Surely, she can come back in half an hour,' he says. 'Pretend you've forgotten something. Send her on an errand.'

'Thomas—'

'We'll pretend we have to discuss Pernilla. We can be quiet.' He hints towards the staircase.

They could sneak away for a quick one, could even go up to the attic. Surely, no sound will travel from up there, all the way to the kitchen, if they keep it down. Of course, Niina will work it out. And she will have the shits. But she'll have the shits when she sees the fridge, anyway. *My best friend's here to help. And I'm thinking about sex right now.* With a sigh and an apologetic grimace, Agnes leaves Thomas for the kitchen.

Niina's busy opening the box. She notices Agnes and holds up one hand, displaying her fingers laden with ornamental silver rings and long, loud nails, the same blue as her dress and hair. 'Not going overboard,' she says. 'Purely keeping with the theme.' Then she fiddles open the lid. It's a two-tiered Princess cake with a marzipan layer in baby blue, decorated with white roses. At the bottom, in a cellophane bag, arm in arm, lie the plastic bride and groom. 'I'll put them on later,' she says. 'You've made room in the fridge, yeah?' She opens the door. 'Apparently, not.'

'I've been somewhat busy.'

'Hand me an apron. I'd better get this place organised. Got drinks too that need to go in. And what the hell is this?' she says, lifting the drenched and dripping piece of knitwear in the sink, then dropping it again.

'You're not staying. Are you?' Thomas hangs in the doorway, sullen-faced.

'Of course I am.' Niina's dress swishes and swishes as she moves around the kitchen. She's taking things out of the fridge that can sit in the pantry for a while, wiping surfaces, moving bottles and jars back and forth. 'You've got a lot of outdated stuff in here, Ness.'

Agnes holds her hands for Niina to pass items to her, but no, Niina ignores her.

'We could do with a bit of quiet time before the madness starts,' says Thomas.

'We or you?' says Niina without interrupting what she's doing. She's a whirlwind. Her shoes click-clack under her quick feet. The two inches heels give her calf muscles shape, and a workout. Most likely she's bought them to go dancing with. The wedding is the warm-up.

Thomas, fingers in his jeans pockets, straightens up. 'Agnes and I were about to have a moment to ourselves.'

'Well, there's no time for your dick, right now.' Niina says it the way you might say, gosh, that soggy zucchini really needs throwing out.

I don't want to be here for this. Agnes fixes her gaze on the garlands, still waiting to be decorated with bouquets. She's got herself sidetracked. She'll need to do them now. What is the actual time?

'You say whatever comes to you. Don't you?'

'No Thomas. I say whatever *needs* to be said.' Niina comes to a halt in the middle of the kitchen, hands on her hips, like a matron pulling the children into line before dinner, telling them to go wash their hands or something. 'I'm helping my best friend get her house ready for *your* family and friends, get her ready for her wedding, and make this her best day ever. And so you're not welcome right now.'

'Who do you think—?'

'You say you need time out? Take it. Aren't some of your family over at the South Hamlet Haven? Go there. Agnes doesn't want to see you until the absolute earliest three thirty.'

'She can speak for herself.'

All eyes on her.

Silence.

The sound of rain on the windowsill outside.

'What time is the wedding, Ness?' asks Niina.

'Four,' she says, staring at the kitchen table corner.

'There you go, Thomas. Now show me how astute you are and piss off.'

Niina is only this rude when she is nervous or drunk. She isn't drunk, and Agnes has only ever seen her nervous selling classics online, with an auction at its last minute. *Patrick? Surely not.*

'You've got a mouth on you,' says Thomas.

'Established fact,' says Niina.

'Agnes.'

Why doesn't she have pockets in these blooming pants? Her hands find the lining of the waist. Agnes tucks all her fingers in there. The surrounding air is thick, so thick you couldn't carve it with a butcher's knife. 'Well ...'

'What?' the other two say in unison.

It seems sex has been the answer all along. She's just been too blind to see it. If they'd been one minute quicker out of that office. But the moment is gone. Niina's right. If there's going to be a wedding, she'd better get on with it. 'I have flowers to finish and—'

Thomas turns on his heel.

Agnes wants to say something to Niina. But she doesn't. She heads after Thomas.

The doorbell pings.

Ignoring this, Thomas crouches to put his shoes on. Agnes steps around him with some difficulty to open the door. It's Patrick in a yellow raincoat.

'Got the right place then,' he says with such cheerfulness she stumbles backwards into Thomas's shoulder. 'Sorry, it's a little early, but don't worry, I brought my freezer boxes.'

Thomas stands, grabs his jacket, and strides out the door without acknowledging Patrick at all, which is rude with Patrick offering a smile and his hand, and ridiculous, considering the colour and size of the man.

'Is it a bad time?' says Patrick.

'Umm ... no,' says Agnes. 'Come in.'

'You'll need to move your car, mate!' That's Thomas at the gate, keys in his hands, eager to leave.

Agnes shoves her feet in the wet clogs and hurries after Thomas, who's getting in his car. She stands in the way as he's about to shut the door. A fine drizzle cools her scalp and skin. What is it with her and water today?

'Some best friend you have,' says Thomas, while strapping himself in.

'She's not herself.'

'I beg to differ.'

'I'll talk to her. But she's right.'

'See you at ten to four. Better keep what's-her-face happy.'

Patrick, who's moved his van a few feet so Thomas can get around him, has opened the side door, and is hauling out a large blue box.

'The food's here,' says Agnes. 'And ... Well ... You're not helping.'

Thomas starts the car, then sits waiting for her to move. When she steps to the side, he shuts the door. Speeding off, he misses her foot with a couple of inches.

Agnes's gut churns with nausea. In the kitchen, sandwiched, she lost her footing, her confidence. Why is that? Australia changed her. At least that's what she thought. But maybe she's wrong. Maybe she was a different Agnes around people who didn't know her the way she's always been. Is she falling into old habits after less than a week in Sweden? Is it too impossible because Niina and Thomas know her in a certain context? Does Villa Solus enforce ingrained habits and expectations? She should be able to choose how she wants to be.

It was a challenge to meet up with Niina in the bookshop. Agnes didn't take the argument head-on but bailed. *I didn't bail. I said my piece and went home.* That's true. She did. *I simply hate arguing.* And now she has done exactly that—with Thomas. She can count arguments between them on one hand. This is the first time she's seen him angry. Is it because he usually gets his way, and today he didn't?

Thomas and Niina in the same room. The thought is ludicrous. Yet, they will have to do it one more time, for the sake of the wedding. Niina will get over it and she'll fake it for Agnes. Thomas knows how to put on the charm. That's his thing—why he's so good at his job. Thankfully, by the time he returns, there will be wedding guests as a buffer zone. Hopefully, both of them will have cooled off in a couple of hours. However, Agnes will have to speak with Niina once Patrick's gone. Niina was right, but she didn't have to be so rude. Her and her foul mouth.

In the kitchen, Patrick's holding the fridge door while Niina carefully places the cake box in its allocated spot.

'Let's keep Mr and Mrs Lundén cool,' she says, tittering. It's a brand-new sound for Niina. Girly. Doesn't suit her.

'You've been introduced then?' says Agnes curtly, which she regrets for Patrick's sake, but hopes Niina notices. She doesn't.

'More or less,' he says. When Niina closes the door, he offers her his hand. 'Patrick Norling.'

She reciprocates. 'Niina Bogati. First name with double i for the sake of my rebellious nature. Kept it singular in the last to keep my cultural heritage untouched, and as an assurance that I'm not a lost cause.'

He leans over, lifts her hand to his mouth, and kisses gently. He doesn't let go either but studies her nails. 'Spectacular,' he says.

Niina giggles. 'The colour? The length? Or my rings?'

'All of it.'

Patrick's a big man—broad shoulders, solid thighs, and hands like dinner plates. With his ponytail and beard, he'd make an excellent bikie or some fantasy warrior. He would look right with leather and hog, or leather and sword. Yet, he's such a calm and collected, quietly spoken gentleman in serving his customers. And here he is, admiring Niina's bejewelled hand, not worrying about the extra woman audience.

'I need to finish my flowers,' says Agnes. They don't hear her. Niina's positively purring. Agnes feels like an intruder in her own kitchen. If not for her flowers, she would leave them to it. She walks over to the table and starts up again, but the enjoyment of creating has left her. There's now no time or space to work meditatively.

'Agnes, we'll rearrange your lounge room and dining and sunroom,' says Niina. 'Our Deli man has offered to stay and help. We've got this, haven't we Patrick?' She titters again. There's no other word for it.

She has never seen Niina like this. Not that she has seen her around many men. Agnes only gets to *hear* the stories of Niina's nightly winnings, as she calls it. 'Great,' she says. If Patrick stays, she's off the hook with Niina. An argument with her best friend isn't something she wants for her wedding day. Agnes leaves her flowers, to go show them how she's imagined the layout.

Pernilla is fast asleep in the cane lounge with her knees up, arms folded on her chest, hands encapsulating her precious phone.

'What's she doing here?' says Niina.

'Please keep it down?' whispers Agnes.

'She's picked a stupid place. How come she didn't leave with what's his name?' says Niina.

'We'll work around her,' says Patrick.

'This is where the chairs will go,' insists Niina. 'And they will be here any minute. So we can't work around her. We need to shove her over to that corner.'

'Can't you start with something else?'

'Ness,' Niina says with gritted teeth. 'It's your fucking wedding day. Can you stop catering to all and sundry? We'll be moving things around in here to make it look nice, to make it fucking practical. And we don't have fucking all day.'

Patrick looks a little stunned.

Yes, Patrick, you've had your ten minutes. This is the real Niina. 'You were over the top rude to Thomas?' Agnes whispers. There, she's said it.

Niina rolls her eyes. 'You really wanna do this now?'

They glare at each other. Of course, she doesn't want to do this right now. Or ever. Definitely not now. The blue behemoth eyeing her is not one to admit to any wrongdoing. In fact, in all the years of them being friends, Agnes has never won a single argument. She won't win today either. Niina is in high form.

'Well, she's a good sleeper,' Patrick says disarmingly.

Agnes turns away from Niina, looks at Pernilla, and there it is again, the feeling she's seen her before, not her, but sort of her.

Years ago, Agnes saw photos of Pernilla as a toddler and a young girl. The few pictures she's seen of her lately have been out of focus, from a distance, or showing her in profile. Right now there is something strangely familiar.

'I'm going back to my flowers,' whispers Agnes. 'Work around her if you can.' She says this more to Patrick and doesn't wait for a response from Niina.

There's a vague niggle, like a word on the tip of your tongue—an almost thought. The best way is to busy her hands and mind. When she least expects it, what's hiding will shape and rise to the surface. She tells Patrick and Niina to arrange how they see fit, then leaves them to it.

Back in the kitchen, she's soon handling the flowers again. Though working fast, not fussing at all, the bouquets turn out fine. Once she ties them to the garlands, the overall effect is natural and whimsical. It lifts her spirit. It's been a strange day so far, but maybe it'll be smooth sailing for the rest of it.

Niina and Patrick come back to the kitchen. Pernilla slept through the entire pandemonium, which Agnes is thankful for. Patrick goes to get platters, trays, and utensils out of his car. Niina offers to help her finish the garlands and ignores Agnes's dismissal.

'He deserved it,' she says, picking up a rose.

Agnes has the urge to hit her over the head with her dad's cast-iron skillet. Suddenly there it is, a flare gun in a dark sky. Out of nowhere, or she supposes, from deep within her. Agnes knows where she's seen that face before—Pernilla, but with an added beauty spot. She might be wrong, of course. There's only one way to find out.

'Would you mind cleaning up the table?' she says and leaves as Patrick walks in.

20
twenty-one days ago

Waking up to a sleeping house, Agnes had done the cowardly and rude. She'd gathered her things, and sneaked out after leaving a written thank you note for Holly and Mick. She'd walked from their house all the way to the marina, booked in at a motel ten minutes from the jetty, showered and then gone for a stroll down to the beach, to sit in the sand. There had been early swimmers, joggers, and dog owners, and everyone greeted her with 'G'day' or 'How ya going' and she smiled and helloed, appreciating the friendliness, even if it didn't mean anyone actually wanted to know how she was going.

And how did she feel? She was disappointed with herself about the previous night, and she wondered what kind of game Guy and Tanya were playing with each other. On the beach, she'd wondered if the two of them ended up together. She'd braved it, texted him, invited him for brunch. He'd said yes.

Now they sat at a table on the balcony, facing the view of Mutton Bird Island with nothing much to say. Guy was solemn, unlike what he'd been so far, looking weary. Agnes regretted waking him and didn't know how to behave. She didn't notice the fingers to her lips, her tongue searching the short nails for any fresh growth. Guy did.

'There can't possibly be anything left of your nails?' he said.

She dropped her hand and clasped both in her lap.

The waiter brought menus, a jug of water and glasses. They barely greeted him and neither of them picked up the menus after he left. Guy who was resting an arm on the table kept moving his fingers back and forth over the plastic surface. Agnes started chewing her nails again. And so they sat for a while, awkward, watching the ocean and people walking by on the path below.

A young couple with a toddler in a stroller stood by the break wall. Though the family was ten metres away, Agnes could see the face of the child, rosy cheeks, big eyes looking out into the world while mum and dad had their heads bent down towards their phone screens, captivated.

There was a faint sigh from Guy. 'About last night ...'

He let the words fade out. He obviously felt he had to explain the situation, make sure she'd not misread him, whatever. Why couldn't they just ignore the previous night? She didn't want to hear about him and Tanya. She wanted everything back to how it was, wished he would joke and be himself. His fingers stopped and started, stopped and started, back and forth.

'About last night ...' he said again.

Agnes kept her eyes on the child, pretending to be lost in the moment. What kind of idiot invites a friend for breakfast and then can't even hold a conversation? The toddler had fine hair that fluttered in the wind. That was her—fluttering fine hair. She should have settled for breakfast on her own.

'Did you enjoy yourself?' he asked.

'It was a fun night,' she said with her best upbeat intonation.

'What's so interesting? And stop biting.' He grabbed hold of her hand that had sneaked back up to her mouth, forcing Agnes to turn away from the child. She tried to wiggle out of his grip, but Guy held on. 'I've wondered about that ring of yours,' he said, holding her hand up so he could look closer.

They sat there for a bit behind their sunnies with the wonky round table between them. His hair was wild. He looked more unshaven than usual. What level of intoxicated had he been the night before? Was he hungover-grumpy? That was such a Niina thing.

'So what's the story?' he asked.

'Thomas gave it to me.'

'Did he?'

'It's a sort of engagement ring from years ago.'

'Is it?' His lips pressed into a brazen smirk.

'Yes.'

'Then why don't you sort of wear it on the more customary finger?'

She swallowed. 'Old habit.'

'That makes no sense.' He slid his thumb back and forth over the ring and rubbed the fake blue stones while still looking at her face, expecting an answer that made sense to him. His hand was firm, dry, and calloused. Warm.

She thought of the previous night's dance, his body moving with hers, and was glad to be wearing sunnies, to be sunburned. 'My parents didn't approve, that's all,' she said. 'They probably wouldn't have noticed anyway, but just in case, I kept it on another finger around them. In the end, I got used to it being there.'

'You said you and him were on and off for years.'

She nodded.

'And you never took it off.'

'I didn't.'

'Why not?'

'I told you. Old habit.' Agnes tried to retrieve her hand, but Guy held it firm.

He examined her short stumpy nails, felt across each fingertip. 'No growth whatsoever,' he said. 'You know, Agnes, not all habits are good habits.'

'I know there's nail stuff you can paint on. But it doesn't work. I chew it off.'

He snorted at that. 'With breaking bad habits—I reckon, see them for what they are and use your willpower.'

'You speak from experience?'

'I do.'

The waiter interrupted. 'I gather you're not ready to order?' he said.

'Give us another minute, mate.' Guy let go of her hand and picked up the menus, handed Agnes one.

It seemed the family was leaving. The young dad was turning the stroller, still watching the phone, and the mum was texting. How many hours of undivided attention did they give that cute little face in the stroller? The baby had chubby cheeks and chubby little fingers that were pointing as he or she made sounds. How was it that a tiny, flat screen was more interesting?

While she studied the menu, Agnes thought of Guy's cryptic behaviour. She wanted him to be the other Guy, the easy-going one. How could she turn this around? She'd invited *him* to breakfast, but she was no good at whatever this was. She should have left him sleeping. 'Have you seen Tanya?' she said. And why did she? And what if he'd say? 'Yep, she's sleeping on Felicity. Might bring back coffee and a croissant.'

'Nope,' he said. 'Why?'

Instantly—relief. So dumb. So childish.

'She's cancelled my lessons.' She'd received a brief text when she got home the night before. Tanya had used the word two-faced, and though that was not a Swedish adage, Agnes understood perfectly well.

Guy looked up from his menu with an expression of smugness. 'I bet she's got the hangover from hell,' he said with a chuckle. 'She'll be good as gold tomorrow, you'll see.'

Agnes nodded. But he was wrong. She'd made herself an enemy.

'Well, I've made my mind up,' said Guy, and lay the menu back on the table.

Agnes felt his eyes on her while she tried to decide. She thought he said, 'All's fair in love and war.' Was that meant for her? What did he mean by that? 'Pardon,' she said.

'I recommend the scrambled eggs,' he said, offering her one of his generous smiles. Had she heard right? Was this a game between him and Tanya?

His persona shifted. It was tangible. As if Guy unzipped and stepped out of the suit he'd been hiding in. It made her think of forensics after they've looked at the corpse—mask and suit off and on with their day. The real Guy returned, laid back and comfortable. If he could put the stupid incident behind them, so could she. And she'd make sure she wouldn't become a pawn in some gambit. She'd stay out of it.

Agnes noticed the young couple had settled at a table not too far from them. The baby was in a high chair. Mum and Dad had put away their phones and were interacting with their child. She forgave them for their previous detachment and smiled approvingly when the mother glanced her way.

Guy poured water into the two glasses and handed her one. 'So she cancelled,' he said. 'No worries. No swimming for you means we can make a day of it.' He had lots of ideas that he shared while they ate. The places were merely names to her, and she honestly didn't care. With him, it would be a good day, no matter where they went.

Guy was busy strapping his surfboard to the roof rack, and she was sitting in the grass reading an email from Niina when Tanya parked next to them.

'Going somewhere?' she asked Guy, as she hopped out, in lycra as always, her hair in a bopping ponytail, and ridiculously huge sunnies. She didn't see Agnes at first. There was a change of energy when she did. Agnes nervously gave her a quick wave.

'Taking Agnes to South West Rocks for the day,' said Guy.

'Is that right? What about your lessons?' She looked down at Agnes.

'I thought. That message you sent me—'

'That? Agnes, I was drunk.'

'I didn't think—'

'Nah, you're on,' said Tanya. 'Ignore what I say when I'm plastered. What's wrong with you Guy? You know what I'm like. I'll see you there at 3 o'clock sharp.'

'We won't be back in time.'

'You'd better be. We're on a mission, aren't we, Agnes? I'm going to have this girl underwater before she goes home. She paid for the lessons upfront, and I've spent the money. There's no going back.'

The two of them eyed Agnes from above, wanting her to take their particular side. Guy had it all planned in his head what they were going to do. Tanya stood with one hand on her hip. Agnes wasn't so sure it was worth *not* agreeing with her.

'Is there maybe time for all of it?'

She received a definite 'NO' from both. At least they agreed on something.

'There's tomorrow,' said Guy. 'Surely a day won't matter when—'

'Oh, but it does,' said Tanya. 'You're here until when?'

'Next Friday.'

'A week is all we have. We've got some serious work to do.'

'Agnes?' said Guy.

The most part of her would much rather go in the car with him. She knew they'd have a fun day. But Agnes felt quite desperate to get on the good side of Tanya, and she was on a mission, and she'd paid for the lessons.

Guy knew he was defeated before she uttered her verdict. 'No South West Rocks today then,' he said.

'Great,' said Tanya and off she went, giving Guy a flick with her head as in *I won*.

21
today

In the living room, Patrick and Niina have placed the two armchairs in a corner each and the leather sofa in front of the bookshelf. All to create space for a bit of dancing later.

The bookshelf is built around one window and takes up an entire wall. The one thing they all shared in the Andersson household was reading. Her romance novels and craft books are jumbled with her father's garden books and assorted biographies, and her mother's books on mathematics and a substantial collection of thrillers or crime.

Her mum had come down with a cold. In those days, the hospital-style bed took up the centre of the living room, and her mother watched dully from her pillow while Agnes searched for something to read aloud. The photo fell out of a book. When she showed her, Irene, who had lost her ability to produce words, croaked her favourite syllable 'No' until Agnes shoved it back into another book. Which book?

She vaguely remembers where she'd stood, but that's no help. Two months ago, when she did her yearly big clean, she rearranged according to alphabetical order. So the book could be anywhere. She can pick at random or be methodical.

Agnes walks over to the left corner and picks out Allende, flicks through the pages. She pushes it in, then pulls out the next to flick through, wishing she'd tucked the photo in her pocket instead. But her mother's bookmarks? You didn't touch them.

'What are you doing?' It's Niina behind her. 'The chairs are here,' she says. 'Patrick's setting them up and I need help to hang the garlands.'

'Can't you do it?'

'What's going on?' Niina snatches the book, Agnes is about to open, out of her hand.

'None of your business.' Agnes pulls out another book, but Niina's quick to snatch that one, too. She stacks it on top, then throws her arm in Agnes's way.

'Are you two arguing again?' says Patrick, entering the room.

When Niina drops her arm, Agnes takes the opportunity to continue the search.

'Garlands have to wait,' says Niina. 'Agnes is too busy airing her books.'

'I'm looking for something.' Agnes flicks through another one.

'Right now, we need to decorate,' says Niina. 'Then we must get started on you.'

'Right now, I need you to leave me alone.'

'It's like after two.'

217

'This can't wait.' *It can't.* She won't bother with her nails. Make-up will do; that's what's noticeable. And the bride running a little late—that's almost the rule. Isn't it?

'I'll help you with the garlands,' says Patrick. 'I'll just get the chairs in first. They'll need a quick wipe down.'

'Thank you, Patrick,' says Agnes. 'I'll only be ten minutes, fifteen max. Promise.'

'No worries. Can I have my assistant back?'

'She's all yours.'

Niina shoves the books at Agnes's chest. 'Here. You keep airing.' With that, she swishes herself out of the room and slams the French doors behind her with a bang. The glass panes rattle. That temper of hers.

Agnes goes as fast as she can. She finds a rhythm. Pulls, flicks, then places it back with her left hand while pulling the next with her right.

The French doors swing open again.

'Where's Dad? Where's Grandma?'

'Guesthouse,' says Agnes without stopping. There's no time to lose, and she's on a roll.

'What guesthouse?'

'The only one we have, The South Hamlet one,' she says with a kind of Niina-curtness.

'Can't you drive me?'

'Ring your father.'

'Not answering.'

'What about your grandparents?'

Pernilla is quiet for a few minutes, texting. Then she says, 'Grandma is in the bar drinking. Dad's having a nap. So are Uncle Leif and Pop. No one else has arrived. You're it.'

'No, I'm not,' says Agnes, and oh, that feels good. 'But if you help me with this, I'll pay for a cab after.'

'That's bribery.'

'That's a deal between two parties.' Now she sounds like her mother.

'How long will I have to dust before you'll get me a cab?'

'Not dusting. Looking for a photo. And until we find it.'

Pernilla sighs, but she gets up. Together, they drag the sofa away to make the books behind available. Agnes doubts they'll find it there, but she can't be sure, and the aim is to silence Thomas's daughter for as long as possible.

Agnes keeps finding actual bookmarks between the pages and plenty of yellow, folded A4s—her drawings. She put one on the fridge once. Her mother took it off. Her mother preferred to flatten them in her books. Any time Agnes opens pages and one of her pictures escapes, sailing to the floor, she lets them. There's no time for unfolding and reminiscing, but they deserve to be collected.

'Did you draw this?' asks Pernilla, who's just found one herself—a house, and a garden inhabited by stick figures with humongous heads.

'Chuck them on the coffee table,' says Agnes. 'And while you're at it, pick the others off the floor for me.'

Five minutes later, Agnes has finished another shelf and is crouching, too. This is fruitless. It would be easier to find a lost pin inside a stuffed bear.

'I found two more,' says Pernilla. 'How come they're in there?'

Agnes shrugs. 'Mum worked all the time. If she'd ever come out of her office, I'd follow her like a shadow and as she sat down, I'd be there placing my latest drawing on her lap, waiting for praise.'

'And she used them as bookmarks?'

'I suppose that's a good thing.'

Agnes has worked her way through the complete Mankell collection. She hoped to find it in one of the Wallanders, but no such luck.

'Photo,' says Pernilla triumphantly.

Agnes holds back her impulse to snatch it out of Pernilla's hand. She leans in to look. It's of her mum and Olga. They're in the backyard, sitting on the garden chairs from her childhood. Her mum sits wide-legged with a bump like a giant egg under a loose dress. 'I'll hang on to this one,' says Agnes, taking it from the girl.

'Is that your mum?' says Pernilla. 'Don't much look like her.'

'No?'

'You're prettier.'

A compliment? Is there an angle?

'Can we go now?'

And that's a yes. 'It's not the one I'm after.'

Pernilla gives up. She collapses in the lounge again and returns to her phone. Agnes will have to stop as well. *Come on. Think.* It's not that long ago.

Agnes steps back and starts skimming over the books she's skipped past. The ones that belong to her or her father. There, between two gardening ones, is a slim paperback about South Hamlet tucked in tight. And just like that, she knows. She'd thought her mum might enjoy hearing about her own town. Agnes pulls it out with one finger, opens the first page, and there it is.

The colours in the photo have faded and yellowed. The background is a lake with a jetty stretching out into the water. Three people, in clear focus, are posing for the camera. The man, in the middle, has an arm around Agnes's mum who'd be in her early thirties, perhaps. It's hard to tell. Holding on to a slouchy hat in the wind, she's smiling at the cameraman. The man is laughing turned to the other woman who has her arm on the man's shoulder. They are both tall, while Irene is a pear-shaped shorty. The other woman is beautiful, lanky, and Pernilla-fragile. Long blond hair wafts breezily around her face, but you can still see it—the birthmark.

Though she had an inkling, an almost certainty, Agnes stares in disbelief. Their mothers, acquainted with each other in their youth? What kind of weird coincidence is that? That explains why Britt-Marie thought they'd met.

'Did you find something?' Pernilla says, from the lounge, disinterested.

'Another one of my scribbles,' says Agnes, tucking the photo inside her bra. She has to know the story of this photo. 'You know what? I give up. How about I drive you?'

'Like right now?'

'Absolutely, but we'd better move the sofa back, or I'll be in trouble with Niina.'

'You already are.'

Niina has sneaked the French doors open. She stands wide and booming blue in the doorway. Her apron is gone. Her face is flushed. 'We're done, so it's—Wow Niina, you're the best, thank you ever so much for working your ass off while I've been doing shit all.'

'I do appreciate—'

'And you're next on my list.'

'Great. I'll be back in a tick. I'm about to drive Pernilla—'

'No, you're not. Shower and hair wash. These are your marching orders. You are dismissed from everything and anything that's not directly related to your personal scrub-up. I'm setting up beauty salon in your bedroom. Brought my mirror and my entire range.'

'I know time's ticking away. I won't be long.'

'Out of the question.'

'Happy to stay,' says Pernilla.

'I can drive you in a minute.' Patrick squeezes in next to Niina, casually laying his arm around her. 'Going home for some beautification of my own.'

'Thanks, Patrick,' says Agnes. 'But I'll drive. I'll be in and out of there in ten or twenty.'

'Not happening,' says Niina.

'I'll just get ready here,' says Pernilla.

It's probably the seduction of Niina's make-up. She does send out a message of being well-supplied.

'Might be better if I drive,' says Agnes.

'Thomas's daughter,' commands Niina. 'You'd better give me your best smile.'

And she does. Her face breaks out in a forced yet charming grin.

'That's a pass,' says Niina. 'You'll be my guinea pig before the bride.'

'Really, I should drive—'

'No,' says Niina and Pernilla.

Patrick walks over giving Agnes a look of sympathy, before lifting the lounge back in place while Niina orders Pernilla to go get dressed in something other than ripped jeans. The girl doesn't argue—gone in a heartbeat. Patrick assures all is under control and he'll be back in good time to serve the bubbly. Agnes nods absentmindedly.

'Upstairs then, miss Andersson,' says Niina. She goes to see Patrick out.

Resigned, Agnes follows. As soon as Britt-Marie arrives, she'll have a one-on-one with her.

In the kitchen, Niina and Patrick have pushed the table to one side and stacked it with necessities—serving plates, utensils, glasses, bottle openers, serviettes, even toothpicks. Underneath the table, they've squeezed two large portable fridge boxes together. They've cleaned up the sink as well. The surfaces are clear. Agnes notices but fails to compliment them.

'Don't open the fridge,' says Niina, tapping it as she walks past. 'Stuff will fall out.'

While Niina waits as Patrick puts his raincoat on, Agnes sneaks upstairs. While Niina does her Pernilla trial, she's going to take ten minutes to herself.

The attic is dim, and the gloomy afternoon outside casts resting shadows around the room. Agnes sinks into her beloved wingback and stretches out her legs, resting her feet on the windowsill. She pulls out the photo again, places it on the armrest, wondering what Britt-Marie will tell her about her reticent mother.

All she knows about her mum is that she came from Norway and that she broke away from her family, but not why. Her dad must have known something, but he told Agnes that her mum's past was too painful to talk about, and if Irene wanted to leave it behind, it was her right to do so.

'How's that for a turn of events?' says Agnes. 'So, who was the man? Just a friend?'

The rain comes at an angle, hitting the side of the house. Drops spill down the window, some slow, some faster. Agnes watches the rivulets, tries to follow them with her toes. She rests her head and thinks about her unusual mother, the distant relationship they had. She'd forgotten about the pictures she drew to get her mother's attention. Now she wonders if—to begin with—her bear-making expressed the same need.

Her mother only came up here once. Agnes claimed the space the year she turned teen, cleared it on her own, and painted the walls without help. She nagged her dad to put up shelves along one wall. Once it was finished, Agnes invited her mother up, and her father too, but it was her mum's approval she craved. Agnes had sneaked the Steiff—her dad's worth-a-mint-vintage bear—from the top shelf in the library, knowing full well she'd be in trouble. She was prepared for a slap from her mother. 'He's my mascot,' she told them. 'I'm going to make teddy bears, not toys—collectables.' Her mother had peered at her for a long time, probably wanting to give her a wallop, but delivered none.

Agnes's first sewing project the previous year had been all about making a bear like the out-of-bounds Steiff. She'd used the teddy her dad had bought for her seventh birthday. She'd pulled fur out, taken out an eye and replaced it with a button, cut holes in his feet, and painted him with brown patches. Her handiwork had shocked her dad. He suggested she'd learn to make one instead. He'd bought her an old

Husqvarna, and she'd taught herself to sew. The first bears were rudimentary designs, first in calico, then plush. Then she'd asked her mother for money to buy authentic mohair from Germany, and her wish was granted. Once she'd made her first, fully jointed teddy bear in traditional fur, she began mutilating them again.

Watching the rain on the glass, Agnes lets her mind drift to a morning she'll never forget, the last morning before her mum left them for good. The three of them. In the kitchen.

Almost sober, her dad's feeding her mum mashed pumpkin with a teaspoon. Her mum obediently and awkwardly chews, then swallows, before producing a smile with half her mouth, orange mash on her teeth.

Agnes's father dabs his wife's lips with a serviette. 'She did it for me, you know,' he says. 'She found him in a box, his body like a sack, moth-eaten, threads stuck out where his eyes had been. Blind, the poor bugger.' Her dad strokes her mum's fine hair, then pecks her on the cheek.

She likes it. Never used to.

'But you mended him. Didn't you, darling? You stuffed him, sewed his ear on, and mended his feet, gave him new eyes.' He finds her hand. The hand that used to be busy tapping away on her keyboard is stiff now. Her left isn't much better. Her dad's thumb, inflamed with arthritis, moves back and forth over her mum's wrinkled, spotty skin. He blinks at Agnes. 'She, presenting me with that stupid old Steiff ...' Tears well up. He lets them trickle down his cheek. 'It was like she put me back together,' he says.

'Go,' says Agnes.

As he stumbles out of the kitchen, her mum follows him with her eyes, straining to turn her stiff neck. Agnes offers another spoon, but her mum won't open her mouth. They can hear him upstairs, blowing his nose. Agnes touches her cheek. Her mother has lost weight. Her sagging skin looks like old leather but is like the softest suede to her palm.

'Mum?' says Agnes. 'You inspired me.'

Pale blue eyes blink at her until her mother closes them. When they open, they are hazel with flecks in them. It's Guy holding a cracker with soft cheese to her mouth. He's whispering something, but it's too quiet, and she's too tired. Agnes can smell the salt and the wood. She lets Felicity's gentle motion rock her to sleep.

22
fifteen days ago

The week that followed surpassed Agnes's expectations. Guy created a routine around her lessons. He'd pick her up from the motel at sunrise. They'd drive for a couple of hours and have breakfast, usually at the end destination or on the way, as they travelled north or south exploring country towns and random tourist spots, headlands and beaches.

If there were good conditions to surf, Agnes would leave him to it. She'd go for long walks, collect shells and venture into the water on her own, to begin with ankle-deep. As her lessons progressed, she became braver. She'd wade around to her knees, or challenge herself to lie down in the shallow, and let the water drag her back and forth while her hands followed along in the sand.

They'd eat a late lunch at some local café before heading home. The rest of the afternoon, Guy would work for Mick. After her pool session, Agnes would walk back to the motel. They'd meet again in the evening for a meal. She'd make sure dinner didn't drag on, and she'd insist on getting back to the motel early. After they'd said goodnight, she'd read, or write her emails—tall tales for Thomas, bits of truth for Niina. Her nightmare was changing. Now the water didn't paralyse her. She'd be moving through it, treading water, trying to break free, and she was able to hold her breath. There was less waking up with a fright.

She assumed Guy and Tanya were seeing and sleeping with each other. She tried not to think about that. And really, she did not know what went on between them. With Guy, she spoke of Tanya only in the role as her teacher. With Tanya, it was all about the lessons. Agnes was keeping out of their complicated relationship.

Tanya was patient, efficient and positive in her teaching and Agnes couldn't believe what she'd achieved in such a short space of time—from splashing her feet by the pool's edge to floating on her back, from resting her face below the surface and holding her breath to crouching underwater, blowing bubbles. Today she was learning to duck-dive to the bottom of the pool. It wasn't going well.

In preparation, they'd practised on the lawn. A group of children had gathered to cheer the two women performers—Tubby and Trim. Tubby made the frog-leap attempts. Trim went for the kicking legs, found the ankles and held on tight while trying to pull Tubby's legs out straight up, trying to force a handstand. Much laughter from the kids.

They were in the pool again, and the audience had dispersed. Tanya had shown her the procedure, step by step, more than once.

'You will conquer this if we have to stay past closing time.'

'Don't you have a class?'

'Yep, so there'll be a shit storm if you don't get with the program.'

'We could start fresh tomorrow.'

'You're going to nail this, you hear me? Again.'

Agnes breathed in, sunk below the surface, angled her arms, thought *down*, then two strokes and somehow she was up again.

Tanya sighed. Then she put her own goggles back on. 'Again,' she said. 'You'll feel my hand on your back, but don't freak out. Promise I won't hold you down, only guide.'

As they went under alongside each other, Tanyas's hand between her shoulder blades added firm pressure. It changed nothing. They tried again and again, but her body refused to assist. Her bum wouldn't tilt up in the air. Her feet refused to be away from the bottom.

'I'll never get this,' she said. 'You may as well ask me to fly.'

They ogled each other, two goggle heads on the water's surface in fluorescent swimming caps surrounded by echoes of voices and water, one head encapsulating iron will, the other wanting to cry.

'Come on, you're almost there,' said Iron-will, doer of all things.

'I'm happy with what I've achieved.'

'You need to finish what you've started.'

'Last week I couldn't even be in the pool.'

'So what?' Tanya spat the words. 'There's more to life than floating just below the surface. You're telling me you're willing to settle for so-so?'

'Couldn't I still learn breaststroke?'

'I don't care what swimming style you settle for. You're here to overcome your fear.' Tanya splashed water on her in frustration. 'Show me what're you made of.'

'I'm not made of the same stuff as you.' Agnes splashed water right back at her.

'Bullshit.' Another splash. 'You're no different from me or anyone else. If you want something you go for it. Don't even try to tell me otherwise. So you want to keep treading water forever?'

'It's too hard.'

'But not impossible.' Tanya pulled off her goggles, threw them out of the pool, then said with gritted teeth. 'Stop wasting our time. Swim towards me. Think chest down. If you panic—which you won't—release the air slowly. Go touch the bottom. Or get out.'

How easy that would be. Agnes was cold, hungry, and couldn't wait to be set free. A hot shower? A big fat yes. But of course, Tanya-the-bitch was right.

'So you're a quitter. Good to know. Meet the Swiss chick who quits.'

'Damn it.' said Agnes. 'I'm Swedish.' Then she took a big breath, and dove towards Tanya, thinking *down*. There was the pressure of two determined hands—on her shoulders first, then lifting her hips up, then her legs, and there she was, upside down. And how fast she reached the bottom. Tanya's hands released Agnes's as hers touched the tiles. It wasn't deep, about a meter and a half, but it was still a total wow moment. A split second later, her legs sank and searched for the bottom of their own accord. She came back up.

'Again.'

Agnes obeyed, and Tanya helped her again. And again. And again. Until the penny dropped. Until her body understood the mechanism. Once it did, she didn't want to stop. Was this what she'd been afraid of for so long—too long? Heading upside down to the bottom of the pool seemed a decent metaphor for the total opposite. It was Agnes, rising.

When she finally came up for a breather, Tanya gave her a thumbs up, looking pretty pleased with herself. 'Now that's a grin,' she said. 'I bet you don't mind me being such a pushy bitch. Don't know about you, but I'm done. Got my five-thirty gym class.'

Agnes got out, excited and disappointed, already looking forward to tomorrow's pool session.

Tanya wrapped a towel around herself and started changing from swimmers to gym gear with impressive speed, devoid of embarrassment. 'Two days to go and what? You'll go meet your dude in Sydney?' she said.

Agnes nodded. She'd suggested a Sunday arrival. Hopefully, Thomas had taken note. They were on Skype that evening to work out the finer details.

'Must miss him?'

'I do.' She didn't. Agnes had trouble picturing Thomas with her in Sydney—anywhere in Australia, really. Thomas belonged to her other life, miles away from there. Light-years.

'I bet he'll be amazed to find out what you've been up to.'

'He will.' He wouldn't. Because he was under the impression that she was on a bus trip. Agnes kept sending him reports of the tour, making up funny incidents with butterfly woman, an imagined couple—Joe & Mary—as well as the rather nasty tour guide woman. Despite moments of misgivings about where her initial fib had taken her and the holiday, she would let it run its course. If she told him that all her encounters with resort pools had cured her fear, he'd think nothing of it. No big deal.

Niina had received the odd, authentic photo. Agnes had sent her one of Guy and true to form, Niina had made unsavoury comments about *the scrumptiousness of the man*.

'Thomas doesn't actually understand my fear,' she said.

'Which you don't have anymore,' said Tanya from underneath the towel, drying her hair.

'True. It's mostly gone.'

'Mostly? You're over it. I watched you.'

'Well, the pool isn't murky. I can see.'

'It's about the seeing, is it?'

'Partly.'

Tanya took a brush from her bag. 'We'll squeeze one more thing in tomorrow. For your last lesson, you'll also learn to dive with your eyes closed. How does that sound?' She pulled the brush through her hair before shoving it in a side pocket.

Agnes sighed. 'Me and my big mouth.'

'Yep, for someone who doesn't say much. Well, I'm off.'

'Wait.' She was undecided, had been for two days. Selfish Agnes didn't want her to come along. Conscientious Agnes insisted she'd invite her.

Tanya stopped with the bag over her shoulder, an expectant look on her face.

'Are you free tomorrow night? I'm taking everyone out for a farewell dinner. I'd like you to come.' A pang of regret collided with her good intentions. 'It'll be Holly, Mick, and the kids, and Guy, of course. As a thank you.'

Holly had invited her and Guy for a barbecue the previous Sunday. She'd been nervous about seeing his sister again. No need. It had been a good-natured evening and rowdy. They'd all played soccer in their backyard—another first for Agnes. She and Holly were equally useless, tripping over each other and their own feet. After dinner, they'd played Monopoly. On Ruby's insistence, she and Agnes had teamed up and ended up owning the stretch leading up to Mayfair and most of the hotels. Ruby had been ecstatic at beating her brother for once, and Agnes had discovered she had a competitive gene in her, after all.

'I don't think I can,' said Tanya.

For a fleeting moment, Agnes thought she saw the face from the nightclub—without the intoxication—that same unguarded vulnerability she usually tucked away behind all her Tanya confidence. It was there and gone again. Selfish Agnes wanted to say, 'Okay.' Conscientious Agnes said, 'You have to come. Please, don't say no. It's my way of saying thank you. It would be so nice if you could come.'

Tanya pondered Agnes's words while the seconds flew. 'All right. Count me in.'

'Great,' said Agnes wishing she'd bought Tanya a gift voucher for a spa treatment instead. Surely she would have loved a good massage.

She watched Tanya leave, downright jealous. She would go back home and all of them would keep living their wonderful lives in the sun. Tanya and Guy would keep seeing each other as friends, or more, and Agnes would become a fading memory. She wished she could stay a little longer, wished Thomas hadn't recuperated yet.

Agnes sat dressed and ready on her bed, waiting for Thomas to call. Needing to be warm for a cool evening, wanting to look her best, she had layered with a top under her new expensive knit. She'd put on some make-up and blow-dried her hair to leave it out for Thomas's benefit. Once she ventured outside, the coastal air would come at her fierce with humidity, forcing her hair up in a bun again.

In order to celebrate her duck diving success, after the Skype call, she'd walk to the marina for a takeaway dinner in Felicity's cockpit, under the stars. Her fear of the pontoon had ebbed, and she had no trouble getting on and off so Guy had lent her a spare key.

She kept checking herself in the wardrobe mirror, wondering what Thomas would think of her tan, wondering if she'd be up to a bit of fibbing if need be. He may ask her about Airlie Beach, which was where the bus tour was at that moment, where she was supposed to be.

The last time she'd seen Thomas, they'd been standing in her hallway, she in PJ's and he ready for the road. He'd stayed the night as he did on his trips south, had arrived late, seemed over tired, not tuned in during lovemaking, and when they talked about their pending holiday—distant. It had probably been precursory flu symptoms. And she'd not wanted him to leave. Though she had lots of work to do before the upcoming show, and they'd see each other at the airport only days later, she had not wanted to say goodbye.

Agnes jumped with fright when the Skype signal came, almost an hour later than they'd agreed on. She'd nodded off against the propped-up pillows. Disorientated she pressed the wrong button, not accepting the call. After a minute, he rang up again.

Thomas on her phone screen—for a few seconds it was like the first time she saw him, the first superficial impression of his good looks, his angular jaw and high cheekbones, his low brows and eyes that saw right through you. Then it was Thomas's familiar face. He looked good for someone who'd suffered the flu. He was on his laptop at his desk.

'Hey. Look at you. Nice tan. Up you get. Give me a twirl.'

She stood and aimed the phone at the full-length mirror.

'You look, W O W.'

She got back on the bed. 'How are you feeling?' she said.

'Pretty good. No complaints.'

He gave her an account of the symptoms he'd had and how much he'd slept. He kept telling her how good she looked. She wasn't used to Thomas going on and on about her like that. She found it annoying.

'So where are you at the moment?' he asked.

Agnes coughed and cleared her throat. 'It's called Airlie Beach.' This was not as easy as writing stories to him. Surely that reeked? But no, apparently not.

'Can't wait to meet up in Sydney.'

'Yeah, that'll be great.' Would it? They'd be checking out the tourist spots. She'd be half-running next to him to keep up. Thomas would stride along Circular Key, taking photos, talking to strangers, telling her stuff about the Opera house, what year they built it, who designed it, how much it cost, and on and on. She'd visited already and read up on it, but that wouldn't matter. He'd have to tell her.

'I've got a surprise,' he said. Then he winked at her, slow and exaggerated.

What did he mean by that? A ring? What made her think that? Agnes wanted to get up and pick up all the clothes strewn across the carpet. The room was a mess from her deciding on what to wear for this, for him. She wanted to hang up, wipe the make-up off, and clean up her room.

'That's all I'm going to say. I'll bring it with me.'

'Okay,' she said, and couldn't think of adding anything else.

A second, proper proposal in Australia, on a beach at sunset or on the steps to the Opera House—that would be his style. Agnes couldn't help glancing at her ring on the wrong finger. Maybe he'd produce diamonds this time. That was the thing, wasn't it? Except diamonds were not her thing. In the past, she'd hinted about how she liked vintage. He wouldn't remember.

'When do you land?' she asked. Without a doubt, he'd forgotten about her suggesting Sunday instead of the original Friday. She wanted a couple of days on her own before he arrived. Well, if she couldn't have that, so be it. She was nervous, that was all. Because she'd not seen him for weeks. Weeks that had changed her. The thought startled her the same way Guy's words, at the airport, had.

'Sunday.'

The relief that flooded was beyond reasonable.

'I want to run this by you,' he said. 'We should add two more weeks. Change your return ticket. There are a few options.' Thomas began reading from his scribbled notes on a piece of paper, dates, and times.

There was a knock on the door. Since Thomas had his eyes on the paper, she sneaked out of bed to open, thinking it was management wanting to tell her something. It was Guy.

'Just making sure you've not fallen asleep.'

'Sorry,' she whispered. 'Got Thomas on Skype, so I'll walk to yours in fifteen.' She wanted to close the door thinking Guy would get her sub-textual 'Give us some privacy' but he just stood there, and sort of nudged the door with his body.

'Agnes, where'd you go?' Thomas's deep voice called out.

'I'll leave in a minute.' Agnes attempted to close the door on Guy.

He sidestepped her with that big grin of his. 'I'd like to say hi.'

'Now? We're, you know, sorting out tickets and stuff.' She leapt to the bed and grabbed her phone, angling it away from the door, making sure *she* filled up the space on Thomas's screen.

'Got a visitor?' said Thomas. 'Is it the tour guide from hell? Are you misbehaving?'

'Umm ...'

'Or that nutty woman?'

'Hey there,' said Guy. He came close to Agnes and stooped down towards the phone screen, his face right next to hers.

His beard brushed her cheek, and he smelled of soap and toothpaste.

Agnes was cooking in her knitted top and underlay. Her brain was working overtime. She could see where this was going. Guy knew nothing about her holidaying fibs. She should have told him, absolutely should have.

Thomas lit up. 'Tell Mary I said hi,' with a confident American accent, loving the opportunity to use his English skills.

'Who?'

'It's Joe, isn't it? Agnes mentioned you in her emails.'

'Right.' Guy poked a thumb in Agnes's side, which made her jump.

'How's Airlie Beach? Heard you had quite a scare while snorkelling.'

'Snorkelling?'

Was her face as flushed as she suspected? Agnes could feel how stiff her smile was, how fake. How to get rid of Guy?

'Yeah, the reef sharks.'

'Oh, them? Nah, all good. I think Agnes here's been making up stories. So I'm Joe and you are?'

'Thomas. I'm sure she's mentioned me.'

'You had the flu?'

'Yeah.'

'Sorry to hear that. You've been missing out mate—big time. Agnes is enjoying herself. We make sure of that. Mary and I.'

'Nice meeting you,' said Thomas.

'Likewise,' said Guy poking his thumb into her again. 'And now, I need to steal her from you. Dinner under the stars tonight.'

Agnes moved the phone away from Guy, pushed herself off the bed and managed a quick whack with her foot on his shin.

'Sorry Thomas, Joe has to go.'

'Got Mary waiting,' said Guy. Picking up one of the dining table chairs, he winked at her.

'Hang on, Thomas,' she said. 'Joe's telling me something.' She turned the phone towards the floor.

'Looks like we'll have to reheat the food,' said Guy. 'But don't worry, I'll take a seat and wait outside. I don't mind.' He grinned at her. 'So am I just a regular Joe, or is it short for Joseph? And in that case, is there a baby Jesus?'

'Close the door, please.'

He did. Agnes still walked into the bathroom and sat down on the toilet.

'Quite a character,' said Thomas.

She produced a tight lip smile.

'So back to these tickets, I think—'

'Can your surprise wait?' She hadn't planned to say it. The words sort of sprung, surprising her as much as Thomas. A sentence had formed and spat itself out, and now what should come next? 'Can it wait until I come home? How would you feel about cancelling altogether?' And there it was.

'What do you mean?'

'I'll be home in ten days.'

'You don't want me to come?'

'Well, you've been sick. Sick and then flying? You know the air-con on the plane. It would be more sensible to stay put.'

'What's going on?'

'I think, if you rest up properly and ... and I can't extend my stay, can't expect Niina to keep looking after my neighbour.' *That was true.*

'But surely, you don't want a week on your own in Sydney?'

'There's lots to see. I'll be fine.'

Thomas was thinking about it, licking his lips. 'I could catch up on work instead.'

'You could.'

'You sure about this?'

'I am.' Two words and a mantle of calm settled on her, draped like warm water on her skin. Oh, she was sure. Agnes had never been more sure. Truth was, she wasn't ready to share Australia with Thomas. This place had become her personal adventure of growth. It was changing her. Agnes still had over a week to enjoy. Not meeting Thomas meant she could stay in Coffs. She wanted to spend that time accomplishing as much as possible in the pool. And Guy had more places he wanted to show her. He'd complained they'd run out of time.

'Sorry, I have to go Thomas.'

'Already?'

'One of those under-the-southern-cross-dinners tonight. You know how it is. They run a tight schedule. Our Draconian tour guide is on us all the time. Punctuality is the motto that runs her life.'

'Right.'

'Sorry.'

They blew some kisses and for once, Thomas was the one, not wanting to say goodbye.

23
today

Agnes sits up, disorientated at first, before she realises she's in her wingback. Someone has called her name. She stands up too quickly and the world spins.

Again, 'A-g-n-e-s!' Niina rarely goes looking, just bellows out your name with the commitment of a foghorn.

Agnes finds the other two in her bedroom. Niina has placed a big mirror on the windowsill and brought up her mum's swivel chair. In it, Pernilla sits dressed in the plummy-coloured dress, the one Agnes picked. Niina is curling the girl's hair.

'I must have fallen asleep.'

'We got less than an hour, so get your butt in the shower.'

This time, Agnes follows orders. Ten minutes later she's in the chair, in her specially bought underwear, hidden under a shabby jersey tunic. Her wedding dress will wait until after Niina has finished with her. They have rolled away the chair from the mirror.

'For the surprise effect,' says Niina.

She and Pernilla are talking music. They discuss bands and gossip about celebrities she's never heard of. While she's been snoozing up in the attic, they've been bonding. Agnes is happy that Niina hasn't pissed the daughter off the way she has the father.

Expendable and separate, she tunes out and instead thinks of the upcoming conversation with Britt-Marie—what might reveal itself and what it all means. *Is it too weird to be a coincidence? Coincidences are weird by default, aren't they?*

'Go easy on me,' she says to Niina, who's working fast and methodical, her fingers smooth and confident, massaging in cream after cream. She's spending time on her forehead. That's good. But she still hopes for subtle. 'It's me and my small wedding.'

'Meaning?'

'I don't want to look fabulous from thirty metres away.'

'See what I put up with,' says Niina. 'You're happy, aren't you, Nilla?'

What's with the Nilla? Niina and Nilla surely deserve—according to Niina's own vocabulary—a puke-stamp.

'She's like a pro,' says Pernilla.

'I'm going for the natural look.'

'Agnes has trust issues,' says Niina.

'I'd rather not have eye-line—'

'Shut up already. And close your baby blues for me while you're at it.'

They'll be rolling their eyes at her while she can't see.

'Did you find what you were looking for?' asks Niina, steady with the eyeliner pen, but overworking it. 'Pernilla said you were looking for a photo.'

'I was. And I did.'

'Meaning?'

'You'll see. Later. Maybe. If you behave.'

'Agnes's got the shits because I told your dad off.'

'Did you tell him off?' Pernilla sounds giddy with admiration.

'I suppose I got a little carried away.' That's her apology, right there. That's all Agnes will get.

'It might be nice if you let *him* know,' says Agnes.

'I'll see. Later. Maybe. If he behaves.'

That makes Pernilla giggle. She's sitting on the bed surrounded by boxes with hair accessories and make-up, painting her nails. Niina has arranged Pernilla's hair in long ringlets and attached tiny fake roses that match the colour of the dress. Despite being edgy today, Niina has excelled. Where would Agnes be right this minute, if it wasn't for her old friend?

'Thanks, Niina,' she says.

'You're welcome.' She isn't easily offended at the best of times, but this afternoon Niina sparkles. Is the reason for that, Patrick? Agnes would love for Niina to fall in love and stop all the sleeping around nonsense. She doubts it's as satisfying as Niina makes out.

'You're obviously not sisters,' says Pernilla. 'Have you got any siblings, Agnes?'

'No, and my dad was an only child. A true local, but no family left.'

'Her mum was a mystery,' says Niina. 'Arrived out of nowhere, in South Hamlet, in the eighties, married Nils, and started up a business. For all we know, Irene was an alien who landed in the forest and found her way to the nearest town. She was a little alien, wasn't she, Agnes? And don't get all funny about it. I loved your mum. But she was odd. There's one in every family. Though some end up with more than one.'

'Meaning?' says Agnes with Niina's exact Gothenburg-intonation.

'I'm not having a dig at your family, though weird doesn't come close. Oh, I'm kidding. Who am I to talk? They had to rescue me out of mine. And no Nilla, before you ask twenty questions, I won't answer any of them.'

Pernilla shrugs. 'I have a weird family too,' she says. 'My pop isn't my real grandfather. My real grandfather sat in prison, and dad won't answer questions about him.'

Niina pokes a finger at the back of Agnes's neck, as a code for, *I bet that's news to you.*

Agnes knows that Thomas's biological father has never been part of his life. She knows he's passed away. So he was in prison? 'Why? Do you know?' she asks Pernilla.

'Nope.'

The first car drives over the gravel. Straight away, Niina rushes to the window.

'It's Patrick. Nilla, run down and open the door for him. Let him know I'll be down in ten.'

'So your groom's dad broke the law,' says Niina as soon as Pernilla is out of the room. 'Should I be concerned?'

'My best friend's past is shady beyond belief,' says Agnes.

'Not my past, my biological family's past. Okay, I'll shut up now.'

'Thomas might feel shame about this,' says Agnes. Shame, she understands.

'I don't know about that,' says Niina. 'But wanting to keep up appearances makes perfect Thomas-Lundén-sense. Anyway, changing the subject completely. Isn't Patrick utterly scrumptious?' Niina is on the finishing touches. She's working fast, impatient to go downstairs. 'I apologised to him about saying fuck a lot,' says Niina. 'Told him it's because I'm nervous for you.'

Agnes snickers. 'You should be able to keep him in the dark for at least another hour, then.'

'You wanna know the truth? I'm more excited about Patrick than anything else about this arvo.'

'I forgive you.'

'It's not like me, you know. While you were away, I walked into the Deli, saw him and walked friggn' straight out. This has never happened to me. You don't get it. This is momentous.'

'I do actually get it.'

'Oh, heck. Sorry. Going on about me when it's your day. How are you feeling?'

As much as she'd like to show Niina the photo, Agnes knows better. Niina could easily take it upon herself to bombard Thomas's mother. 'Like my fridge,' she says.

'Filled to the brim with bottles of bubbly, chocolates, and a big blue cake, or trying to keep your cool?'

'Just a lot of stuff in here,' says Agnes, tapping her temple, not giving Niina the appreciative giggle she's waiting for.

'You've been acting strange all day,' says Niina. 'Might be normal behaviours for brides. I lack experience in that department.'

Her fingers are fidgeting with loose strands around Agnes's face. It tickles in a delicious best-friend-fussing-over-you kind of way. Niina has tried so hard. A wave of gratitude floods Agnes. She'll always have Niina. 'Once we're finally there with the celebrant, it'll all settle in my head,' she says. 'Shit. We didn't remember music. I forgot about—'

'All under control. Where would you be without me?' says Niina, pushing the chair and Agnes to the mirror. 'One bottle of hair spray, a dozen elastics and a million hairpins. Flipping heck, I'm good at this.'

More make-up than Agnes would normally wear, yet she knows Niina has held back for her sake. Miraculously, her hair has volume and ringlets and bounce and gorgeous white flowers throughout. Shame that her mum and dad aren't there, that there's no other family.

'It's … I look …'

'Got nothing to say? Well, that's the usual, so in that case, I've failed.' Niina puts her fingers to a pin, starts pulling it out slowly.

'I love it,' says Agnes. 'Love it. Love it. Love it.'

In the mirror, Niina wiggles her eyebrows at her.

Another car arrives. They peer out of the window. It's Annie from the boutique, stepping out of the car with a man Agnes has not seen before.

'I invited a few extras,' says Niina. 'Annie's met a new guy. He's a photographer. Thought that would come in handy. So I said he could come too. The more the merrier, right? We can't have Thomas's clan take over.'

'How many?'

'A manageable group of friends. And no, I didn't bribe them. They reckon they like you. Well, the ones who can recall who you are.' She giggles at her own wit. 'All right, I bribed some of them, said you'd do a strip show on the table once the groom's too drunk to notice.' More giggles. 'Oh, they've come for a bit of fun. Who doesn't like a wedding? I told them it was a secret surprise for the bride. I think that's like a totally new thing. The photographer is getting paid. My wedding gift.'

'Really?'

'Yep, but be careful with your make-up.' She takes hold of Agnes's hand. 'Save hugs and tears for after. Okay? And he'll do the shoot after the ceremony, up on the canal, between the rain pours. And if the rain doesn't stop, he said he's got his big wet wedding umbrella. Got it all figured out.'

'Wow. Niina.' Agnes smiles at her friend's beaming face in the mirror. 'And when did you invite these extras? On such short notice.'

'Tuesday.'

Niina has been at her all this time, to not go ahead with this. Agnes can't work her out.

As if reading her mind, Niina says, 'I gathered, if you'd cancel we'd have an engagement party instead or just a party. Wedding? Party? What difference does it make?' She winks. 'Don't worry, Agnes. We'll fill them all up with Champagne. Get them nice and relaxed. You'll be fine.'

It's strange to see so many cars parked in her driveway, and up and down her quiet street. This is a first, at least in her lifetime. A fresh wave of nervousness overwhelms her. They'll all be watching her. She supposes they'll want to hear her and Thomas say the vows. That'll be like being on stage, the only advantage, she doesn't have to face the audience.

A taxi arrives. Thomas steps out before helping his mum. Britt-Marie's walking as if fuelled already. Two more men come out of the cab. Agnes assumes they're his stepdad and uncle.

Agnes points. 'That's Britt-Marie,' she says. 'Please, send her up to me. As in now.'

24

fourteen days ago

The so-called farewell dinner had been a success, thanks to a generous menu and Guy's and Holly's family anecdotes from their growing up on the land, with another four sisters and plenty of misadventures. Agnes couldn't understand how you could leave a close family setting. Holly answered that. A road trip to see the coast changed her course. She had every intention to go back and marry her high-school sweetheart. Instead, she met Mick.

'And Guy met the Pacific,' said Tanya.

Agnes was glad after all she'd invited her. Tanya and Guy had seemed on edge to begin with, but that faded away within minutes. Despite jokes needing explanation, and memories shared between everyone except her, Agnes didn't feel like an outsider. And she was still the favourite with Ruby, who kept smiling at her from across the table, giggling and asking her knock-knock jokes whenever there was a gap in the conversation. The atmosphere had been warm and friendly, until now.

Since her Thomas Skype, Agnes had known the arranged dinner would not be a farewell. She could have put it off until the following Thursday, but since they'd all agreed to come, she kept the booking. Agnes, who'd hung on to her surprise during the main meal, dropped the bomb with the desserts and coffee. The change in temperature was immediate.

'Staying another week?' said Holly. 'What happened to meeting up with Thomas?'

Holly, who'd been nice all evening, as well as last Sunday, wanted her gone, wanted Guy to work full shifts, not just afternoons. The Swedish tourist had taken up too much of his time. Why hadn't Agnes thought of that?

Nathan must have picked up the change in his mum. He sneaked the much argued over phone back on his lap. Mum and Dad didn't seem to notice.

'Change of plans,' said Agnes. 'He's not coming.'

'So seeing a bit more of OZ or staying put?' Mick asked.

'When was that decided?' said Guy.

'Not sure,' she answered Mick. 'Last minute,' she said to Guy. She could have told him the night before, but she'd wanted to surprise him with the others. 'I know you need to work. I was hoping for more pool experience.' She looked at Tanya, who said nothing, focusing on her cake.

Agnes had assumed she'd be for it. After all, she was making good money. When Agnes had told Guy what the hourly rate was, he'd rolled his eyes, said he could've tipped her upside down for free. 'That's if you have time, of course?' she said.

'Yeah. Maybe not, hey.' Tanya didn't look up.

Ruby disengaged from her chocolate mousse. 'Does that mean we get another farewell dinner next week?'

'You'd like that, wouldn't you?' said Guy, ruffling her hair.

'I want to come back here. Love this.' Her chin told just how much.

'I'll be busy next week,' said Guy. 'But we could use the weekend to travel further, do a couple of nights.'

No one said anything after that, which made Guy's words hover like a foul smell. Holly was eyeing her, weighing her up, sipping her coffee. Agnes felt awkward. A brilliant evening had shifted.

It made her think of a game she had as a child—a maze gizmo under a plastic cover, so small it fitted in her hand. Five tiny silvery balls rolled around a colourful surface with five small dints. The idea was to roll the balls into them. Her mum claimed it was all in the wrist. She'd take it from her young daughter, have the balls settled in no time, and place the gizmo on her desk. Agnes would pick it up and the balls would instantly roll. She could never manage more than one ball. She'd hated that thing.

'Excuse me, I need the ladies,' she said.

'I'll come with you,' said Holly.

Instead of the ladies, Holly guided her out the door into the dark, round the back of the restaurant where the noise of it dulled and blended with the mull of the ocean. One spotlight from above gave the top of Holly's head a glow and cast strange shadows on her face. Agnes could see her cheekbones, but not her eyes.

'I know it's not my business,' said Holly. 'But I gotta ask.'

Agnes couldn't get the darn silver balls out of her head.

'Are you done with Thomas?'

'Am I done?'

'Is it finished? Is that why he's not coming? Because you broke it off with him?'

'No.'

Shaking her head, Holly crossed her arms. 'Why are you doing this, Agnes?'

'Doing what?'

'This. Staying longer, wanting more time with my brother. What is it you want?'

'It's not what you think.'

'Is that right?'

Agnes felt like crossing her arms too, as a mode of defence against both Guy's sister and the evening chill. She shoved each arm into the other's sleeve and hugged herself. 'I'm going home next Friday.'

'Another eight days is a long time.'

Eight days was too short? 'If you're worried that somehow I'll make him go to Sweden, you've got it all wrong, Holly. I mean, Guy has a mind of his own.'

'Yes, he does.'

'So ... I don't understand why you're angry with me.'

'It's not just about Guy leaving us all again. It's what you're doing to him.'

'What? I mean, I beg your pardon. I'm not flirting with your brother.'

'Is that right?'

'I'm trying to get him and Tanya back together again.'

'Are you now?' Holly scoffed.

'That's why I invited her tonight. I don't know all that's gone on between her and Guy, but I'm sure it'll work out.'

'I'm sorry, Agnes, to be so blunt. But seriously, have you got shit for brains?' Holly was tramping on the spot, cold perhaps, and agitated.

Agnes tried again. 'There's no point in Thomas coming when I have a week to go and I can promise you, Holly, I am no threat to anyone.'

'Don't take me wrong. You're a nice person,' said Holly. 'I quite like you, actually. But you're hurting my brother. You hearing me?'

'You got it all wrong. Him and I—'

'Agnes, he's in love with you.'

'He's not. You know nothing. You're his over-protective sister who treats him like one of your kids. We are friends, him and I. That's all. Friends.' Agnes had gone too far. She'd raised her voice. They both had. Holly might be used to that, but she wasn't. The taste of sour coffee, cheese, and sugary sweet in her mouth made her feel sick. 'I'm sorry I've upset you,' she said. 'You've been kind and hospitable and I'm being rude to you.'

'This isn't about me. Go home, would you? Why prolong this?' With that, Holly turned and walked off.

Agnes wasn't sure what to do after Holly left. She didn't want to follow her, didn't want to face the others. It would be obvious that there had been some kind of altercation. The words 'he's in love with you' played on repeat in her head. How could Holly get it so wrong? With the pinballs rolling, she headed for the break wall. There were no lights, and Agnes stopped by the massive rocks, where she stared into the roaring black. The night sky was thick with clouds. There was no moon, not a single star, and the southerly wind had a numbing bite in it. She was shivering.

'Agnes.'

She turned at the sound of Guy's voice. His dark silhouette striding toward her filled her with both gratefulness and dread.

'There you are. Brought you this.' He handed her the jacket Holly had lent her. He waited while she put it on and zipped up. Then he said, 'What's going on? Has Holly upset you? What did she do now?'

'Nothing. She's done nothing.'

'She's all flustered. She must have. You don't have to protect her.'

'I'm not.' Agnes wished they could go for a walk up to Mutton Bird Island in the dark, run off some of the dessert and have a laugh. Though she'd probably vomit if she actually had to run. 'About what I said in there ...'

'Yeah, what's going on?'

She sighed. 'Well, I told Thomas not to come.'

'I'm glad.' Guy lay an arm around her and their jackets squished against each other.

'Thing is ...' What was the thing? What should she say next, to make it right? Holly's words rolled around in her head. Guy was a friend, a good, good friend.

'We could go to Armidale if you want to see something other than the coast, meet my parents, and my other crazy sisters,' he whispered in her ear. 'You could stay over on Felicity.'

Then he kissed her cheek. His lips lingered, warm on her cold skin.

Holly wasn't wrong.

She was.

This was her cue to pull away, say something. Instead, Agnes let his hand bring her face to his, her mouth to his, his lips on hers. The scent of chocolate mousse. She opened her lips and allowed him in. The pinballs rolled quietly and obediently into their slots.

Guy kissed differently to Thomas, probing in the most delicious way. He kept his palm on her cheek and it was as if it alone held her up, kept her body from giving way under the power of his tongue in her mouth.

Why are you doing this? Not Niina. Holly.

The pinballs started up. Agnes dropped her head. 'I'm sorry,' she said.

'Don't be.' He tried to tilt her head up again, but she withdrew from him.

'Sorry, I shouldn't have done that,' she said.

He went quiet. The light from the restaurant windows didn't reach them here, and she couldn't see his face. All Agnes saw outlined was a man with broad shoulders and hair tousled by the wind.

'Can I ask you something?' she said.

'Ask.'

'Have I been sending you ... messages?'

'As in ...?'

'Have I been flirtatious?'

He didn't answer straight away. Then he said, 'No, I wouldn't say that.' He took a small step closer. 'It's obvious you have feelings for me.'

'Not *that* way.' Agnes took a step back.

He laughed softly. 'I think you do.'

'I shouldn't have kissed you.'

'But you did.'

'I'm sort of engaged. I've got Thomas.'

'Yet you've told him not to come.'

'I can explain.'

'The kiss?'

'A mistake.'

'Is that what you tell yourself? Pretty good at lying all around then.'

She'd not dealt with the fibs the night before. During their shared dinner in Felicity's cockpit, wrapped up in blankets, she'd bombarded Guy with questions about Felicity, sailing in general, all the places he'd been and travelling in general, skilfully avoiding the incident in her motel room. Guy had looked at her curiously more than once, but he'd not probed.

'You've lied to him and yourself, Agnes. I'm sure you like me *that way*.' He took another step.

'I'm sorry, Guy, if I've come across deceptively. Niina says I don't get it.'

'Get what?'

'Men. Women. How it all works.'

Guy snorted. 'You need to see, that's all. See what's true. Tell me. What is it about him?'

'I don't have to tell you.'

'But you could. If you cared enough.' He took another step and so did she.

'He knows me.'

'So what? I know you.'

'We go back a long time,' she said. 'Like you and Tanya. We have a history, shared memories, a past. I thought I'd never meet anyone, and then I did. I had a bit of a trust issue.'

'Trust? Interesting word.' He snorted again. 'You've been making up stories for him.'

'It was immature, but I didn't want to worry him.'

'Because you're not to be trusted. Because I'm right.'

'No, I—'

'I know what I see.'

'You are wrong.'

Guy had slowly been taking small steps towards her and she'd been doing the same away from him. Now he stopped and so did she.

'You know what, Agnes? I'm not playing this game anymore.' He shoved his hands in his pockets. 'You know where I am if you change your mind. I want you and when you're done lying to yourself, come see me.' As he brushed past her, Agnes's hand went up and touched the back of his jacket, light as a feather. He didn't notice, or he didn't care. His silhouette walked off, along the break wall blending into the night.

It stunned her. It wasn't what she'd expected—at all. The pinballs vanished. Holly's words vanished. There was nothing.

Then there were footsteps behind her.

'Where's Guy?'

Agnes nodded in his direction. 'Gone, to Felicity.'

'He's got my phone again.' Agnes could tell Tanya wanted to run after him. 'Thanks for dinner,' she said. 'It was generous of you.'

'The least I could do.'

'And sorry about the swimming and—'

'Don't worry. My fault.'

'Make sure you keep it up.' Tanya gave her a quick kiss and a loose hug. 'If I don't see you before you go, have a good life.'

She watched Tanya hurry off in the dark with bag and jumper under her arm. Probably there would be some kind of comfort-friends-with-benefits-sex between her and Guy tonight. The thought made her queasy.

She and Mick argued over the bill. She stood her ground until he gave in and let her pay. Then he gave her a firm double squeeze. Nathan gave her a loose hug. Holly's lasted longer than she'd expected.

'I love you,' whispered Ruby in her ear, her elf arms around Agnes's neck.

'I love you too,' she whispered back.

Actual tears came as she walked back to the motel. How had she not seen this coming?

25
today

When Thomas's mother knocks, Agnes is all set, waiting with the photo in hand.

'Look at you,' says Britt-Marie. Her languorous consonants remind Agnes of her dad after too many jiggers of whiskey. 'Where did you buy it?'

'I didn't. I made it.'

Britt-Marie's 'Oh' is not intended as a flattering remark.

Agnes doesn't care. She's happy with the dress that's hung in her wardrobe in a protective bag for years. It's a high-waisted a-line in a gorgeous cupro with v-neck and trumpet sleeves, no lace, nothing complicated.

'Your dress is lovely,' says Agnes. The pale pink softens her mother-in-law-to-be.

Britt-Marie and Irene—the idea of them as friends is nothing short of unfathomable. Niina and Agnes complement each other somehow. Her mum and Thomas's mum make Agnes think of single negative magnets forced on each other.

'You wanted to see me?' Britt-Marie scans the bedroom with a superior eye. 'Not really customary, but I suppose it's all very casual today.'

Agnes rolls the swivel chair toward her, keeps it steady, and invites her to sit. Then she hands her the photo. She's keen to see the reaction when Britt-Marie spots the resemblance and committed to not giving it away herself, to wait for the moment. Britt-Marie holds the photo with delicate fingers. She's chosen the wrong pink for her nails. Epic clash, as Niina would say.

'I recognise this,' says Britt-Marie.

'Don't need glasses?'

She shakes her head. 'Laser. Where did you get this?'

'Where is this?'

Britt-Marie shrugs. 'Somewhere, northwest of Stockholm. It was a road trip. I'll have to show Leif. He won't believe this.' Then she looks at Agnes inquisitively. 'Who gave you this?'

'You mean, Leif, as in your brother?'

'That's him, between us girls.' Britt-Marie is frowning, swaying her head slowly. 'He nagged me to come along and keep Karl company. I'd met him before. I was already smitten.' She stares past Agnes, into the past.

'Karl? As in Thomas's biological father?'

'He's the one taking the photo. Gosh. That brings back memories. How come you have this?'

'A road trip, you said?'

'They'd both made friends with her. What was her name? Leif saw Karl as competition so my job was to keep him busy, which I did. With success, I might add.' She gives Agnes a look as if they're best friends swapping romantic encounters with each other. 'Leif had a serious crush on her. What was her name? And most girls fell for Karl.' Britt-Marie lifts the photo again. Then she eyes Agnes and back at the photo. 'That's not ...?'

About time. 'My late mother,' says Agnes.

Britt-Marie drops the photo back on her lap and peers up at her. 'So, that's why I thought we'd met. You don't look alike really, but there's something about your eyes.' She scrutinises Agnes's face for a moment. 'That's extraordinary,' she says, blinking. 'That's right, Kerstin was her name. So she was, is, was your mother?'

'Not Kerstin—Irene Andersson both before and after she married my father.'

'I knew her as Kerstin,' says Britt-Marie. 'Berger, if I remember right. Kerstin Berger.'

Niina has changed her name too. She's never revealed the original and never talks about her childhood. What did Kerstin Berger leave behind?

'So she changed her name?' says Britt-Marie. 'She was unusual.'

'And my mum dated your brother?'

'Not for long. She dumped him. We never knew what happened to her. The year after this photo was taken, she was gone. This is most peculiar.'

'Were you close? You and my mum, I mean.'

'Not exactly. I was protective of my older brother, and I found Kerstin odd, quiet, brooding. I would even say calculating.' Britt-Marie is tipsy enough not to notice if she offends Agnes or not. Then again, she didn't let that bother her, sober. Agnes has to admit she's nailed her mum.

'Did you know much about her family?'

'No. Kerstin was this mysterious Norwegian who'd cast a spell on Leif. She was older than him, older than all of us.' Frowning at Agnes, she says, 'You're younger than Thomas. He was born the year after this photo was taken.'

'Mum was over forty by the time she had me.'

'You know what?' says Britt-Marie. 'I'd like to tell Leif before you walk down the aisle. Can I borrow the photo?' She pushes herself out of the chair with some difficulty. 'And I think Thomas should know.'

'Actually, I will tell him myself,' says Agnes, snatching the photo out of Britt-Marie's hand. 'Leif is yours. The groom is mine.'

Britt-Marie nods, dumbstruck, and a little unbalanced in her heeled shoes.

'So Thomas was born the following year,' says Agnes. Can I ask what happened? You never married.'

'It didn't work out.'

'Why?'

'Oh, it's old hat,' says Britt-Marie.

Agnes will have to go out on a limb. Thomas hasn't told her. Again, it has been Pernilla. Again, she might get the girl into trouble. *Sorry Nilla.* 'Was it because he went to jail?'

'Jail?'

'He went to prison. Didn't he?'

'We don't talk about that. I wouldn't have thought you'd—'

'I know.'

'I should go.'

Without a second's hesitation, Agnes slips past Britt-Marie, placing herself in front of the door. 'I don't want to ask Thomas, don't want to upset him,' she lies. 'But I think it would be helpful if I had a clear picture.'

Britt-Marie offers a doubtful face. 'Karl's never been part of our lives.'

'I'm about to marry your son. And I need to know.' *How's that for authority?*

'Thomas never knew, as a little boy,' says Britt-Marie with a sigh. 'As he got older, he nagged me. When I was about to marry, I decided he should know who his biological father was.' She looks down at her synthetic nails and lets her fingers interlock as if in prayer. 'I suppose, I thought, he'd like his new dad better that way. You could say I had selfish motives?'

'I'm not one to judge,' says Agnes.

Britt-Marie gives her an earnest, appreciative look. 'I was pregnant when they charged Karl. Throughout the court case, would you believe, I would have said yes. Except, he never asked. When he went to prison, I visited for a while. Leif kept telling me Karl was not the man I thought he was. They'd been friends sort of, but Leif wrote him off. In the end, I moved on to create a better future for myself and my little boy.'

'What was the crime?'

'He was a thief, but the rest was an accident. And they pinned something else on him too.' She looks at Agnes with unfocused, glassy eyes, as if she's about to burst into tears. 'You haven't met my husband yet, but he's a good man. He has loved Thomas like a son.'

'I'm sure.'

'He's probably wondering where I am. He and Leif won't believe this.' Britt-Marie hints at the photo in Agnes's hand. 'No one in the family understood what my brother saw in her. We all thought he was better off. He married a wonderful woman who's sadly not with us anymore.'

'Sorry to hear that,' says Agnes, ignoring the insult of her mother.

'This is like a one-in-a-million-coincidence,' says Britt-Marie, stepping closer to Agnes. 'Who'd have thought Kerstin's daughter would one day be my daughter-in-law?' She studies Agnes's face. 'Now that I know. Yes, you look a little like her. But I think you have a rather different personality to Kerstin.' Nodding in agreement with herself, she says, 'You're softer, Agnes? And I don't know if anyone's ever told you this, but you have this sanguine look about you.' She places a gentle thumb on the corner of Agnes's lips. 'Here, a little up. No resting bitch face. That's what they call it, isn't it? Lucky you. Yes,' she says, still nodding, 'I think you'll be good for my son.'

Agnes steps aside, astonished at the change in Britt-Marie. Is this acceptance? Becoming part of Thomas's family may actually work out. All they need is time to get to know each other. 'Before you go,' she says. 'What was his crime?'

Britt-Marie stops with her hand on the door handle and shakes her head. 'I don't think ...'

'I'm about to marry him, Britt-Marie. I deserve to know.'

'Don't tell Thomas, I told you. Let him tell you in his own time. And don't be surprised if he never wants to talk about it.'

'Okay.'

'It was a heist gone terribly wrong—armed robbery. But Karl never meant to kill anyone.' Then she opens the door and slips away.

26
thirteen days ago

After a long night of tossing and turning, processing how on earth she'd misread Guy and screwed everything up, Agnes rose to a Friday, grey and thick with clouds—both the sky and her. She left her pre-paid card in the phone, in case Guy would want to contact her. She lost count of how many times she picked it up and sat with her thumbs resting on the keys. The phone stayed silent.

The tour bus would pass Coffs Harbour, at midday, but Agnes didn't consider jumping on board. She didn't want to go to Sydney, couldn't go to Sydney. However, she walked up to the bus stop to retrieve her cabin bag. Walking, she discovered, soothed the persistent nausea. When the driver had to pull a dozen bags out, she didn't bother apologising, and she ignored the glower from the tourist guide.

The passengers seemed worn out. Butterfly woman was asleep. Agnes saw her colourful headscarf flattened against the glass. She would never see her again in her life. It made her sad how people cross paths with you and play their part in your story, only to be gone again. Agnes, too, would become a snippet of memory to Guy and his family—'That Swedish woman, what was her name?'

Agnes walked past the pool. Her brand-new swimmers were in her retrieved cabin bag. But she couldn't find the energy. Instead, she dawdled back to the motel, dropped into a supermarket on the way, and bought the biggest box of chocolates she could find. Agnes spent the rest of the day with in-house movies. She half slept and half watched, film after film with no idea of character names, what was at stake, or if it worked out for anyone in the end.

27

twelve days ago

Saturday midday, after another restless night, Agnes opened the blinds and window to cool air and clouds like fluffy giants that sped across the sky. Australian autumn at its best, declared the motel receptionist, as Agnes walked out the door, wearing the sneakers Guy had picked for her, and Holly's sunnies. She would head to the marina to see if she was brave enough to face Guy. He wanted more than a platonic friendship. She couldn't offer that, but she had to explain herself. On the walk out there, she practised what she'd say, her stomach churning.

The discovery that Felicity's spot was empty came like a punch to the gut. While she couldn't eat—not counting chocolate—, couldn't sleep, couldn't sit still, Guy was out on the ocean doing what he loved the most. She hated him for it.

Agnes walked up Mutton Bird Island as fast as she could, which set her legs on fire. She'd been up once before with Guy. He'd pointed south and north, given her the names of all the beaches, the ones they'd visited, the ones she was still to see—but wouldn't now. It had been a windy day with hair blowing around their faces and them laughing a lot. The southerly today was obnoxious, teasing her. The line of the horizon lay endless, the ocean dark. Somewhere out there was Guy, all on his own. Or with Tanya?

Back at the motel, Agnes changed her phone card. But when she saw all the failed Skype calls from Thomas, she swapped cards again. She ordered a pizza delivery. Ate one piece. Then she walked across the road to the supermarket and bought another box of chocolates.

28
eleven days ago

Sunday it rained. Agnes stayed in bed with her cold pizza and her sweets, the remote at the ready, flicking through channels like her life depended on it.

She thought of Guy on Felicity, sailing through the wind and the rain, and wondered if he thought of her. She thought of Thomas believing her to be in Sydney, discovering all that the city offered, but didn't write him any emails, because she couldn't bother with fabricating any more lies.

And the truth? She'd let herself get caught up in something of a holiday crush. She'd sat on that bus not wanting to depart, and not admitting to herself why. Jumping off the bus feeling so deliriously independent and wild had only delayed the inevitable, made it more painful. And worse, she'd done to Guy what Holly had warned her about. Strange as it was, Guy wanted her. Whatever that meant. Well, there was no going there. That was a Niina thing. She had Thomas at home. At the moment, Guy seemed to have a hold, but that was the thing with holiday romances, wasn't it?

Guy would most likely be back that night. Tomorrow he'd be working with Mick. She would have to try again, to talk to him, or she could write him a proper letter, leave it on Felicity with his keys, and all the borrowed clothes.

29
ten days ago

By Monday, her old nightmare had clawed its way back, and Agnes sat up startled twice during the night, clammy with cold sweat. In the morning, she woke up on edge but determined. She would not let her last days seep like sand between her fingers. Today she would not analyse a thing. Today she'd achieve. She ate the last of her stale pizza before walking to the pool.

It was a quiet morning, with mainly retired men and women doing slow laps. Agnes went to her familiar corner and changed into her own swimmers and Holly's rash vest.

It was her first time without Tanya, and she'd not been in the pool for three days, but she felt confident. Getting in was fine. Wading, holding her breath under the surface, treading water were all fine. Her ingrained fear seemed strange now. Clear water didn't freak her out anymore. She would absolutely attempt a duck dive. There were a handful of other swimmers around her. The next time one came free-styling past, Agnes took comfort in that and the opportunity. She dove, touched the tiles, and came back with such a sense of achievement that she let out a selection of

Swedish swearwords loud enough for a handful of people to turn their heads her way.

Agnes couldn't stop diving after that. She alternated with pushing from one wall across to the other and even went a little deeper. In her last lesson, Tanya had planned for her to try swimming underwater with her eyes closed. When she'd forgotten, Agnes had not pursued it. Well, damn it. This was it. She took off her goggles. Before fear could grab hold, she breathed in, closed her eyes, and dove. She focused on aiming straight down, her hands reaching towards the pool floor. Her fingers touched the tiles. Then she was up again. It was over in seconds. Agnes wanted to laugh out loud, scream even. Her fear was gone. Gone.

She spent the rest of the day at the pool, had snacks from the canteen for lunch before getting back into the water. She blocked out Guy and Thomas for the moment of pursuing the magic of water. Cool jelly liquid, heavy with slow motion—how had she been so afraid? She would definitely take lessons when she got home. The seamstress would become a swimmer.

Strolling back to the motel with tired limbs, she had an idea. It was better than talking or writing. It would be a true thank you for all that Guy had done for her. She would give Felicity new covers and curtains. After visiting a handful of shops, she found one that stocked tape measures.

With her heart pounding in her chest, Agnes walked out to

Felicity that afternoon. Guy should still work another two hours. This was going to be a surprise, and if he was on his boat, she'd have to wait until the morning.

He wasn't there.

Guy always left the forward hatch half open for ventilation, and it was easy to open. Dropping into the boat was like immersing herself in the holiday that would soon lie behind her. The scent of Felicity and Guy—her wood varnish, tea tree oil, and diesel, his soap and cologne—was as familiar as an old friend. Feeling the time pressure, not wanting him to walk in on her, she drew pictures of all seats, with measurements, fast and methodically.

Agnes spent the evening working out material and researching where to purchase all she'd need. She still couldn't bear talking to Thomas, so she took the easier way out—emailed photos of Sydney icons, found a few travel blogs, copied and pasted words about her experiences, and apologised for having lost her Swedish phone card somewhere in her luggage.

30
eight days ago

Agnes didn't wake until early Wednesday afternoon. Pulling the thick blinds aside, it was clear she'd missed another blue sky day, of swimming, and walking on the beach.

She'd spent her entire previous day sewing. She had caught a taxi to the fabric store and made the driver wait while she chose material, bought threads, sewing tools, and a middle-of-the-range sewing machine. At the motel, she'd ordered in another pizza, rearranged furniture to make room, and set up her own sweatshop. By the time she'd ironed the last curtain, it was pitch black, and she'd drifted off to sleep as the sky changed from black to mauve.

Her well-ironed and neatly folded covers lay stacked on the sofa, with the extra throw cushions and blankets she'd bought. She could pack them in a box and drop them off last thing before she left for the airport on Friday. It would be less scary, but not satisfactory. She wanted to be the one transforming Felicity. When he got back to his boat that afternoon, she wanted the surprise to be immediate. That didn't mean she had to be there when he discovered his new lounges. To see the surprise on his face would be something, but it would also be nerve-racking—to face him again. No need to decide yet.

Agnes covered up her hollow eyes and sunburnt face with make-up and put on a new silk shirt from the cabin bag. She got a cab to the marina.

Felicity was warm with the sun beating down on her deck and Agnes was already overheating with anticipation, so she took her silk shirt off and found one of Guy's T-shirts. It looked clean. Still smelled of him.

Agnes began pulling the seats out of their faded half-torn covers. Dust wafted around her. If only she was able to open the companionway hatch, but Guy had locked it from the outside. Stubbornly, Agnes pulled all the covers off and then stuck her head out through the hatch at the bow just to breathe some fresh air. She kept going, squeezing the uncooperative seats into their new outfits, sneezing and sweating with a fine layer of dust on her bare arms.

Guy's tiny mirror showed dank hair, smudged mascara blending with the dark under her tired eyes, and a shiny face as if she'd smeared her skin with oil. She'd leave as soon as she was done, and send him a text to let him know the new interior came from her. If he hated it, he need not reply. Even if he didn't hate it, he'd need not reply. If he considered texting her back, he'd have time to figure out what he wanted to say. So would she.

She had only two covers to go when Guy's shoes landed outside on the cockpit floor. What was the time? The dread was instant. She was an intruder. He'd made himself clear and nothing had changed for her. She was going home the day after tomorrow. What was she doing here?

Her gift seemed suddenly presumptuous—something Holly would do. Agnes regretted her entire project. She froze, holding on to a half-naked seat cushion while listening to Guy opening the hatch. What would he think of the turquoise blue and the scatter cushions in bold Marimekko patterns? What if he hated it? That would be a great farewell gift—dressing Felicity according to her tastebuds.

'I thought I could hear something,' said Guy as he moved the last of the wooden panels that made up the hatch.

She squinted up at him, not even able to produce a 'hi'.

Guy looked wide-eyed at her. 'What the ...?' He took the few steps down into Felicity while looking at her handiwork. His beard had grown. His jeans and T-shirt were tattered and splattered with paint stains. He was so close, Agnes had to look away. This was how he made her feel. The cool air from the open companionway was pure delight on her flushed face.

'I measured up the other day, while you were at Mick's.' Her voice sounded shaky. At least to her.

'Sneaky.' He gave a crooked smile. 'So I take it you see me as a colourful guy?' Then there was his big grin, so generous, so irresistible.

'What do you think?'

'Luv it.'

His words went through her entire body, drained her of all the anxiety and tension. Her hands steadied, and she continued pushing the fabric over the seat again. 'Phew,' she said.

'Need a hand?'

'No, almost done.'

But he picked up the last cover, anyway.

'I need to apologise,' he said. 'I was unfair—'

'No, you weren't. If anyone should apologise, it's me.'

He didn't respond, and Agnes didn't know what to say after that, so they worked alongside without talking. They gathered up the old fabrics and rolled them into a few lumps. While Guy took them to the bin, Agnes sucked up most of the dust with his handheld vacuum cleaner and arranged the cushions. That was that. Now what?

'Hungry?' he asked when he came back.

She was starving. Guy went to buy fish and chips. Agnes freshened up, borrowed some of his cologne, and put her shirt back on. They settled on a seat in the cockpit where the breeze prickled her neck. Guy opened the wrap between them and food had never tasted so good. She eased into the comfort of him.

Guy cleared his throat. 'It seems to me we both want to apologise,' he said. 'I say let's forget about it. I have an idea.'

She glanced at him.

'Sailing,' he said.

'Sailing?'

'I was a jerk, and I'd like to redeem myself.'

'No need.'

'And you owe me.' He patted her thigh. 'It'll be smooth as. Promise you.'

'You mean now?'

'Perfect afternoon for it.'

The thought of going out on the ocean almost made her regurgitate the chips. But suddenly there were the words from Tanya, about treading water, floating just beneath the surface, settling for almost. 'You win,' she said. 'But I'll need to let my food settle or you'll have me hanging over the railing.'

Guy prepared Felicity and educated Agnes in the most important aspects. He was the captain and his words were orders for her safety. Not that she wouldn't be safe, he assured. 'As long as you don't head-butt the boom.' He went through calls and responses they'd use for tacking. 'Again, to make sure you don't head butt the boom.'

An hour later Felicity was motoring out with Agnes sitting close to Guy, layered up in his jumper, windcheater, lifejacket, and beanie. Once they were out of the first small harbour, she had to hold Felicity into the wind. 'Don't worry,' he said. 'She'll go nowhere.' While Agnes did that, feeling quite sailor-like, Guy raised the mainsail. He pulled hard and fast and was back in the cockpit before she knew it. Then he turned Felicity and her sail flapped less and less, filling with air until it sat taut. Guy navigated his boat through the outlet, and there, in front of Agnes, spread the vast horizon, and the mass of steel blue sea.

'Not much swell.' Guy placed a hand of comfort on her knee. 'Go with it, Agnes.' Then he switched off the engine, and there was only the wind, and the swell, and Felicity moving, lulling, creaking.

All those years in her attic chair stitching bear's paws, watching boats glide past in the canal. Never in her wildest, weirdest daydreams would she have thought that she'd one day be sailing. Puttering along the canal would already have been a stretch—but sailing! There was tension in her shoulders and down through her spine, but she focused on her breathing, slow and steady.

'I'll get you to hold her while I raise the jib,' said Guy.

She watched his shoulders at work, his arms, his hands. In fact, Agnes took in Guy's entire body while he focused on getting his jib up. She couldn't help wondering what he looked like naked.

Felicity picked up speed, and Guy took over the steering. Agnes sat as close as was physically possible with the tiller between them. Guy was right. It was a little like flying. She avoided looking into the water, kept her eyes on the horizon instead. Guy, too, wore sunnies and beanie, his curls escaping below the hem, fluttering in the wind. He was sitting with his legs stretched out, glancing from her to the sails, to the ocean and back to her—grinning. She was glad she'd said yes to come along. It was a privilege to see Guy in his element, see the truth of the man.

After a while, her body loosened and Agnes released the grip she'd had on the edge of the seat. She closed her eyes and listened to the sound of water against the hull, the squeaking and grinding of Felicity as she laboured against the forces of nature. After another little while, Agnes challenged herself to embrace what surrounded her. She purposefully thought of Felicity immersed in the massive body of the Pacific. How small the boat was, how small they were. She marvelled at Jessica Watson, who'd sailed around the world all on her own, and the ones before and after her.

Agnes thought of the young men, boys even, who throughout history had gone to sea, who'd lived their entire lives on wooden ships. She thought of the dead sailors buried in oceans over the centuries, of how they'd been sewn inside hemp sacks made heavy with weights, how their makeshift coffins had been catapulted, into the deep void, sunken to the bottom, hidden from the world in the deepest graveyard of all. The muscles around her heart tightened, as well as her hands to the seat's edge. But she kept going. Her father begged her attention.

She opened the portal she'd kept closed for so long, allowing the images of her dad in the last moments of his life—infused with alcohol, soaked clothes and boots like heavy boulders to pull him downwards. She saw him splashing about, confused, searching for something to hold on to, his head going under, swallowing water, and up again. How long until he gave up?

And she not wanting to get out of her warm bed, thinking it too much of a hassle to rug up and go fetch him, lead him home. If she'd not rolled over and forced her eyes closed when the door slammed, if she'd run after him, he wouldn't have fallen in, he wouldn't have drowned. Her tears came and she let them. They kept coming, but they dried easily in the wind. The tears were about the loss, not the guilt.

The guilt wasn't something you released through tears. When she was five, she'd once pinched the Steiff out of her mother's office, and given it a bath in the kitchen sink. It had taken weeks for the bear to dry out. Her mum had warned her the mould would eat him from the inside. Guilt was like that—mould that ate you from the inside.

Agnes recoiled when Guy's hand touched her knee.

'Are you all right?' he said. 'Mind going walk about again, hey?'

She nodded, glad to be interrupted.

'We'll be tacking our way home. Let's take your workload up a notch.'

Guy showed her how to release and pull the jib sheet on the winches when to bring home the main sail and when to release. Agnes found it wasn't too complicated or too strenuous. It was fun. When the wind picked up and Felicity heeled, Agnes loved it, all of it, and could not believe how close she'd been to missing out.

The sky had turned pink by the time they had secured Felicity in her berth. Guy found Agnes, one of his smaller-sized fleece tracksuit pants and a hoody, which she put on while he stowed sails and tidied up the deck. Then he changed into a tracksuit as well. With bundles of towels, soap and shampoo, they walked to the marina's shower facilities. Agnes sneaked her icy hand into his warm one. In the hot shower lathering her body with his soap, she imagined her hands were his.

They strolled to Felicity in silence, connected through entwined fingers. Onboard Guy led her along the deck to the bow. He crouched to open the hatch. The night air was cool and smelled of kelp. Speckles of lights illuminated the dark—lanterns from other boats, the street lamps along the boardwalk, the noisy restaurant, and Coffs Harbour in the distance.

His hand touched her ankle and helped her out of one shoe, then the other. She let her fingers through his damp hair. When he stood, her hands followed along his shoulders and arms. She whispered or thought to herself 'I want you'. He pulled her into a kiss, his lips soft, enclosing, wanting. Agnes had the same sensation as the first time, the bones in her body softening, giving in to gravity.

They pulled apart, and he wiggled out of his own shoes before lowering himself through the hatch. When it was her turn, his hands found her waist. Agnes's bare feet landed on a fluffy duvet that smelled of tea tree and damp wood.

Guy slid off the bed. 'Back in a tick.'

There were pillows at the head of the bow, and Agnes sunk into the wadding spread her limbs, and breathed deeply. Outside the open hatch was the world, and they were a million miles away, lowered into a universe of their own. There was only now.

Guy came back with a flickering candle in a lantern that he hung on a hook above.

They lay on top of his bedding and kissed and probed, finding their way under each other's clothing—her fingers through his chest hair, following the outline of his muscles, and shivering when his hand found her breasts. Later, she watched him pull her tracksuit pants off, smile at her, and ask for permission. She smiled back, nodded.

It wasn't a first, but he gave her time, all the glorious time she needed. It was like floating, like being pushed effortlessly through still water waiting for the inevitable wall. Then she was holding her breath, rising from the depths, rising and rising. It made her laugh with tears as it waned off.

The rest of their clothes came off and Agnes took a turn, certainly not a first, but she'd never had such a strong desire to give the way he had. Later again, when finally he moved inside her, she felt as if she could breathe properly for the first time in her life. She let her voice out. Freedom.

They lay in silence for a long time. Once their skin felt the bite in the air, they crawled under the duvet. She drowsily remembered Guy leaving—to raid the fridge as it was. He came back to feed her some bread and cheese that Agnes chewed half asleep. She was tired, probably dehydrated, and her body ached from days of walking and tension. She remembered him sliding under the duvet, spooning into her, his breath on her neck, the weight of his arm around her. Soothed by Felicity's soft creaks, the steady lapping of water against her hull, and the chiming masts outside, Agnes slept deeper than she'd slept since long before her dad passed away.

31
today

Agnes is putting her boots on when Niina barges in with two glasses filled to the brim.

'It's fake.' She winks at her. 'Yours, that is.'

'Have you seen Thomas?'

Handing her a drink, Niina inspects Agnes from feet up. 'If looks can kill, there'll be a lot of cleaning up corpses in about half an—' She stops mid-sentence, regretting her word choice.

Agnes smiles, pretending it doesn't register. 'Thomas,' she repeats.

'Don't worry, he's alive and kicking, seems happy. He should be. Pompous dick. Kidding Agnes, I'm kidding. I haven't hit him over the head yet. You'll be proud of me. I apologised. Sort of. Him and I, we're cool again. No need to stress.' Niina clinks her glass to Agnes's. 'Good thing I've actually written a proper speech,' she says. 'I'll do my best to keep my foot out of it. But no guarantees. As Patrick says, under-promise and over-deliver.'

'I'd like to talk to him?'

'Who? Patrick?'

'Come on Niina.'

'Stop worrying. It's all good vibes downstairs. People are mingling, and Thomas is doing his best to charm. I must admit, he's got the gift when he wants to.'

'That's great. Could you go find him, send him up?'

'He'll have to wait his turn.'

'It can't wait.'

Niina huffs at her. 'I want a few minutes with my weirdest friend before she becomes a Lundén and too much of a snob to talk to me.'

'All right,' Agnes puts her glass on the side table. 'I'll go find him myself.'

Niina sighs. 'I had things to say to you in person, but obviously, I'm not wanted. Will keep it for later then, add it to my speech. Prepare for mawkish.' She halts in the doorway. 'The celebrant will be here in ten, so make it a quickie, but not *that* kind.' She shuts the door with too much force when she exits.

Agnes doesn't have the patience to wait. Seconds after Niina, she walks out the door. There's a lot of noise downstairs, people's voices fading, shoes on the floorboards, the sound of chairs. They're moving out to the sunroom. Good. She should be able to find Thomas without announcing herself.

Halfway down the stairs, she meets Pernilla on her way up. The girl comes to a standstill, two steps below. For once Agnes is the taller one.

'Wow. You look hot.' The girl offers a stunning smile. Her unexpected words sound genuine. Niina has waved her magic wand while Agnes wasn't looking. 'I was coming up to see you.'

'What's the matter?'

She hesitates, and there is a similarity with her father—the tilt, the jaw, her eyes. 'About today... ' she says, dropping her head, sliding her fingers up and down the handrail. 'I was mostly mad at Dad. I ... said some stuff.'

'It's our fault. His and mine. I should have made an effort a long time ago,' says Agnes. 'I could've asked for your number, called for a chat.'

'I wouldn't have talked to you.'

'No, I guess not. Still ... I've been a coward.'

'Marrying Dad is pretty brave.'

'Because he snores?'

They both giggle.

Agnes takes a step down, and Thomas's daughter takes a step up. They hug. It's fast and uncertain, but it is a hug. Niina's signature perfume fills Agnes's nostrils.

'My two favourite girls.' There he is, at the bottom of the stairs, in grey suit-pants and vest, shirt and tie, hands in his pockets, looking all suave and relaxed.

'See you guys,' says Pernilla. She gives her dad a quick hug before leaving them.

Thomas takes Agnes's hand and leads her down the steps. 'You look sensational.' He draws her close, kisses her neck. It's barely a distraction. 'I'm saving the proper kiss for after,' he says. 'See, I'm being romantic. But we should get a move on. They're all seated. This is it, babe.'

'No,' she says, shaking her head. 'Thomas, we have to talk.' With that, she opens the door to her mum's office.

'This again,' he says, following her in. 'Look, I'm sorry I lost it earlier. No need to pull me into line.'

She's forgotten about that. It's insignificant now. She closes the door behind them and holds out the photo. It probably is a totally weird coincidence. But there is, of course, the niggle that it isn't. Agnes observes his eyes intently as he takes it from her. It definitely throws him.

'Where'd you find—get this?'

'Strange coincidence, isn't it?' she says. 'You know who they are. Don't you?'

'Mum, and my uncle.'

'And the other woman?' says Agnes, not taking her scrutinising eyes off him.

He's licking his bottom lip. And he's blinking.

'That's my mum,' she says. 'I found this in a book. The photographer is none other than your father. It's from a camping trip the four of them took. Your mum fell in love with your dad on that trip. Did you know that?'

Thomas sighs. 'You've been talking to Mum?'

There's a knock on the door before Niina pokes her head in. 'It's time, guys. We're waiting.'

'I'm sorry, Niina,' says Agnes. 'We're going to need a few minutes.'

'We don't *have* a few minutes. You're wanted.'

Agnes frantically shakes her head at her. 'Not now.'

Niina raises an eyebrow, but surprise, surprise, obediently closes the door again.

Thomas parks himself in the visitor's chair. 'What did Mum tell you?'

'Well, she explained why she never married your dad.' Agnes has more or less promised she won't bring this up. Well, she has to know. *Sorry, Britt-Marie.* 'True, he never asked,' she says. 'But he also went to jail for armed robbery, for killing someone.'

'You should've come straight to me,' says Thomas.

'Why have you kept this from me?'

'Not something I dwell on. Quite the opposite. But I should've told you.'

'That's not really what bothers me,' she says, walking over to him. She taps the photo. 'This does. I mean, what are the odds? Our mothers knew each other. It's not a coincidence. As she says it, she knows it. You'll need to tell me the whole truth, Thomas.'

He leans forward, exhaling, flicking the photo back and forth over one thumb. 'It's *not* an accidental happening,' he says finally. 'It's a long story. Can we do this after the ceremony? I think the celebrant is under time pressure.'

'The celebrant will have to wait.' Agnes doesn't know if it's her new height in the awesome lace-up boots, her pretty hair and make-up, or how comfortable she feels with a little cleavage. She will not back down for Thomas, Niina, or the celebrant. Her curiosity is more important than wedding matters. 'I'm all ears,' she says.

Thomas nods reluctantly. 'Do *not* tell mum, about what I'm about to tell you. Promise me.'

'Sure.'

'No, not sure, "I promise". Say it.'

Agnes sighs, then repeats his words.

It takes another minute with Thomas thumbing the photo. Then he says, 'Mum doesn't know that I reconnected with my real dad when I was eighteen. She doesn't know I visited him in jail and kept visiting him once he got out. I'd take him out for a meal. A few years later, he was riddled with cancer. She doesn't know I was with him when he died. Liese knew he was in prison and that he passed away. Pernilla knows nothing, of course.'

You really don't know your daughter. 'How come you never told me? And what's it got to do with my mother?'

He shrugs. 'It's not the easiest thing to tell you because, frankly, it's going to sound a little creepy. Anyway, I suppose I'd better.'

'Yeah, you'd better.'

On cue, there's another knock, then Niina in the doorway again.

'Five,' says Agnes, holding up fingers. Something in her tone obviously strikes a cord, because Niina leaves without a word. Agnes closes the door again. 'Get on with it. There won't be a ceremony until I've heard the connection.'

'I used to visit Dad, and he never said much. We never had a great father-son relationship. It was, you know, superficial. It was after the diagnosis, after he knew he wouldn't make it, he started talking about Kerstin, or Irene. Turns out, they were in a relationship.'

'Our parents? Dating each other? No way.'

'Yep.'

'After she went out with Leif?'

He nodded. 'No one knew.'

'And when your mum fell pregnant?'

'Then too.'

Her mum having an affair is a jarring thought. The love Agnes witnessed between her parents was always a one-way streak, her dad doting on her mum, never the other way around. Is this why? Had she already met her man in Karl? Did her mum leave a tragic love story behind? Is that why she went back to Norway? When she found out he'd killed someone.

Thomas interrupts her thoughts as he continues. 'Dad got all obsessed about finding your mum towards the end. I offered to help him.'

'Did he know she changed her name?'

'He knew she came from Norway originally. He suspected she went back there. It took me ages to find her. Turned out, he was right. She went back, changed her name, left Norway, and married a Nils Andersson. Dad was on his last leg and I couldn't find her. Too many Anderssons.'

'And yet here you—'

'There's more. After my father died, looking for Irene became an on-and-off hobby, sort of. I met Liese and got busy working, but I'd search online from time to time. Then bang. One day years later, there she was. She'd won some kind of business award.'

'That's true she did, more than once too.'

'By then, I was a dad myself. I was busy, but it sparked my interest. So I looked up the address the next time I passed South Hamlet. When I finally found your house, I didn't know what to do. I parked my car at the end of your street and sat wondering if I should go knock on the door. Then I saw you come out. You jumped on your bike. And ... I followed.'

'You knew. You knew I was in the bookshop?'

Thomas gives her an embarrassed nod. 'I thought you'd find this bit creepy. Can you understand why I never told you?'

'Yes, it's a little creepy?' *Romantic perhaps?* It could make for a paperback novel. Niina could write it, change all their names, make it lighthearted and quirky like a rom-com. Get rid of the backstory with Karl in it. But if you took Karl out, Thomas would never have come into her life. *A man who killed someone and had a thing for my mum. That's disturbing.* No wonder her mum took off.

'I was living with Liese. I had a daughter. The timing was shit. But there was something about you. I'd wanted to meet your mum, tell her about Dad. But after meeting you, everything changed. It became about you.'

He places the photo on the desk. 'Understandably, your mum didn't particularly like me.'

'Did she know who you were?'

'I think she knew almost straight away. I look a bit like dad. And dad had really pissed her off, getting my mum pregnant and—'

'Shooting someone.'

'Exactly. Irene didn't want her daughter to have anything to do with Karl's son. And who can blame her?'

'Is that what you argued about that time?'

'She told me to keep away. After that, I tried to sort things out with Liese. Didn't work.' Again, he looks at her with that pleading, boyish face of his. 'Things we do for love,' he says.

'Your biological father shot a man dead,' says Agnes, more to herself. Does it change how she feels about Thomas? After the day she's endured, her emotional connection to anything or anyone is figuratively drowning under an overload of details. Overwhelmed is the word she's after. Having a bit of nail to chew on would be desirable, but Niina has painted what there is with some kind of see-through protection, and they're all chewed to the quick. *Does it or does it not change how I feel about him?*

He peers up at her, unflinching. 'I can't fix the past. Karl did the time for it. And it was a mistake.'

Thomas chased her and put up with her parents, didn't want to elope because it would upset them. It was she who shut him out after her mum's stroke. She told him to keep away.

When Agnes glares back at him, saying nothing, he adds, 'I understand you're shocked. But please don't hold my dad's crimes against me.'

'Did you plan to tell me, at some stage? It's not nice to keep secrets from your spouse.' *Who am I, to talk?*

There's another knock on the door. Niina's head again. 'That's way past five minutes,' she says. 'Your celebrant is getting testy.'

Thomas searches Agnes's eyes, offering a wordless apology, asking—are we done?

Is she done? There's more she wants to know. He may have found family connections in Norway. Well, that at least can wait.

'This will be some love story to tell the kids one day,' he says.

'We're coming.' Agnes stretches out a hand to him.

'In two minutes, that music will play. Just so you know.' With that Niina's gone again.

Agnes walks close to Thomas. He places his hands around her waist and rests his forehead on her chest. There's the familiar aftershave, his shampoo this time, and, as always, Don Diego—the fragrance of her twenties, of her youth, her love life.

'It's been a strange day,' she says.

He only breathes on her skin.

'We are rushing it,' she says into his thick hair. 'But flippin' heck, let's go get hitched.'

32
seven days ago

Agnes woke as the morning sun touched the closed hatch, diffusing pale light over their nest. Guy was sleeping with his back to her. His hair was a tangled mess, and he was snoring. There was a gap between them. No skin touching skin. She lay perfectly still, breathing the dank air, keeping her arms warm along her body. The lantern dangling above her head that had cast seductive shadows the night before was, she realised, battery-driven plastic—not the real thing.

The magic realm of Felicity and Guy vanished. Her thumb found the old ring on her finger, and the veridical world claimed her back. There was Thomas's 'You don't want me to come' and Guy's 'You've been lying to the man', then for good measure Holly's 'Seriously, have you got shit for brains?' Holly nailed it. What had she done? What would she say to Guy when he woke up? How could she face Thomas? The queasy emptiness in her stomach wasn't hunger. Guy would wake up and she wouldn't know what to say. She was flying home tomorrow.

With a frantic heart beating hard in her chest, Agnes slid out of the bed careful not to wake Guy up, got into her clothes without making a sound, and managed with some difficulty to slide the main hatch open enough so she could crawl out. She tiptoed over to the bow and fetched her shoes, kept them in her hand and slunk off the boat. Up on the break wall, she put her shoes on. Then she ran.

In the motel room, Agnes turned her phone off, worried that Guy would wake up and text her. In the shower she longed for him, wanting him to be on his way over, hoped he'd sleep for another hour at least, and willing him to knock on the door. She'd become the queen of contradiction—not the queen, the clod.

Agnes lay the two phone cards on the table. Then she pulled her ring off, revealing a fine white line around her finger. She placed the ring next to Thomas's card. *Shit, shit, shit.* Someone was going to get hurt.

Leaving the phone behind, she set out for the beach. The tide was high, and her feet kept sinking in the waterlogged sand as she strode north. The wind tussled the hair around her face and forced its way through the knit, prickling her skin. Now and then she stopped and closed her eyes, breathed in the briny air, trying to organise her thoughts, facing the unembellished hard-hitting truth.

She was pretty sure Thomas was going to pop the question. Had suspected that for days. Against all decency and common sense, she'd involved herself with Guy. Guy who could never be more than a holiday crush. They lived worlds apart on so many levels. Geographically, yes, but he was also a traveller at heart while she was a homebody. He sailed and loved adventure. She made teddy bears, for goodness sake.

But he was kind, laid back, and funny. He'd figured out her body on the first go. With Thomas, it was different. She'd always thought it good. But now, after the previous night, Thomas was … less. That was cheap. Wasn't it? That she would consider sex in the equation.

I would. Niina's voice, on cue.

When she reached the end of the beach, she found a flat rock under a Pandanus. There, Agnes sat watching the ocean caressing the beach, the water devouring the sand in endless rhythm—break, rush in, withdraw, break, rush in, withdraw, break, rush in, withdraw …

Guy was impossible. It would never work. Her parents were gone, but she had her best friend and her neighbour. She had her home, her life over there. This could never be anything more than a bittersweet dream.

The tide had turned by the time she admitted to herself that she was in love and there was nothing she could do about it. Moving to Australia. Was that an option? Was it complicated? Would he consider Sweden? What would he do there? Why did she even think they had a future? Had he even considered one with her? But last night had been special, hadn't it? Holly had warned that her brother had fallen in love. And so had Agnes. So what if she didn't have the answers? So what if Guy was the opposite of simple? She didn't care.

Agnes began the long walk back to the motel. She had to eat and explain herself to Guy. She would need to go home and break it off with Thomas. It wasn't something you did via Skype. She could change her ticket though, extend one more week, one more week with Guy, and then go home. What if she told Thomas she wanted to see Darwin, or perhaps Uluru? She had become a deceitful bitch.

Back at the motel, she put the Australian phone card in, expecting texts from Guy. There was nothing. Though she'd left him hours ago. The truth hit. She'd left *him*. He'd woken up with her gone. What was he supposed to think? She rang, but he didn't pick up. She wrote him a brief text.

> Sorry for leaving. Had to sort my head out. We need to Talk.

She went next door for a late breakfast while waiting for a reply. There was none. Poor Guy must have gone to work wondering what happened to her. It was possible his phone was flat, or he was too busy.

Too excited to sit still and wait, Agnes returned to the boutique where she'd been with Guy. There she spent an hour and a generous amount of dollars on both Niina and herself, not bothering to try anything on. After that, she found a men's store where she bought new T-shirts for Guy, a dressy shirt and a pair of jeans.

While shopping, she found it easier to not worry about the silent phone, but as soon as she was back in her motel room, it bothered her. Had she upset him? But she had apologised. She sent him another quick text, saying sorry again, asking him to message her.

As much as she dreaded it, Agnes finally swapped her phone card over. Thomas would still be fast asleep. She would have to ring him later. More lies coming his way, but she couldn't avoid it. Her heart sped up at the mere thought of telling him she was about to stay a little longer. There were lots of missed Skype calls and a text with sad faces wondering why she wouldn't pick up. And there was a recorded film clip. Though a small voice insisted she'd leave it alone, Agnes pressed play.

Thomas was sitting in his lounge, dressed in a suit and tie. On his way to the office, was her initial thought. This time he wasn't using his laptop but the phone, which he held on a selfie stick. 'Hey, babe,' he began. 'I've been ringing you like mad.' He fiddled with the stick, concentrating on getting it right, then back to focusing on the lens again. 'I've decided, I can't wait. Been trying to nail you down, but you're not answering your phone. What can a desperate man do?' He offered her his saddest eyes. He wasn't all *that* serious. Still, it made her feel awful.

'A film is acceptable, right?' he said. 'You can keep it as a souvenir. By the way, this is take two.' With that, he pushed the coffee table towards her, slid off the lounge, and got down on one knee. He cleared his throat while lifting the selfie stick higher up, looking up at her as if she was standing or sitting in front of him. Part of her wanted to turn it off, but she didn't. She kept watching.

'Ness, it's been a long time coming because of circumstances that don't matter anymore. The only thing that does matter is … that you say yes.' He put a small box on his knee and set out to open it with one hand, his eyes fixed on her.

Made no sense, but she flushed. She'd slept with another man, and Thomas was proposing. It was possible Thomas had been putting this film together while she and Guy … She was an awful human being. Awful.

'This worked fine on my first take,' he said. The selfie stick sunk a bit while he focused on the box. His fingers could not pry it open. It looked like he was going to have the shits. Agnes was sure she could hear him swear before he was all smiles again. The selfie stick went back up. 'OK, it'll be a surprise,' he said, holding the box up to her. 'All good. Come home, see what I found you.' After that, he sat for a bit, looking at her, fingering the box. 'Miss you,' he added before pulling the phone low and turning it off. The screen froze on the box in his lap.

She'd known it, and yet it was a shock. After all this time. What she'd wanted for years was finally here. Now she'd have to find a way to say, 'Thanks, but no thanks.' Staying another week? Out of the question. She had to go home. The bare thought of telling Thomas she was breaking off their relationship made her sick to her stomach. She longed to see Guy, who wouldn't be home for hours yet. Swapping the phone cards over again, Agnes considered catching a cab to Mick's workshop, then quickly decided that was too needy, too presumptuous. She would do the next best thing. Agnes sent Guy another text.

I'll meet you on Felicity.
On my way now. I'll wait
for you there.

33
today

Niina hands Agnes the bouquet. She's remembered to wind the silk ribbon around the stalks. Agnes kisses her on the cheek, hoping Niina understands how much she appreciates her being there. And then Thomas wraps an arm around Niina and pecks her cheek, too which Niina receives gracefully. Wonder of all wonder, thinks Agnes.

'I'll see you on the other side,' says Niina. She winks at them and leaves.

Agnes and Thomas wait in the kitchen. He's calm and sturdy, holding her hand in a firm grip. There's a lot of noise in her head—all these fresh revelations. Behind their long and complicated journey hides the one of Irene and Karl. Agnes has never thought of her mother as passionate, but maybe she was. In her youth. At least with one man. A criminal.

Her mum told her once that if she married Thomas, she'd keep her one child out of the trust fund. It's never made sense. Now it does.

Did her father know any of it? He never approved of Thomas, either. He went along with whatever her mum said. Such a pushover.

'Don't worry, Agnes,' says Thomas, tightening the grip on her hand.

Then the music starts. Niina's wedding song for them. Of course, she'd pick this one. And it's Agnes's own fault. They heard it on the radio one time in her car, and Agnes confessed that was the song she'd like for walking down the aisle. Niina had scoffed and called her a nerdy romantic. Niina is, however, a friend who pays attention to the details in her nerdy friend's life. When Niina assured her earlier, that the music was under control, Agnes thought nothing of it. She should have been paying attention. If only she could call her back and ask for a different song, but Niina is waiting with the other guests.

The first words and guitar through the boombox dim Agnes's mind of clutter, and point the spotlight on the man she's kept at arm's length all week—or underfoot. *Thinking Out Loud* belongs to Guy.

They pass the dining room table. Among Patrick's platters of delicacies, on a high glass stand, their cake commands centre stage. The bride and groom stand at a slight angle, and Agnes shrugs off the urge to reach over and fix them. She and Thomas continue through the lounge room, cleared for dancing. Ahead of them in the sunroom, ivy garlands hang from the ceiling, voile drape along the windows, and on every available surface, candles warm the gloomy afternoon. People seated in crammed short rows are all turned, watching them.

She should be in awe of the moment. She should be *in* the moment. But Agnes is on the dance floor with Guy's arm around her, she's lowering herself into Felicity with his hands on her. There's Guy crawling up towards her, his hair a wild mess, his beard tickling her skin. They're kissing. They are moving together—*Not now.*

There are at least thirty faces looking at her. Most of them she's never seen before. Agnes is forcing a smile. The corners of her mouth tremble. Being the centre of attention makes her self-conscious at the best of times. Here she is, thinking about someone other than the man walking next to her. What if they could all watch her thoughts like a video clip above her head? She and Guy naked, in the middle of lovemaking, or whatever it was. If it wasn't love, it was at least insanely satisfying. She has to give him that.

Britt-Marie whispers to her brother. He nods, can see the resemblance. Pernilla's smiling, filming them with her phone. Even though the day has started worse than bad, Agnes believes Thomas's family will give her a chance. It's the beginning of something new. Yet Guy's pestering her. *No, I'm pestering myself.* She is—with a man who took her for a one-nighter.

The celebrant, a pudgy man, eager-faced in no-rim glasses, is waiting for them in front of the French doors, where Patrick and Niina have created a rather nifty, make-do-archway with the garlands hanging loose from the ceiling. A dark man in a slim fit suit stands on one side, Dennis, whom she met years ago in Stockholm, who made fun of her dialect through an entire dinner. Niina and Patrick are the last on the right. The maid of honour's red lips show off her whitened teeth, in all their glory. That's one radiant face. Niina holds a mobile in her hand, controlling the music that way.

Thomas and Agnes come to a halt in front of the celebrant. The music fades and changes to instrumental. *Thank God for that.* There's shuffling behind them, chairs scuffing on the floor, whispers and then quiet, except for the faint sound of a single willow flute, Niina's choice of ceremony music. It's a little eerie. Agnes closes her eyes to focus on what the celebrant is saying. It won't register.

Someone's at the front door. Olga. Niina will have to worry about her.

Agnes is flat-chat rushing down a highway towards a turn-off. *I am doing this.* Let's get hitched, were her words. But this is madness. This is a frenzy. Why the rush? *It's romantic and totally mad.* She glances up at Thomas, who glances back. His eyes are deep-set and almond-shaped. His long brows frown ever so slightly.

What does her face look like to him? Her eyes? Like she's seen a ghost. She's behind the wheel of a speeding vehicle with seconds away from the exit lane. *Stop freaking out. For Pete's sake calm down.* Keep going straight ahead or veer off? Is this what cold feet actually feel like? She forces a smile and Thomas turns to face the celebrant again.

Agnes stares out through the glass, trying to control her breathing. A silent mast is gliding past on the canal. Someone's heading for the Baltic Sea, for open waters.

If Guy takes on the contract for the summer, he'll be going past up there. He won't know which house is hers. And he won't care. She'll be no more than a passing thought. If that. Agnes hopes the canal will be a stupendous disappointment to him. She hopes the canal will bore him out of his wits for weeks.

Of course, it will. The first time will be a novelty, sure. But there's no freedom. You puff along with your motor for days on end. No sails. No wind. No moving ocean underneath you. He will hate it—the predictability, the quiet bore of it. Once that initial excitement fades, he'll be desperate to sail elsewhere. Why would he even consider something as drab as a dug-out channel of still water?

To Guy, she was but a novelty. Thomas followed her into a bookshop. He's waited—for years. He's flawed. But she knows his flaws. She knows him. They must have another go. She can barely remember walking in here. That damn song. You're supposed to remember your wedding day. Apart from Pernilla with her phone, did anyone film them? Has anyone let Olga in? Can they start again? They have to start again.

Agnes squeezes Thomas's hand tight. It's *her* wedding. And his, of course. But she's the bride. Surely, they can do a take two. Niina will need to dig up a different song. Explaining the situation—Thomas will make it happen. He'll make it funny, make everyone laugh. He'll deal with the celebrant.

She squeezes a second time, and as hard as she can. There, she has his attention, his eyes on hers, his irises enlarged in the dim light, like small portholes. She's about to whisper to him, suggest a take-two. But then, in the literal blink of an eye, truth lands like a stone, breaks the surface with a solid splash, sends out ripples, sinks and settles like an anchor.

Agnes knows next to nothing about the anatomical explanation of the eye. Light hits the retina before changing into electric signals that travel via the optic nerve to the brain to be translated to images again—she knows that much. But what about the interpreting of these images, understanding them? What about the pupil-to-pupil exchange between people? What about the seeing, as in knowing someone? The intricacy of interpreting images correctly must happen somewhere inside the brain. Some images, deemed unimportant, are brushed over. The eye transfers the visual all right, but the brain isn't paying attention. And if the brain isn't paying attention, then the eye is nothing but a sterile camera lens.

34

seven days ago

If eyes truly were windows to the soul. How had she not seen the deceit in his eyes? Agnes lacked discernment—obviously. Because she'd missed it. She'd drowned in them the previous night. She'd thought he'd drowned in hers. He was a first-class con.

Agnes wasn't thinking that when she opened the metal gate to the pontoon. Those thoughts came later. When she opened the gate, nauseous guilt over Thomas weighed against excitement and relief. She longed for Guy, knew she needed to touch him and hear his voice.

Guy would be at Mick's workshop and wouldn't be back for hours, but she had no peace of mind to stay at her motel any longer. If she had to wait, Agnes would rather wait on Felicity. She would lie down on the duvet and think of the previous night. Unless, of course, guilt got in the way.

Relief flooded her when she saw the companionway open and heard his radio playing—louder than usual. She would first apologise about taking off in the morning. Then she'd explain why, and they'd talk things through. Agnes didn't call out. Deep in thought, she climbed down the steps.

Felicity was not a long boat. You could see from the galley through to the bow. Agnes saw as she passed the table. On the bed where they'd made love sprawled Tanya. The duvet lay draped over her, partly covering bare skin. She was obviously wearing no more than, possibly, undies. Is that what she did when Guy wasn't here? Did he know she was treating Felicity as if it was still her boat?

Though Agnes saw, she kept her momentum. It took seconds for the brain to register. By the time the command to stop came, she was there, right in front of her. They both stared.

Tanya pulled the duvet up further, making sure her breasts were covered. 'This is embarrassing,' she said. 'Thought you were Guy coming back for something.'

'Guy?'

'He just left.'

It made no sense, no sense at all. 'Not working today?' Agnes asked, her voice that of a puberty boy.

'Me? I'm on this evening.'

'I mean Guy.'

'He will be for the rest of the day. We just had a long lunch.' She looked away, smiling to herself and said, 'I forgot how good he is at long lunch.'

A roar and heat shot up from the soles of Agnes's feet and up through her entire body. She couldn't work it out. The plastic lantern moved ever so slightly. You'd think it was still, but it wasn't, not completely. She wanted badly to punch it off the hook.

'We're back together,' said Tanya with a sweetness that made Agnes want to smack her in the face, using the lantern. 'I've got a good feeling, too. It's different this time. I suppose you played a part.'

Guy wouldn't do this. He's not like that. He's not.

'Gosh, I've really given you a fright. Wait. I'll put something on.' She rummaged under the cover and pulled up a red lace G-string, which she quickly shoved under the duvet again.

Agnes left her to it and walked into the salon. Her entire body was trembling. Her eyes were on fire. She blinked and blinked and sneaked a quick hand up to wipe her eyes. So she'd misunderstood everything. She'd been a complete dumb-ass fool. He'd accused her of playing a game with him when the opposite was true. She'd believed what she wanted to believe. He'd said he wanted her. He'd said nothing about loving her. Agnes pressed fingers into her eye sockets.

'Been shopping?' said Tanya, coming up behind her.

Agnes didn't answer. The bag in her hand with Guy's clothes neatly wrapped in tissue paper proved her level of dumb-ass gullibility. Not only did she let him take her to bed. She bought him clothes for his effort.

'You wanted to see Guy?' Tanya threw herself down on a lounge. She was wearing his hoody, the one Agnes had worn the day before. 'By the way, we love these.' She stroked the seat. 'So sweet of you.'

The turquoise blue covers she'd spent hours sewing, wanting to give back, wanting to make Guy happy, wanting to leave something of her behind. It had been an honest gift. Seeing Tanya sitting there triumphant and satisfied—and Agnes knew exactly how satisfied—made her want to scream, to beg, to whisper, 'Please no'.

'I slept with him last night,' she said, feeling every bit the bitch she was. It wasn't fair to spill the truth to Tanya. Despite her jealousy about the time Agnes and Guy spent together, she had been nothing but kind to Agnes. It was cruel and yet Agnes wanted to hurt her, wanted her to feel the pain of betrayal the same way she felt it.

Tanya looked uncomfortable and sad.

Get a grip. It's not her fault. 'I don't know why I said that.'

'It's OK.' Tanya sat curled in the lounge, playing with her toes, not looking at her. 'He told me he slept with someone, not that it was you, but I'm not surprised. I wish it hadn't happened. I mean, with you, of all women.' She reshuffled her body, straightened her tanned, toned legs. 'But he's sorry about it. And we've been a bit all over the place, you know, him and I.'

He was sorry? Sorry? 'It was a dumb mistake,' said Agnes.

'I know. He said. So you're okay?'

'Me?'

'He wanted to get back at me, you know. Something I did before he went overseas last year. Our stupid shit. He wanted to get even.'

He wanted to get even?

'You sure you're okay?'

'I'm fine.'

'I'm sorry if he misled—'

'I didn't know the two of you were … you know,' said Agnes. Her voice had a tremor to it as if she'd just come out of an ice bath, shivering. And yet she was overheating. 'Thought it was friends with benefits arrangement, nothing more. So … I'm sorry about that.' Agnes breathed slowly through her nose, focusing on calming down the rage inside.

'It's okay. I'm okay. Kind of deserved it. We're good, me and Guy. We're good.'

'That's good then.'

'You're okay?'

'Yes, yes. I'm fine.'

You wanted to see him?'

Indeed, she'd said that. Agnes thought of the clothes. Considered chucking them in the bin on her way out. 'Merely came to give him this.' She put the bag on the table between them. 'For services rendered,' she said with her most cool and detached voice. And then she left.

Tanya didn't call after her, didn't say, 'Bye'. They were both finished with each other.

Agnes walked all the way to the motel with a screaming noise inside her head, her heart beating at top speed, and her body shivering.

In her room, she sent a short text to Guy, to let him know she knew. Then she threw her cabin bag on the bed and started packing. Agnes rolled her garments tight, tight with trembling hands, and frantically shoved them in. She was meant to fly out the next morning, but the thought of having to stay in Coffs for one more hour was unbearable. No, she'd catch a cab to the airport and grab the first available seat.

Agnes slid her old ring back on her finger. God, she'd been stupid. She had Thomas at home, for goodness' sake. Guy had seen her for what she was, gullible and easily impressed, easily manipulated. When she'd jumped off that bus purely from his word 'Stay', she bet that had fed his ego. And Holly she was clueless about her own brother. Here she was, being protective of him when he was a Casanova.

Agnes packed up the room in no time. Holly's belongings went in her shopping bags. She left them, and the sewing machine with the receptionist, assuring her that someone would come and pick it up. Holly could keep the sewing machine, sell it, or give it away. Agnes didn't care.

Her thoughts were racing around the entire time. She moved from the previous day on the ocean to the night with Guy, to the day's turmoil. The words of Tanya 'I forgot how good he is' kept torturing her—the thought of them enjoying sex while she'd been picking out clothes for Niina. It was, of course, appropriate. What she'd done to Thomas, Guy had done to her.

The drive out to the airport, the small talk with the taxi driver, the checking-in, were all done with this noise in her head. Once she'd gone through security, she found a corner to herself. Two hours had passed since she'd left Felicity. Not one word from Guy. Deep down, she'd expected something from him—a call, a text, a weak apology, a poor excuse, something.

When Agnes stood in the queue to board, she forced herself to let it go. She sent him the terse message she'd ended up with after countless efforts of writing and deleting, rewriting and deleting.

Some stuff for you at the motel. $1000 in the pocket of Holly's jacket, in case my suitcase shows up. Send to address included. You warned me about the Australian ferals and bugs. Seems the worst creepy crawlies walk on two legs. Time to go home and marry the love of my life

Then Agnes took the card out of the phone. She flicked it in the bin before handing over her boarding pass. It was time to grow up.

35
today

Thomas's eyes are fixed on hers. But he doesn't see her, never has. Guy did. His brain registered and interpreted her correctly. As much as he betrayed her, he saw her from the very first time they met. Even if she was his way to get even with Tanya, Agnes doesn't care. There has to be another man in the world who sees her for who she is, someone capable of remembering even fundamental basics such as, how she likes her coffee, how she hates the word Babe, how she loves slow sex.

She can't settle for Thomas, no matter how fantastic this new revelatory back story is, no matter how good his mother thinks she'll be for her son, or that Pernilla has thawed, that there's a hint of a budding friendship. Thomas is second best. Second best is not good enough. Walking out on him, leaving him in front of all these people will in Niina-vocabulary classify as bitch stamping yourself. So be it.

'I can't do this.' Agnes's voice is a quiet whisper, drowned by the lofty tones of the Swedish north. She hears herself. No one else does.

Thomas frowns. Unsure.

'I cannot do this,' she says again with her heart hammering hard in her chest. Her pulse booms so loud in her ears, she can't hear the flute anymore. Heat's rushing from the bottom up. She's a tomato-faced bride, pumping adrenaline, gearing up for flight mode.

'Agnes, what's going on?'

'I'm so, so sorry, Thomas.' And she is. He's done his best. This is her worst. She could have spared him this if she'd listened to reason, listened to Niina, or her own doubt. Because it has been here all along. Shame on her for going along with this. Shame on her for not having the guts to call it off.

'You're only having a moment,' he says. His other hand on her shoulder is like a bag of sand. 'It's fine. It'll be fine, babe.'

The celebrant lets his last sentence fade out. Then he waits, looking at his papers, his watch, at them, then back to the papers. Thomas clutches her hand as if his force can change her mind. Agnes won't be able to make him or anyone else understand, can't make a speech to explain herself. She has to get away. She wants to push the celebrant aside and open the French doors. Air. She wants fresh air.

'You need to let me go.' She works on their hands, probing hers out of his. His fingers hang on, long and strong and stubborn.

'No, Agnes. You're just freaking out. It'll be okay.'

'Let me go.' Agnes snaps hard and her hand slips out of his. She loses her balance and staggers backwards into

Niina before pushing her aside, dropping the bouquet. She stumbles past everyone, lucky not to fall over. Niina calls after her as she runs through the house.

Agnes isn't proficient on heels and has gained an impressive speed by the time she reaches the hallway. Parked right in the middle, between her and the front door, is her giant leather suitcase. The shiny new thing she said goodbye to at check out has returned, scuffed, but in one piece. Agnes flings her hands out to break the fall.

She lands her knees on it, toppling it over and herself. For a split second she expects Guy to make his appearance, saying, 'Look what I brought you.' Then there's the familiar swish and click-clack behind her.

'I bet that hurt,' says Niina, before offering a hand to help her up.

Once upright, Agnes scrambles out the door onto the porch. The driveway and street are quiet.

Niina follows her out, closing the door. 'What happened in there?' she says.

'Do you think it was the courier? Doesn't he want a signature?'

'What courier?'

'That's my lost suitcase.'

'Oh. Nah, he's not a patient man. He never waits if I'm serving someone. Mind you, if he'd committed to waiting for the "I do", he'd end up covered in cobwebs. We all would. Oh, that reminds me what the heck is going on. You busting for the toilet?'

The thin dress is as cold as the air, and goosebumps prickle Agnes's skin. 'What do I do now? I can't go back in there.'

'And I repeat. What's going on?'

'I'm an idiot. That's what's going on.'

'Yeah, yeah. But could you narrow it down for me?'

Agnes glares at her.

'Oh, Agnes, just bloody well, say it.'

'You were right.'

'Meaning?'

'You've been right all along.'

Niina pretends there's an audience gathered around the porch, nodding, smoothing her skirt out, sweeping one hand in Agnes's direction. Then she says smugly, 'And there it is.'

'Can you take this seriously?'

'I am. This is seriously good news.'

'What do I do now?'

'You need to talk to him.'

'I need time to think.'

'He deserves an explanation.'

'I need everyone out.'

'A job allocated to me, no doubt.'

'Would you mind? I need to take a breather and clear my head.'

'Can I send *his* people and keep ours?' She finds Agnes's hand and starts moving it about. 'Dance party?'

Agnes snatches back her hand. 'Are you kidding?'

'Okay, okay. I'm sorry.'

'I'm going for a walk before he comes after me.'

'Hang on.' Niina opens the door. Agnes can see Thomas in the kitchen. It seems Patrick's blocking his way. Niina grabs her duffel coat and hands it to her.

'I'll do my best to sweep the place clean of guests,' she says. 'Don't disappear. I expect you back in half an hour at the absolute latest.' Then she closes the door.

Niina's woolly coat is many sizes too big. It smells of her perfume and tobacco which is gross and reassuring at the same time. Agnes hurries down the steps and through the front gate as a new energetic bout of rain starts. Well, she isn't going back in now. Her poor boots.

She considers her car or Niina's at first, but people will leave, and they'll notice her. Or Thomas will come looking. So off she trudges, up the gravel road to the canal, avoiding the potholes as best she can.

The realisation of what she's done dawns on her. She's walked out on a perfectly decent man because she doesn't think he knows her well enough, or worse because Guy bestowed her with a better orgasm. *No, that's not how it is. This is how it is—I wanted someone who didn't want me and now I don't want someone who does. I'm a cliché.*

Niina's woollen coat fails as a barrier against the rain and is getting heavier. Why would she wear this coat on a day like today, and why not hand Agnes an umbrella instead?

Agnes pulls the hood over her head, but it's getting damp. Apparently, today she's to remain wet.

There's a large pothole to her right—a few inches deep. Resolutely, she steps into it. Agnes watches as muddy water soaks into her boots, staining them grey, drowning her feet in the cold. It's pure relief. Come to think of it, her dress could do with the same treatment. It has hung in her wardrobe for years. For what?

She jumps and stomps her feet. Sprays of water chill her bare legs. Instant dark specs shower the fabric. One heel lands on a rock, and she waves frantic arms so as not to lose her footing, though it would be quite fitting to plunge her entire self. Wonder of all wonder, she finds her balance. Agnes keeps clomping and splashing, thoroughly enjoying the destruction of her wedding outfit.

She holds Niina's coat up as well as she can. Niina doesn't deserve to have it ruined. However, if she ruins it, Agnes will go out and spend an absolute fortune on whatever coat takes Niina's fancy. Within minutes, spots and streaks and splatters cover her dress. Pleased with the result, Agnes steps out and keeps walking, her boots sloshy inside, her anklet stockings slippery under and around her feet.

She will take a walk in the rain, and come back drenched. That's how she will face him, and his family if Niina can't make them leave. She's humiliated him, so why not some of the same dished out for her?

Agnes steers towards the lock when, through the drizzle, she sees Olga on her way to their back gate. When Agnes calls out, the old woman hurries up the stairs again, waving at her. Olga marches to the wooden bench and Agnes dashes over, glancing towards the house, hoping not to be seen. The many burning candles light up the dark glass veranda, and figures move about in there. Hopefully, Niina is rounding them up and sending them on their way, cleaning up the almost-bride's mess.

Agnes seats herself next to Olga. Despite the damp coat and dress, the wet seat is a shock to her buttocks. She keeps her hands inside the pockets where it's a little dryer.

Olga has not dressed up. Underneath her clear plastic poncho, she's wearing jeans, a jumper, and, of course, the life jacket. There really isn't much more to Olga than a little head of grey hair and a worried face. She's breathing fast and fidgeting with her hands. Water is dripping from the hem, and rain trickles its way along the creases of her plastic covering, creating tiny waterfalls.

'Your phone's not working,' says Olga. 'I should've come earlier.'

'You missed nothing.'

'I was scared,' she says. 'I'm sorry.'

'Do you need to see a doctor?' If Agnes has to take her to the hospital, that means she can take a breather and escape facing Thomas. Leave it for later. But does she even want that?

Olga shakes her head inside the too big unmovable hood. 'You married now?'

'No.'

'Good,' she says with obvious relief.

'There won't be a wedding.'

Through the plastic, she grabs at Agnes's arms. 'I saw him that night.'

'Who?'

'When Nils fell in ... ' Olga groans, as if in pain. Then she bursts into tears.

Agnes forces her hand out of its warmish hiding and wraps her arm around Olga's cold, slippery, and bony back. She rubs and waits, willing her dear old neighbour to settle. Down at the house, a couple of cars are starting up.

Olga finds a handkerchief in a pocket and blows her nose. 'He was there. I saw him.'

'Did you see my dad?'

'Yes, and ... your man.'

'Thomas?'

She nods.

Poor little Olga. She's confused again.

'I recognised him today. That walk,' she says. 'He stood right next to Nils. They argued. And Nils fell in and he, Thomas, just stood there and watched.'

Agnes thought she was cold before, but now—though it may have been a dream—Olga's words chill like ice.

'Where were you, Olga?'

'On my way to the bridge. I'd seen your dad staggering along, talking to Irene, how he often did. I used to watch him.' Her voice is thick and quiet. 'I'm a poor sleeper.'

'I didn't know.'

'He was so drunk that night. You used to come looking for him. I used to watch the two of you. But you weren't there, so I was going to help him home. It was dark, but I could see them. They started arguing. And then Nils fell in,' The next words are only just audible. 'Don't know if he pushed him,' she whispers. 'But he stood there watching.'

'Are you sure?'

'I closed my eyes until it was quiet.' She's rocking back and forth, her hanky held tight in her hands. 'I didn't save him. I closed my eyes. Oh, Agnes.' She sobs uncontrollably again, and Agnes rubs her back.

'You were scared, Olga. You couldn't have saved him.' And that's how it was. Neither could Agnes. Olga was too petite to drag Nils out. Agnes would have drowned with him.

'I walked home thinking I'd imagined it,' says Olga with a congested voice. 'When they found Nils ... I didn't want them to put me in that place again. *They* told me it didn't matter. *They* said I'd end up in that place again?'

'Did they?' says Agnes, giving extra rubs.

'Today, when he came walking. *They* told me to leave, told me to be quiet. But I knew I had to tell you. It's my fault. I did nothing. I—'

'No,' Agnes cuts her off. 'Dad was drunk. You are not to blame yourself.'

That night, Olga didn't call Agnes or emergency. When Agnes phoned *her* the next day, a frazzled Olga hung up on her three times. And she withdrew after that. Agnes thought it was grief, only grief.

'I don't want to go to the hospital again,' Olga whispers. 'Now I've told you.'

'You won't have to go anywhere. Promise.' More cars are leaving. How long has it been? She gives the elderly woman a hug. 'I don't like to leave you like this, but I need to go, Olga. Why don't you come with me, see Niina, have a cup of tea?'

'No darling, I'm going home. I feel better now.'

Shivering, Agnes waits while her neighbour rows back across. Did Olga actually see Thomas that night? With her dad? In the past, she and Olga often met at the bridge whenever the older woman wasn't up to rowing. Since Agnes's father, they have both avoided the lock. The two of them have shared similar ghosts.

Why would Thomas even have been on the canal that night? Surely he'd not come to see her? In the beginning of her mother's illness, he did that—parked closer to town and walked along the canal to theirs. But he'd text her first. She'd sneak him inside, up to the attic. The stealth visits ended the night her father walked in on them, armed with his rolling pin and chef's knife.

They tried occasional dates on a Sunday if Niina could come over. Thomas would book their motel room, and Agnes would join him for a couple of hours. That worked okay until Irene woke up one late evening, discovering her daughter gone and refusing Niina's help.

After that, Agnes rarely bothered. The night her father drowned, she and Thomas had not had a date since February, and she'd only seen him briefly when he—against her wishes—had dropped in for a visit a summer morning, a few weeks before her mum's death.

So why would he be on the canal? He wouldn't. Would he? Olga must be mistaken. Did she see Nils fall in, and imagine the rest? Then again ...

Once Olga is up on her own pier, Agnes heads back with one thing on her mind—the truth.

36
today

Apart from her own car, there's only Patrick's, Niina's, and an Audi. She thinks it's Dennis in the driver's seat which must mean he's waiting for Thomas.

Her house is dry and warm and savoury. There are voices coming from the living room. Agnes hangs Niina's now leaden coat on a hook, before unlacing the boots with awkward fingers. She's pulling her benumbed feet out with some difficulty when Pernilla comes out of the guest toilet. The girl looks like she's been crying. She's definitely been drinking. Underaged, yes, but it wouldn't be the first time, and Thomas's daughter is not Agnes's responsibility.

'Can we talk?' says Agnes. Then she walks into the toilet, dragging Pernilla with her.

Agnes locks behind them. They stand close, jammed between vanity, wall, and toilet. Pernilla's breath is sour and her eyes glazed.

'Was it me?' says Pernilla. 'Is that why you're not marrying dad?'

'No. No. God, no.'

'He's upset. Acting all cool, but that's all fake.'

'I know,' says Agnes, glancing at herself in the mirror. Her mascara has ended up underneath her eyes. She looks as if she's sobbed for an hour. Niina's carefully applied foundation has gone blotchy in the rain, and her camouflaged scar stretches a long pale *hello* across her forehead. Her once-in-a-lifetime-romantic-curls have returned to dead-straight wet strands glued to her skin while random hairpins and tiny white roses still hold on for dear life.

'Towel, please,' she says.

'There aren't any,' says Pernilla, pulling a strip of paper from the roll behind her instead.

Agnes wipes as well as she can. As the soft paper wets, it falls apart. *Useless crap.* 'Look, you and I had a rough start,' she says, picking soggy bits of her skin. 'But I promise you, what happened in there, that was all me.'

'Have you changed your mind?'

Agnes turns the tap on and rinses her hands, then shakes over the sink before wiping them resolutely on the bodice of her dress that's still clean and almost dry. *How to approach this?* She has no time to waste.

This is going to sound strange,' she says. 'Could I have a look at that phone calendar of yours?'

'Why?' Pernilla presses her phone tight to her chest.

'I need to check something.'

'Why?'

'I'm after a date, that's all.'

'Is this about dad? Will it help you change your mind?'

Agnes cringes internally when she, without hesitation, says, 'Yes.'

Pernilla puts her code in. 'What date are you after?'

'Can I have a look?'

'You tell me and I'll find it.'

'Let me have a look.' This is Holly speaking to Nathan or Ruby—or Guy, for that matter—pulling them into line. 'I need to have a quick look at some dates, nothing else,' she says.

Reluctantly, Pernilla hands it over.

Agnes scrolls through the previous months. She has to lock her elbows to keep the phone steady. There are all kinds of capital letter abbreviations. 'They're all about your dad?' she asks.

'No,' says Pernilla. 'I have a life.'

There it is, 12th of November, and Pernilla has written S H. Agnes's heart thumps furiously in her ears. 'Do you keep track of what time of the day it is?' she asks.

Pernilla shrugs. 'Sometimes.'

She's written a name there as well. 'What does that mean?' asks Agnes.

'Oh, that was a mate's eighteenth. It went belly up before midnight, so I rang Dad to pick me up. Mum had a girl's night. I didn't know then, but he obviously came here to see you. I had to take the night bus to his. Only just beat him home. The

335

night buses take forever. When Mum found out, she was mad. That's when things started going ape shit between them.'

Agnes keeps scrolling back and forth, thinking. She moves forward, taking mental note of all the days with S H marks. They start up in December, not long after her father's funeral, and are pretty regular. There's S H over Easter. And there's a few in a row beginning the day she flew out. He was in South Hamlet? 'Your dad had the flu, didn't he?'

'Yep, barred me from coming over. Didn't want me to catch anything. Don't know why he couldn't admit he was coming here. I didn't think so then ... but it's kind of cute that he missed you that much, that he'd rather be sick at yours,' she says. 'And even if you don't have a wedding today, doesn't mean you have to break up.'

Pernilla looks like a lost little bird, but Agnes abstains from hugging her. She's just betrayed her trust. 'Pernilla,' she says, 'Make sure you never settle for someone who doesn't see you.' She touches her cheek with gentle fingers. 'You.'

Pernilla frowns at her.

Agnes hands back the phone, and before the girl can say or ask anything, she unlocks and goes to find the girl's father.

Britt-Marie with husband and brother hover around the dining table. The men are half-heartedly hand-picking from Patrick's food platters. Britt-Marie is drinking. They're not talking but probably eavesdropping on the muffled voices coming from the next room. It sounds like Thomas and Niina, with some Patrick thrown in for good measure.

Agnes's almost in-laws don't notice her in the doorway. She would have loved a talk with Leif about her mother, but the timing couldn't be more askew. There's only one person she needs to confront, and she wants to avoid all the others. She should sneak away, out the front door, and get back into the house through the sun-lounge.

Before she has time to make the move, Pernilla calls out from the hallway that their taxi has arrived, and all eyes land on Agnes. What follows are awkward minutes of introducing herself to Thomas's step-dad and Leif while also apologising *and* bidding them farewell. The interaction between her and the entire family is solemn, stiff, and perfectly awful. Thomas, who joins them, treats her like air, then follows the others out, but she knows he'll be back. He wants an explanation. Well, so does she.

She'll need to contain her emotions, not let them run amok with her. Agnes has always thought Thomas clever. Now she suspects his clever is a Machiavellian strain that demands a cunning determination to match—if she is to sift the truth from the lies.

'Time to talk,' he says, marching towards the sunroom.

'We'll go out for a smoko,' says Niina. 'We'll be just outside. Okay?'

'Great,' says Agnes and quickly pats her warm arm as she walks past.

Thomas, with hands in his pockets, stands in the middle of the room. He's surrounded by disorderly chairs scattered about having a party of their own. The flowers and the candles contrast the insipid afternoon coming at them through all the window panes. As soon as she closes the doors, he erupts.

'You made me look like a complete and utter dick. Why? Why screw this up for us after all this time? Seriously, what's going through your head? This is what we wanted. You've been fine all week, but you had to freak out on me today, in front of all my family and friends, in front of my daughter. What's happened to you?' Thomas doesn't expect an answer, doesn't pause for her to give one.

'I get it,' he says, adjusting his pace, continuing in a slower fashion as if explaining to himself. 'I know what happened—too much, too soon. We need to slow down. Forget about marriage for now. We just got engaged. Let's enjoy that. We'll go to Greece. Chill. Two weeks in the sun—it'll be great. We might have a summer wedding unless we tie the knot on one of the islands. How romantic would that be?' He gives her an uncertain smile and walks towards her. 'Just a thought,' he says. 'Don't worry, no rush.'

She moves to the side and past him, making sure there are plastic chairs between them, not taking her eyes off him. 'Where were you the night my dad passed away?'

His face smooths out and readjusts.

'Actually, don't bother. I already know the answer to that one.' She can't be sure of anything. Bluffing is the approach now. 'I'll ask you this instead,' she says. 'Did you push him?'

'Did I what?'

'Did you push my father into the canal?' Her voice is calm. Internally, there's a raging sea.

'What are you going on about?' He walks closer while she walks backwards, pulling chairs in front of her. Then he stops, lifts his hands up in the air as if she's pointing a gun at him, and backs off, creating more space between them.

Agnes stands where they stood, less than an hour earlier, ready to say, 'For better, for worse.' There are hanging garlands of ivy on either side of her. The leaves are curling, and the clusters of flowers drooping. They would have been cut from their stems early that morning. Have been dying ever since. How sad a sacrifice—to wither away before their time, for no reason at all. 'I have two witnesses,' she says.

'I don't know what you're talking about.'

'Bullshit.' Her choice of word and volume shocks him. So out of character. Her father was out of character on the booze. The day her mum suffered her first stroke, Agnes met Nils-the-drunk for the first time, complete with vocabulary and agitation. If need be, she can be her father's daughter without the alcohol, and if that doesn't work, she can be her mother's. 'I want an answer,' she says. 'Evidently, the truth.'

Thomas seems unsure.

They eye each other while he decides which way to go.

Then his shoulders slump. 'I didn't push your dad,' he says with a sigh.

'What were you doing on the canal?'

'On my way to see you.'

'Did you argue with him?'

'He was smashed, could barely walk up—'

'Again. Did you argue with him?'

Thomas shakes his head almost imperceptibly. '*He* argued. And he stumbled.'

'Why didn't you help him?'

'I'd had a few drinks. I wasn't that switched on.'

'Come again?'

'There wasn't enough time. I was too far away.'

Stay calm. 'I don't believe you,' she says.

'I wasn't in my right mind. Hesitated. It all happened too fast.'

'You watched my father drown, too busy thinking of how it would benefit us?' She spits the words. His diamonds have to come off. They're like poison around her finger. Agnes yanks in panic when the ring won't pass over her knuckle. She wets the finger in her mouth, before forcing off with her teeth. When she throws it at him, the ring clatters across the floor, and disappears beneath chairs.

'You have no idea how much I regret that night.' Thomas turns away from her and walks up to the glass panes, pulling at his tie.

Agnes takes in his butt in the chinos, the outline of his back, his shoulders and biceps. She's loved this man for years, but she doesn't know him any more than he knows her. *Blind? You bet.* 'Not sober enough to call for help,' she says calmly. 'Sober enough to drive back to Stockholm.'

Thomas struggles with his tie knot, enlarges the noose and pulls it off over his head. 'Honest. I didn't push him. He ran at me. I moved out of his way, not realising what was behind me. He fell in. Sunk. It was over in seconds.'

She thinks about that night. She—comfortable in her bed while a few hundred meters away in the chilly autumn night, he watches her father drown.

'I should've ... I am sorry ... so so sorry.'

What about the other dates? 'You were here while I was away,' she says. 'How did you get in? Did you make a spare key? You did, didn't you? That day we went to North Hamlet. You drove my car and carried my keys around. While I looked at suitcases, you disappeared. Did you do it then?'

341

Thomas keeps his back to her. He's trying to undo the tie knot. Apart from that he's perfectly still.

'You weren't sick?' The question becomes an answer. 'At the airport, all that coughing in my ear—such an actor. You wanted me out of the house. You wanted to snoop? For what? You wanted to know what I'm worth. Is that it? You didn't withdraw any funds. No need when a quick wedding was more profitable. Are you in financial strife or you're just thinking long term?'

There's a sigh from him.

'I should call the police for break-in and possible manslaughter. This needs to be properly investigated.'

Thomas turns around. He's finally released the knot. The tie is blue at her request, to match the poor cornflowers. He rolls it into a tight bundle and throws it. Mid-air it uncurls, falls on a chair and slides off. 'You're getting ahead of yourself, Agnes. Before you ring any police, I should fill you in on the not-so-minor details.'

She glares at him, wondering if they actually could charge him with anything.

'Do you know the real reason your mum changed her name?'

Her mind halts. His words send another cold shiver up her spine.

'See, now I have your attention. You might prefer to sit down for this one.'

He waits.

She remains standing.

'Okay. Here we go.' Thomas pauses for two seconds as if waiting for a drum roll. 'Your mum was my dad's accomplice in the robbery of a jeweller in inner-city Stockholm in 1982. Yes, you heard me right. Kerstin didn't see it fit to wait two minutes for my dad when he got tangled up with the security guard. What did she care? She drove off. Bailed on him. If his getaway car hadn't taken off like that, he wouldn't have gone to prison.'

Agnes wants to call him a liar. She says nothing.

'Your mum escaped that day. She disappeared with cash and a small but valuable collection of diamonds while my dad rotted in jail for eighteen years only to be diagnosed with cancer, and rot in palliative care until he gave up his breath. So go ahead, fetch the authorities, and I too will have information to share with them. What was it you said? It needs to be properly investigated.'

It's such an incongruous claim. Yet instead of a punch to the gut, it's like the turning of a key. There was something mysterious about her mum. Although she struggles with the image of Irene doing a runner from a crime scene with stolen goods on the seat next to her, Agnes knows instantly and instinctively this was her mother's secret. How had she lived a long life with her dad, holding on to a lie like that?

'Karl didn't think Kerstin would be savvy enough, or have the guts, to sell the stones. After all, she was just a bookkeeper. Karl told me your mum was odd, the kind who would hide them in her mattress. He was dying, and I took it upon myself to find her, to set things right. You understand the diamonds didn't belong to her.'

All these years. So much tumbles around in Agnes's head. The truth is like those 3D images that were all the rage for a while, where you had to move a page back and forth until the erratic patterns aligned until the actual image came into focus. Thomas stands with his arms crossed, waiting for her to see it. The picture is sharpening.

'So, you and Mum didn't argue about me? You argued about stolen goods?'

He shakes his head slowly. 'Your mum refused to acknowledge any of it. I showed her the photo. Didn't matter. No, that wasn't her. I was mistaken. No, what she wanted was to get me away from you. So, it was actually about you, about me pissing off, out of your life.'

'You did for a while.'

'A financial agreement.'

'She paid you off to keep away?'

'Monthly instalments,' says Thomas, unfolding his arms.

'So that's why you didn't want to elope? You came back, though. Why?'

'I told you. It started off with diamonds. Then you got under my skin.'

'Mum saw through the charade. She knew you kept seeing me, didn't she?'

Thomas shoves his hands in his pockets. 'Irene called me, said it was time to settle the score. She'd hand over the diamonds, and if I didn't keep away from you after that, she'd come out with the whole truth, which would make me an accomplice, sort of. Your mum was going to arrange for you and your dad to run errands for her, get you out of the house. Two days before my meeting with her, you rang me from the hospital.'

'Her stroke?'

He nods. 'Luck has never been my thing. That photo? Thought I'd chucked it.'

'So you came to visit, not for my sake. You came to see if my mother still had all her marbles?'

'No, I came for you too, for both. I was torn.' Thomas shoves a chair to the side, bends down, and picks up the ring, then parks himself in the chair in front of her, a metre away.

Shaking her head at him, she says, 'Wow, me or diamonds, or me *and* diamonds? So you got me out of here, to fine-comb the place?'

He looks up straight into her eyes. 'I needed closure, had to know if there was anything left of what was rightfully mine.'

'Why send me half across the world?'

Thomas gives a short laugh at this. 'You're such a homebody. I needed a few days. A bear show was the perfect solution. There just happened to be one in Australia.'

'And all that b-s about meeting me in Sydney?'

'I had every intention.'

'Unless you found what you were looking for, I bet.'

Thomas looks down at the ring. It looks so small in his palm. He shakes his head. 'It's more complicated than that,' he says. 'You don't get it.'

'You got rid of me to find out what I'm worth. My odd mum was—surprise, surprise—proficient enough to find buyers. You thought I was worth marrying. I'd say, I pretty much get it. Did it take you long to weigh up the pros and cons? Seems to me the diamonds were your preferred wish, so tying the knot with me, or rather with the trust fund, was Plan B.' The irony isn't lost on her. She's tempted to inform him how he was *her* Plan B.

'Actually—'

'Shut up.' She says with a stone voice. She came so close to marrying him, so close. And she's felt bad for him—guilty.

Just like Guy, Thomas has played a mind-fuck game. Agnes doubts there's a word for her level of credulity. One man's mind-fuck was for the sake of another woman, one man's for the sake of diamonds.

From a distance, the glassed sunroom must look serene with the tiny flames, the ivy and flowers around them, the drapes. From a distance, anyone would assume the bride and groom are taking a break after having entertained guests, shared a long dinner with speeches, and danced for hours.

Thomas turns the ring over and over between his fingers. 'I know it looks bad, Ness, but—'

'You don't get to call me that,' she snaps.

He licks his lips before continuing. 'I know it looks bad, but hear me out. Yes, the diamonds became an obsession, but there's so much more. You are good for me. We could share this—the legacy of our parents.'

'You're delusional. See yourself out, or I'll call Patrick to assist.'

'Can't you see how unfair it is? My dad didn't rat on your mum. He could have, but he didn't. You'd have nothing if it wasn't for him.'

'Go,' she says, putting up a hand waving him off.

'You owe me.'

'P-a-t-r-i—'

'I'm going.' Thomas gets up. 'This is not over,' he says.

'I've changed all my passwords!' is the last thing she calls after him before the door slams.

Thomas has sucked the last bit of energy out of her. A vacuum replaces the sense of freedom she felt mere minutes ago after hearing the truth about her mother. It's as if she's come out of a storm. She hasn't capsized, but her sails are torn, her rudder's broken, and she's definitely head butted the boom.

37
today

He has a spare key. Agnes sighs. She doubts the locksmith will come until the earliest Monday. An entire weekend knowing Thomas can walk in any time is not a riveting concept. She'd better get her hands on it now. That's the immediate issue. However, a new lock won't solve Thomas. This isn't over. It has only just begun. She owes him.

Does she though? Or does she owe the authorities? And if so, how much? Villa Solus already belonged to her dad when he met her mum, but what if she can't afford to keep it? And what about her financial support? How do you stop an illegally funded trust fund?

'Oh, Mum, what have you done?' she says to the door as she passes her mother's old office. Her mum with her award-winning business virtuosity grew the family's nest egg with stolen goods. It's decades ago and maybe no one cares anymore. Except for Thomas, of course. But it isn't right. Is it?

Agnes finds gumboots and car keys. On her way down the steps, she runs into Niina and Patrick, glued to each other under an umbrella that he's carrying protectively.

'We got caught in the rain,' she says. 'And just so you know, we haven't heard a thing. We saw Thomas get into the best man's car. Niina has an arm around Patrick and an empty glass in her other hand. She sounds tipsy. Both of them look flushed. 'Are you okay?'.

Agnes nods

'Let's eat. We are peckish, to put it mildly. Then I want to hear all the latest. Think I've earned it. Oy, Agnes. You going somewhere?'

'Thomas has a house key of mine.'

'You need a jacket.'

'I'll only be a minute.'

'Our cars are in your way,' says Patrick, and he's right. 'I might as well drive you.'

'We'll all go,' says Niina. 'They have a little bar, so cute. Do you like Piña Colada?' she sings to Patrick, who plants a kiss on her cheek. She laughs.

They pack into the front seat of Patrick's van, Niina in the middle, looking quite excited.

'I never liked him, you know,' she says. 'But Agnes, you are a drama queen. Just so you know.'

Agnes says, to Patrick, 'Niina tipsy or Niina sober, without fail honest.'

Patrick drops her off, and she leaves them to search for parking. Agnes hurries along the stone terrace of the resort-like guesthouse, checking through the windows into the restaurant. A little early for the kitchen to be open, is her guess, but it looks like Thomas's wedding party has gathered around a long table in there. She hopes Thomas isn't with them, hopes he's gone up to his room. She doesn't want to face that crowd again. Unfortunately, Agnes hears his voice as soon as she walks into the vestibule.

The receptionist is busy on her computer, so without a word, and before hesitation gets the better of her, Agnes veers into the restaurant. It's empty except for Thomas's group and some lonesome drinker in the corner of Niina's cute bar. Self-conscious in her flat hair, mud-spluttered dress, and her gumboots, Agnes strides determinedly across the room. She'll make this swift and be out before Niina shows up to nag about her cocktail, or worse, pick her own argument with Thomas. No thanks. The day has been long enough.

Thomas sits on the short end with his back to her. He seems to be bantering with Dennis about some shared antics. You wouldn't think he's not long been stood up at the altar.

Resolute, Agnes walks up to him, her heart ticking at double speed. It'll be over in minutes, she reminds herself. Everyone except Thomas has noticed her. They all watch. Dennis leans in closer to him, says something, and Thomas flicks his head around.

'Changed your—'

'Key,' she interrupts. He was going to say, 'Changed your mind?' to make light of it. That is so Thomas—sitting here, making small talk, making the afternoon fiasco a humorous event. What has the extraordinary showman told them? Oh, what the heck, she doesn't care. This is the last she'll see of his friends. Agnes closes her fists and straightens her back. 'My key,' she says again.

Without another word, Thomas gets his key ring out.

The silence is awkward. The old Agnes would keep her head down now, check out the carpet, but damn it, she's done nothing wrong. While he slides her key off the metal loop, she challenges herself to out-stare anyone who's game to take her on.

His immediate family is missing. These are friends of his, people she's not met before. Except for Dennis. These strangers have dressed up, set this day aside, driven the hours, and paid for their accommodation. Agnes sincerely hopes they'll at least enjoy their dinner and tomorrow's breakfast.

As she gazes around the table, they pick up their menus or turn to the next person, not meeting her eyes. One woman offers a closed-lip, faint but definite smile as if she's happy for her. Dennis does not look away, so Agnes ends there. It feels like minutes ticking by, but she doesn't back down, blinks slowly with a neutral face, as if bored, until he gives in, checks his cutlery, straightens the fork. Finally, Thomas holds out the key.

'Agnes.'

She knows that voice, that way of saying her name, the English twang. Thomas looks past her. They all do.

'Joe?' says Thomas.

In one swift move, Agnes grabs the key with her left hand, then swings around, and smacks him hard with the right—open palm on his cheek.

Guy doesn't flinch.

'Ouch,' says someone behind her.

'What the heck,' says Thomas.

She almost swings around to smack him in the face too, except Guy has all her attention now. Because indeed—what the heck?

He's wearing the jeans and shirt she bought for him. His beard has been shaved to perfection. His hair is shorter, which has made his curls even curlier. They have a shine to them. He's checking her out too, isn't exactly smiling, but wants to, she thinks. Guy looks younger than she remembers him.

Agnes presses her stinging palm to the cold satin of the dress. 'The suitcase? That *was* you?'

A quick nod.

He's come all this way? 'Taking on that contract, then?' she says coldly.

'It depends. But that's not—I've come to explain.'

'Well, I'm warmed up,' she says. 'Suppose I can muster another round. But Guy, whatever story you're about to tell me, it'd better be good. Believe me, the competition is stiff.'

'She set you up.'

'What are you doing here, Joe?' Thomas asks.

Guy doesn't take his eyes off her when he answers. 'Got a room for the night, and name's not Joe.'

'Who did what?' says Agnes.

Guy looks embarrassed. 'Tanya dropped in that morning, swapped phones behind my back, and hers was flat, except I thought it was mine. I had to get to the workshop. Couldn't find the charger either. She'd snitched that. Anyway, she got your messages. Knew you were on your way to Felicity. Set the scene up. I didn't know she wanted to get back with me. For real. I'm an idiot. Blame myself.' He touched his cheek. 'Deserved that.'

'She swapped phones?' says Agnes, trying to keep up with the logistics.

'When she came clean, I almost punched her lights out. I would have if she'd been a bloke. Except if she'd been a bloke, she'd never been able to pull that stunt.'

'But if you had her phone ... Surely you could have found a charger?'

'I did in the end, Mick found one—'

'Tanya had my number on her phone. You could have rung me.'

'No, Agnes. She had deleted all traces of her Swedish competition. I can assure you.'

Agnes can feel herself staring. She must look dumb-ass-dumfounded.

'Waking up with you gone, I assumed you'd freaked out a bit, and needed time to sort through stuff—me and ...'

He nods towards Thomas. 'I had to get to work.' There's a moment's silence before Guy starts up again. 'I was angry with myself for having a flat phone, which is not something I do. Once charged, I realised it was hers, but she didn't take my calls. Avoiding me on purpose, naturally.'

Agnes thinks back to Tanya dressed in Guy's sweater on Felicity's revamped lounge, touching the cushions, telling her how much they appreciated what she'd done.

'I got hold of her that afternoon after I'd been to the motel,' says Guy. 'Found her at the gym. Your last message came while we were arguing.'

'So you never—?'

He shakes his head.

'She and you didn't—?'

'Nope.'

Agnes lets his words sink in. How did she get it all so wrong? How was she so easily deceived? She should have seen through Tanya and trusted herself about what had happened the previous night. 'And you came all this way—'

'I had to see you in person. Is that too bonkers?'

'Kangaroos in the top paddock kind of bonkers,' she says. *They never had sex.*

'Holly's sentiment exactly,' he says. 'You two have that in common. Sensible women.'

'Did you come all this way to tell me how much I'm like your sister?'

He shakes her head slowly. 'How about six months while I'm here for work? See what happens. I know it's not the best idea ever to date someone at the other end of the world.'

'Not the worst either.' She smiles, and it feels so good to smile at him. 'Yes to six months,' she says. 'See what happens.'

'Australian feral creep, was it?' Now he grins. 'And for the record, I did call, once I finally had my phone.'

'I thought you belonged in the garbage.'

'Don't blame you,' he says. 'I found your landline too—continuously engaged.'

'Mostly off the hook, actually.'

Guy shrugs. 'Didn't matter. I was coming after you anyway. Your suitcase arrived at my sister's just in time—a bonus. Ruby sends her love.'

'I knew it,' mutters Thomas behind her. 'I knew you were having it off with some tosser.'

Agnes pretends she doesn't hear it. 'Let's get out of here,' she says.

Guy holds out a hand. The connection is instant as if no time has passed since she lay next to him on Felicity, as if they just made love. He walks backwards. She follows. But then there's another thought, and she stops. 'You dropped my suitcase,' she says. 'Why did you sneak out again?'

He chuckles. 'Wouldn't you, if you arrived in the middle of marriage vows? I thought it was time to accept defeat.'

'What about, all's fair in love and war?'

Guy cocks his eyebrows, and squints at her in a sort of are-you-for-real kind of way. 'Listen here,' he says with mock sternness. 'I stood in your hallway listening. And I considered barging in, demanding a minute with the bride. But then I thought of how you left without confronting me.' He flicks his head in Thomas's direction. 'He and you had a long past. You told me that more than once. Tanya set you up, no doubt about it. And your words about marrying the love of your life, I assumed them no more than a stab at me. Then I got here. Not even a week and you were already walking down the aisle. Well, that made me think I was the fool for coming after you. I'm only human, and no man wants to lose face. So I came back here to drown my sorrows. I was rudely interrupted when this lot arrived. Despite the language barrier, it was obviously a disgruntled wedding party. When Thomas showed, I thought, the wind might have turned in my favour, and so I was finishing up, waiting to make sure the bride wasn't joining them. Then you walked in.'

'No man wants to lose face, you say.'

'If that's all you took from that rant, of course we don't.'

Agnes lets go of his hand. 'Only be a minute.'

She returns to the table, to Thomas—who has his back to her again. When she bends down close to his ear, he jolts with surprise. She sort of whispers, but loud enough for the others to hear. 'His name's Guy,' she says, smooth as velvet. 'I slept with him once. That one time was better, a lot better than the total sum of all the times with you.' She straightens up, turns on her gumboot heel, and even though Agnes never walks like that—she makes sure to swing her hips.

'What did you say to him?'

'Tell you later.' She winks. Agnes has never winked in her life before.

Guy fetches his jacket from the barstool, leaving the last of his whisky. As they walk back into the vestibule, loud laughter comes from Thomas's table. The one laughing the loudest is the almost-husband. Compensating is Agnes's guess.

'I've got friends waiting,' she says, pulling Guy with her outside who insists she'll wear his jacket. Once they've passed the windows into the restaurant, Guy stops and brings her close, puts her palm to his lips then gently pecks her fingertips.

'Do you know the real reason I came all this way?' he says. 'Your poor nails. New regime starts tomorrow. I'm taking you shopping for the most toxic concoction we can buy over the counter.'

'I know how to rule them in.'

'Them?'

She smiles up at him. 'You.' They kiss, and his mouth is wood and whiskey, warm and delicious. She longs to lie naked with her cold skin to his heat.

'We have proper food if you're that hungry.'

Niina and Patrick stand on the path a meter away, smiling.

'Meet Niina,' says Agnes. 'Best friend and total nut.'

'Nuts are good for you,' says Guy.

'Yep,' says Niina, 'All that hearty fat.'

'Patrick,' says Patrick.

'And we're starving,' says Niina.

Getting naked with Guy will have to wait.

Agnes returns to Villa Solus, in Guy's rental with the fan on full force and heat. Once home, she doesn't bother getting out of her dress. Somehow, it seems appropriate to keep going, and she's dry, if rigidly draped.

They eat and drink and rave about Patrick's food. Agnes doesn't know who's the merriest. She and Guy keep gazing at each other. Now and then they reach across the table to clasp hands. Agnes sits with her legs up, her cold feet on his chair, tucked between his thighs. He has a very warm crotch.

Niina recounts the day they've just had—from her perspective. She's witty and funny, has them all in stitches. When she reaches the part where the guests leave, when the vanished bride returns upset, Niina waits expectantly.

Agnes doesn't hesitate, not even with Patrick, who's proven to be a good friend in a few scant hours. She doesn't talk about her father's drowning. It's too raw. But she tells them all about Karl, the bank robbery, and the diamonds that her mum used to set her family up—for life, pretty much. Niina says she'll be researching the robbery the following day. So will Agnes.

They end up in a long discussion about what should happen next. Thomas will continue to be a problem, no doubt about it. No one knows anything about trust fund matters. They all assure her it'll work out somehow. Agnes is too elevated to allow the dilemma to bring her down. Not today. Not on her wedding day.

'Maybe I'll disappear to Australia,' she says.

'Not happening,' says Niina.

'We'd love to have you,' says Guy, who's massaging her feet under the table, sliding his hands up and down her calves.

Agnes beams at him.

'I'm willing to fight you over her,' says Niina. 'But first we need exquisite sugar. I've waited all day for a delicious bite.'

She hands Agnes a knife to cut the cake where the bride now stands alone, having had the groom broken off and chucked demonstratively in the rubbish bin by Niina. Half of a suit-clad arm still holds on. Agnes cuts and places a piece on each plate. While handing them out, Niina declares she's going to slice up the rest in smaller pieces and freeze.

'The cake will last until Christmas,' she says.

That gets her and Agnes giggling. The giggle turns into laughter, and Agnes laughs so hard she ends up on the floor, and almost wets herself. It's not even that funny. But then again, it is.

While Niina makes everyone, in particular herself, a strong brew, Guy asks if he can see the bears. 'I'd like to meet the critters I've been lugging around the world.'

'She's bloody brilliant,' says Niina.

'To the attic then,' says Agnes.

Guy carries the suitcase up, and the others follow with the coffees. They gather around the working table. Agnes pins in the lock code.

She packed the suitcase with great care, and the bears are still firmly in place, wedged in with each other. Their furs have flattened from weeks squashed together, but they're all intact, no loose limbs. One by one, she places them on the table. The others pick up to admire. Her teddy bears are back and she'll start sending them out next week, making some of her own untainted money. The sense of lightness that comes, surprises her.

'They look authentically old,' says Patrick.

'So much work goes into them, you won't believe it,' says Niina. 'Agnes rips into them with sharp objects. I've seen her in action. A quiet psychopath is what we're dealing with here. But she's won awards, you know.'

'They're heavy,' says Guy.

'Steel shots,' says Niina matter-of-factly. 'Weight gives them value, a sense of quality. Isn't that right, Agnes?'

Agnes nods, offering Niina her most generous smile. 'Weight and value,' she says, winking at her, hoping Niina gets it—how much Agnes appreciates her. Then she glances at the three of them, picking up her bears, moving their limbs, talking and laughing. She's never had a group of friends in her home, ever. There's only been Niina. It's a good feeling, makes her warm and gooey inside, almost teary in a good way. She picks up the last bundle to distract. 'This big boy is the one that inspired them all,' she says, unwrapping him.

'He sure looks like he's been through the wars,' says Guy.

'Don't be fooled,' says Niina. 'The antique ones cost more than an arm and a leg.'

'Oh aye,' says Guy. 'But this one's priceless.'

'You bet,' says Agnes.

Guy seriously knows more about her than Thomas ever did. She shivers at the thought of how close she came to marrying him. It's like someone pulled her out seconds before drowning. No, that's incorrect. She pulled herself out. She gives a sigh of satisfaction, and the others look at her quizzically.

'Oh, nothing,' she says. 'I sat over there in that chair this morning.' Agnes points. What she knows now compared to then. She's about to say something along those lines, something profound, but Niina interrupts.

'Only Ness would think to start her wedding day with stitching up a bear.'

Mysterious are the ways of the mind. All the paths that crisscross and loop around each other. Guy watching her right now, with a grin on his face. It reminds her of when he sat across from her in Felicity when they sailed. And the word stitching? Agnes's mind travels at lightning speed from sailing to dead sailors stitched up and buried. She pulls her sewing kit from the side pocket in the suitcase, and out of that, her fine scissors. Agnes turns her dad's bear over, finds the back seam.

'What the?' says Niina as Agnes snips him open.

To everyone's amazement, Agnes pulls out the stuffing, piling it on the table. Then she reaches deep inside the bear's belly with two fingers, feels it immediately, and pulls out a satin bag with the knot loosely tied in a bow. Agnes gives Guy the honour, passes him the pouch to open, and cups her hands. Out they tumble, some small, some not so small, some rather large, round ones, oval ones, squares and hearts—glittering prisms of pure carbon.

Hours later, she wakes and stretches an arm across the sheets. Flat and cool. She flicks the bed lamp on. His clothes lie draped across the swivel chair. Agnes puts on his shirt and goes in search. She finds him in her attic.

On the shelves, the contours of bears line up, in the middle slumps the Steiff, hollowed, relieved of his burden. Guy is in her wingback chair. His outstretched legs gleam from the night's full moon. Agnes picks up the bag of diamonds still on the table. When the floor creaks under her naked feet, his hand shoots up, waves, and waits for hers.

'Usually takes a few days to reset the body clock,' he says, offering her to sit.

He's stark naked and superbly comfortable. Agnes drapes her legs across the armrest and leans her head onto his shoulder, dropping the bag in her lap. She places a palm on his bare chest, brushes her fingers across his warm skin, and breathes him in.

'Love the chair,' he says.

'Another heirloom from my dad.'

'Did your mum stitch this up as well?'

'No,' she says with a giggle. 'I reupholstered last year. No jewels. Only dust.' She picks up the bag again, holds it up, lets it sway so the satin glimmers. They'd all agreed. Why involve the police, when it was three decades ago? The Insurance company and Karl had paid their due. Thomas will get the diamonds. Hopefully, he'll be happy with what's there.

'You're doing the right thing,' says Guy. 'Will you keep one for yourself?'

She drops the bag to the floor and sits up to look at him, his illuminated face, his eyes where she wants to drown. 'Funny fact about me,' she says touching his cheek, feeling him hardening under her. 'They're not at all my thing. Never were.'

'No diamonds for Agnes,' he says. 'I'll keep that in mind.'

If you enjoyed Jasper's story, please consider leaving a review on Amazon, Goodreads, or your favourite book platform. Word-of-mouth and reviews help readers discover new books. Thank you for reading.

SCAN CODE FOR AMAZON REVIEW PAGE

SCAN CODE FOR GOODREADS REVIEW PAGE

If you'd like to receive my monthly newsletter and stay in touch:

SCAN CODE FOR FREE EBOOK

Acknowledgements

THANK YOU

Linda Cole, for cheering me on from the start, for listening endlessly to my plot ideas, for reading draft after draft—and everything I've ever written. For your genuine interest, honesty, and patience. Anna Fitzgerald, for always being so keen to read my manuscripts and other bits and pieces, for your thoughtful feedback, kind spirit, and positive vibes. Jenny Margetts, for your keen eye, and studious assessment. Tamily Harling, for your optimism, and for being your honest, energetic self. Rachel Faith, for your generous and fruitful gift of a writing retreat. Camilla Croft, for your reassuring and helpful letter to me. Mike Burke, for your endless insightful advice and for finding me online. Babita Surendran, for scrutinising selected scenes, and for your encouraging words to me that I'll never forget. Leonie Harrison, Di Frost, and Kay Derham, for our little critique group. My wonderful ARC readers. My parents, Anita Hörberg and Bengt Axmacher, for giving me a love for books, and my father for insisting I should write. My younger sister, Katarina Axmacher, for your sharp graphic artist's eye and helpful suggestions. My elder sister, Elisabeth Philippidis, and my niece, Sara Young, for making me think I could do it too. My editor, Laurel Cohn, for fantastic workshops, one-on-one advice, and excellent structural editorial work. My daughter, Emma. for reading and believing. My son, Jesse, for your general enthusiasm. My youngest, Hannah, for your brilliant illustration. Wayne, for listening and suggesting and listening, for always giving me space to pursue my passion, to do what I want to do, be who I need to be, and for having my back. You more than anyone know the doubt that creeps in, the overwhelm, the struggles. Thank you for being there through the good, the bad, and the ugly. You are the best. Last but not least, Banjo, for keeping my feet warm.

About the Author

It took a migration across continents, half a century, and everything from dish-pig to boutique owner before Charlotte faced her persistent aspiration and deepest fear—pursuing writing. Charlotte grew up in Sweden, but lives on the east coast of Australia with her husband, in the house they've built, not far from the beach where they first met. The children have left the nest, but Banjo has successfully planted his speckled paws inside the door, and attached his exuberant personality to their hearts.

Charlotte is an award-winning author who writes contemporary character-driven drama about everyday people and their conundrums, weaving in romance, mystery, and unexpected twists. When not tapping away on the keyboard, Charlotte goes about her daily life pretending *not* to be thinking about writing and obsessing about anything and everything story. She's working on her third novel.

To connect with the author, please visit
www.charlottefrench.com.au

The Secret Life of Jasper Scragg

His Betrayal is About to Sprout

Hoping to revive their wilting marriage, Jasper and Zoe have relocated to the small town of Woolloolobah for a new life. After many gruelling years of trying, Zoe has finally given up on having a baby. Deep down Jasper's relieved. He's no father material.

Three months ago he proved to be no husband material either.

All Jasper desperately wants is to bury his infidelity and be the man Zoe deserves. But his good intentions derail when his one-night mistake pops up with news that lands him in an impossible conundrum.

So the lies begin.